Keeping Carmen Ruiz

Alyson Root

J&M Books

Published by J&M Books

Lytchett House, 13 Freeland Park, Wareham Road, Poole, Dorset, BH16 6FA

Print ISBN: 978-1-917785-01-3

Ebook ISBN: 978-1-917785-17-4

Developmental Edit & Cover design by:

Tara Sullivan, The Write Gal Co.

www.thewritegal.com

Copy & Line Edit by:

Linda Slate

Proofread by:

Morgan Bonito

To healing hearts and loving fiercely.

1

Carmen

"If you like piña coladas... and something, something champagne, doo du du doo. If you like piña coladas... and then fucking in the rain, doo du doo doo."

"Enid, *por favor*. I'm begging you to stop, or at least learn the words to the entire song. Hell, even the correct lyrics in the chorus would do."

Carmen was ready to pull her hair out. For three and a half weeks, she'd endured Enid's enthusiastic rendition of that song—every morning without fail.

"Yeesh, you're cranky in the morning." Enid continued to sway her hips to the imaginary beat.

Carmen dragged the palms of her hands over her face. "I'm not cranky. I'd just appreciate it if you picked a different song—one you knew, maybe?"

"But I'm making piña coladas. It's appropriate. Do you want one?"

"Enid, it's nine-thirty in the morning."

"It's five somewhere in the world. Plus, it's more like a breakfast smoothie."

"It has rum in it!"

"Pirates drank rum for breakfast."

"I hate to break it to you, but you're no pirate."

"Says who? You don't know me!"

They stared at each other for a beat before Carmen cracked up. "You're nuts, old lady."

"And you've got a bug up your butt. The whole point of our girlie get-away was for you to relax, right?" Enid didn't allow Carmen to say anything before she barreled on. "But so far, you've done zip to chill the fuck out. I've offered you gummies, a bong, special brownies—"

"Maybe *you* need to chill out on the green stuff, Enid."

"Why? I'm Zen as fuck!"

"Look, I know I need to relax, but that wasn't the purpose of this vacation. I need time to work out how to get myself right in here," Carmen sighed, tapping the side of her head.

"Fine, but being uptight solves nothing."

"You just want me to drink in the morning with you."

"Damn right. Look, I even put a tiny umbrella in it! We're on holiday, champ. Time to act like it."

Carmen rolled her eyes playfully. Taking the elaborate cocktail from Enid, she took a tentative sip. Holy cow, it had enough rum to *sink* a pirate ship.

"Shit, I think I gave you mine. Here, this is the ball sack version."

Carmen choked on the remaining liquid in her mouth. "Ball sack version? What the hell does that mean?"

"It means the wimpy version. I refuse to use the word 'pussy'. I was talking to Samantha—you know, the hippie chick in the room down the hall. Well, she was telling me about the patriarchy's use of feminine body parts. How 'The Man' uses the word pussy to degrade and belittle. I was so taken with her speech, I vowed to never use the word pussy again unless it's describing my lady garden."

Talking with Enid was always a revelation. Carmen could count on her to keep things interesting. Sometimes, though, she'd like Enid to give her a heads up. A little warning would be nice; Just enough for Carmen to prepare herself for such topics of conversation.

"And let's be honest, if any part of the body is weak, it isn't the mighty vagina, is it? No, it's ball sacks. One nudge and they shoot right back up inside the body."

It was way too early for this. Sucking on the candy-striped straw wedged in her cocktail, Carmen could only hope the rum was at a sufficient level and Enid's ramblings would eventually stop Carmen from cringing.

Enid drew greedily from her own straw, her eyes twinkling with mischief. "She's a les-bi-friend, too."

"Who is?"

"Samantha the Hippie."

"Do not set me up, Enid, I'm serious."

"I'm trying to get you laid, not married. I've been bumping uglies with Ralph for two weeks and look how relaxed I am."

"Who the hell is Ralph?"

"The hotel manager. Oh, the things that man can do with a—"

"No, nope, stop. Do not finish that sentence."

Enid scoffed but didn't go into any more detail. "Alright, no sexy time with Samantha the Hippie. Are you at least using the vibe I bought you?"

Thrusting her now empty glass towards Enid, Carmen waited patiently until she had a fresh glass of rum-infused *breakfast smoothie*.

"Enid, I appreciate your efforts to help me relax, even if they are highly invasive on your part and very uncomfortable on mine."

"It's still in its box, isn't it?"

Damn right it was. Carmen couldn't contemplate getting handsy with herself while using a toy Enid had bought her. Over the last few weeks, Carmen had seen the old woman as a grandmother figure. Grandmothers didn't dole out vibrators—not the ones Carmen had heard about, anyway.

"It is. Now, can we move on?"

"Fine. What's your plan?"

"Plan?"

"Yeah, to 'get yourself right up there', as you put it."

Setting the cocktail on the breakfast bar, Carmen let her gaze wander to the large, floor-to-ceiling windows of their hotel suite. The view was incredible and very conducive to calm and tranquility...if you weren't sharing it with Enid.

The past three and a half weeks had given her time to think. Most of her thoughts had been about Molly, if she was being honest, but some were also about Mateo and Faith.

There was nothing more in this world Carmen wanted, than to feel truly safe. No amount of money would completely do that. Even so, Carmen had amassed a nice nest egg for later in life. What Carmen needed now, and for her future, was to feel safe in herself. Molly, Mateo, and Faith were her family and her home, but until Carmen learned how to feel safe within herself, she could never move forward.

Her mother dumping her as a baby was the root of it all. Carmen had been to therapy enough to know where her trauma came from. The question was how to deal with it, once and for all. In Carmen's mind, there was only one way: she had to find her birth mother. She was the only person who could give Carmen the answers she needed.

Breaking her gaze away from the cerulean sky spread across the length of the suite, Carmen took a fortifying breath. "I think I want to track down my mom."

Enid set down her own drink and sat by Carmen. "Are you sure? I'm not trying to put you off, sweetie. I just want you to be one hundred percent certain before taking that step."

"I need to know why—why she left me."

"I get that." Enid squeezed Carmen's knee. "It's going to be a tough road. Do you think you should call Mateo?"

It was the logical step. Mateo had been with Carmen since they were young children. He knew what she'd gone through, but Carmen had to do this alone. The last thing she wanted for him, was to drag up any unresolved issues.

Mateo had never wanted to know about his biological family. As far as he was concerned, Carmen was his sister, and she was all he needed. Now, of course, they had Faith and Enid, and maybe even Molly, but for a long time it was just the two of them.

For the most part, Carmen hadn't entertained the idea of looking for her mother any more than Mateo had, but as the years went on and she still found herself struggling to lead a healthy life, she couldn't stop the thought from popping up.

Mateo had worked through his trauma and was happy. Carmen couldn't say the same. She needed closure, and that meant she needed to dig into her past.

"He needs to concentrate on Daniel and Faith right now. If I find anything, I'll let him know."

Enid gave her a withering stare, but Carmen wouldn't budge on this. Her issues were her own.

"Fine. So, any ideas where to start?"

"I'm going to visit the fire station where she left me. Maybe they keep records or something. It's a start."

"So, the vacation is over?"

"Not at all. You stay as long as you like Enid. You and Ralph enjoy yourselves. Drink more breakfast smoothies."

"And leave you to do this solo? I don't think so, slugger."

"What's with the sports lingo? Champ and now, slugger?"

Enid barked out a laugh. "I didn't realize I was doing it. Ralph calls me 'champ' and 'slugger' when he nuts."

"Oh my God, nooooo!" Slamming the rest of her drink, Carmen stalked off to her bedroom. Loud music was needed to help drown out Enid's last words.

There it was; the pinpoint on Google Maps showing Carmen where she was left as a baby. That colorful little teardrop couldn't know how painful it was just looking at it.

If she was going to do this, Carmen had to get over the rush of emotion that clogged her throat and misted her eyes when she imagined her mother placing down the basket holding her and walking away, never looking back.

It was just a building. It shouldn't hold any power over her after all these years. It wasn't like Carmen remembered being there, so it shouldn't be too difficult to pack a bag and head to the firehouse where it all started, right?

"Enid?"

"I'm in the hot tub. Ralph is here, too."

"Great," Carmen grumbled. "Okay, we'll talk when you're free."

Not a chance in hell she was going to get anywhere near whatever those two were doing.

"I'm heading to the bar," she called.

If she couldn't enjoy the suite, Carmen figured she might as well take advantage of the sun at the hotel's bar.

Nearly four weeks in the hotel and this was only the second time Carmen had ventured out. It surprised her how disjointed she'd felt when she and Enid left Seattle. They weren't leaving forever, but sometimes it felt that way.

Maybe it was the possibility that Carmen, at least the version Mateo and Faith knew, had left for good, because Carmen was resolute that when she returned home, she would be a different person, one way or another.

"What can I get you?"

Carmen jumped, unaware the bartender had spotted her waiting. She'd completely zoned out. "Beer, please. Whatever you have on tap."

Settling on a tall stool at the end of the bar, Carmen took a cleansing breath. The morning's conversation with Enid needed exorcising from her mind. Several beers were in order.

Cringing at the thought of Enid and Ralph desecrating the suite's hot tub, she made a mental note to call reception and request a deep clean. There was no way she would even dip a toe in that thing before it had been thoroughly sterilized.

"Hi, can I buy you a drink?" The voice next to Carmen's right ear was soft and shy.

Turning to face whoever had approached, Carmen swallowed thickly. Did Molly have a twin?

"Hi...um, thanks...I've just ordered. Can I get you one?" She hadn't meant to ask that, but the sight of this very alluring woman had Carmen all out of sorts.

"I'd like that. I'm Angie."

"Carmen."

They fell silent, waiting for the bartender to return. Placing Carmen's beer on the bar top, he turned to Angie, who ordered the same beer as Carmen.

"How long are you here for?" Angie asked.

"Oh, um... a few weeks. But I might have to leave earlier." Carmen needed to talk to Enid so they could plan the next leg of their trip. She wanted to leave within the next two days. Her courage was hanging on by a thread, and the longer they stayed in the security of the hotel, the more likely Carmen would chicken out.

"Are you going home or on to somewhere else?" Angie asked before sipping her beer. The thin line of white foam on Angie's top lip momentarily distracted Carmen. "New Mexico," Carmen blurted. "I'm going to New Mexico for a few days with...um, with my friend."

"Are you here long enough to have dinner with me?"

"Carmen, there you are. Good God, woman, there was no reason to fly out of the suite like that. We weren't having sex. Ralph ran out of Viagra so we're on a hiatus until he can get his prescription filled."

Slowly closing her eyes, Carmen sucked in a lungful of air before bursting out laughing at the absurdity of Enid. God love that woman. All the tension she had been feeling up to that point, dissolved in a fit of giggles.

"Enid... meet Angie," Carmen gasped.

"Hello, dear, it's lovely to meet you. My, aren't you pretty?"

"Oh, thank you." Angie blushed with a shy smile on her very lovely face.

"I didn't mean to interrupt. I just wanted to let you know the coast is clear. Ralph has a shift."

"Good to know. Do you want a drink?" Carmen had finally calmed down. As much as she complained about Enid, she couldn't have come on this trip without her.

"No thanks, I'm going to see if Samantha the Hippie is in her room. She offered to decorate my leg. See you later. Enjoy yourself."

Carmen could have done without the exaggerated wink Enid gave her.

"Decorate her leg?" Angie chuckled.

"Enid has a prosthetic leg. Usually, she carries her gummies in it."

Angie's shoulders shook with laughter. "Are you for real?"

"Oh, I'm for real. She's a character."

"She's the friend you're traveling with?"

"Yeah, we came here for her seventieth birthday."

"That's so sweet."

"She's a great friend and she deserved a vacation."

"So..." Angie spoke, letting her words hang.

Ah, the dinner invitation. Carmen was tempted, no denying it, but what was the point? She and Enid would leave in a couple of days. A one-night stand wasn't what Carmen wanted anymore, and the fact Angie resembled Molly so closely was a little creepy.

"Thank you for the offer, I really appreciate it—"

"But you're going to say no, right?" Angie smiled.

"I am."

"That's cool. Will you have another beer with me before you go?"

"Sure." Carmen smiled.

As soon as Carmen finished her second beer, she readied herself to go back to the suite. As pleasant as Angie's company was, she needed to talk to Enid.

"I enjoyed talking to you. I hope you enjoy the rest of your vacation."

Angie grinned. "You too. Could I give you my number?"

"Okay, sure." What was the harm in taking Angie's number? It's not like they would actually talk. Carmen knew that as soon as she left, Angie would move on.

Angie punched in her digits and then hit the call button. Carmen glanced at Angie's phone, which was lit up with Carmen's number. She wasn't expecting her to do that.

"There, now we can message. I enjoyed getting to know you, Carmen. And, honestly, I would love to hear more about Enid," she laughed.

"Okay," Carmen answered dumbly. "I...I should go. Bye, Angie."

With a quick smile, Carmen bolted for the elevators. What would she do if Angie *did* call? Carmen wasn't in the headspace for it, and most importantly, the only woman who occupied her mind was Molly Parsons. She was partly the reason Carmen had left to get her shit together.

For the first time in her life, Carmen could see a future with a woman. Molly had captured her, even before they'd met. Hearing people talk about Molly had intrigued Carmen. When they finally had met, Carmen could hardly keep her tongue in her mouth.

Angie won't call. Relax.

Carmen peeked around the suite door, hoping Enid had told the truth and she wasn't about to walk into a septuagenarian sex party.

"Enid?"

"Outside."

Carmen made her way to the sliding doors. Enid lay on a sun lounger in a tie-dyed one-piece, large sunglasses covering most of her face.

"Want another drink while I'm up?" Carmen asked. The reason she hadn't sat down immediately, was because she'd spotted Enid's prosthetic leg, painted with new artwork, and had needed a minute to adjust.

"There's a batch of margaritas ready in the fridge," Enid called lazily.

Rolling her lips to stop herself from blurting anything out, Carmen occupied herself with making two margaritas.

"Here you go."

Enid pulled herself up, resting her sunglasses on top of her head. "Like my leg?"

Of course Enid would point it out as soon as possible. "Um... it's—"

"Fabulous. I'm going to wear shorts for the rest of the stay. That bad girl needs showing off."

"Do...um, do you think people in the hotel will appreciate seeing so many vaginas?"

"Why wouldn't they? Fifty percent of the fuckers have them. Samantha is so talented. Look, she even drew mine." Enid pointed to a very detailed drawing on Enid's ankle. "That's hers," Enid continued, giving Carmen a guided tour of her prosthetic. "I had to describe you to her before she could attempt yours."

"Please tell me you do not have a version of my...you know, on your leg."

"Of course. Look, it's here."

"Enid, of all the things you could have drawn on your leg, why vaginas?"

Carmen was lost for words. Samantha was, as Enid said, a talented artist by the looks of things. But really? Vaginas on a leg? Why?

"I told you earlier, I'm reclaiming the word 'pussy'. Look how magnificent they are."

What was the point of arguing? Enid would always do Enid things. If she wanted multiple bushes on her leg, then fine. It was just unfortunate Carmen would be the one who had to walk next to her. There was zero chance of Carmen being able to hide her mortification.

A change of subject was mandatory. "Are you okay to leave in a couple of days?"

"No problem, sugar. Where are we going?"

"New Mexico."

"Is that where you were born?"

"Well, it's where I was dumped." Carmen couldn't stop the bitterness seeping in.

"And that's where you will get some answers. Positive thinking, darling."

Clenching her fists, Carmen nodded in agreement. Yes, she would get some answers and then go home. Simple.

2

Molly

Laying prone, staring at the ceiling, Molly absentmindedly tapped her fingers on her belly. Should she, at the very least, message Carmen to tell her she was still in Seattle? She wasn't just in Seattle; she was in Carmen's house—in her bedroom.

Enid was aware of the situation but had promised to keep it a secret. Carmen was going through "stuff," and Molly didn't want her presence to detract from the work Carmen needed to do on herself; not if it meant Carmen would give them a chance to build a relationship.

Mateo had insisted Molly take Carmen's room for the duration of her stay, which was still open-ended. Almost a month had passed, and Molly was no closer to figuring out what she wanted to do. Coming to Seattle had been the right call. Molly wanted to be closer to Faith, to get to know her niece better, and have some permanence in her life.

Faith wasn't Molly's sole reason for moving to the rainy city, though. Carmen Ruiz played a large part in her decision to possibly relocate. Their time together, although short, gave Molly a glimpse of something that had been missing in her life for a long time.

The plan had been straightforward: turn up in Seattle and win Carmen's heart, or at least get her to agree to a date. Was it an omen that the plan was already going off track?

Mateo and Faith were being tight-lipped regarding Carmen's need for space. Molly knew it was something to do with Carmen's past rearing its head in her present, but that was it. A small part of her hoped Carmen's need to sort things out was because she wanted to try a relationship with Molly. Maybe that was just wishful thinking, though.

Ugh, she would drive herself crazy if she continued to lie around, trying to guess what was happening with the beautiful Carmen Ruiz. No, Molly had to do something proactive.

Heaving her body off the bed, Molly shuffled to the kitchen. The Seattle weather was wreaking havoc with her immune system. Jesus, was she coming down with the flu?

"Girl, you look like crap."

Halting at the kitchen door, Molly did her best to shoot daggers from her puffy eyes at Mateo. How dare he sit there in his pink robe with perfectly coiffed hair, and skin that looked like soft caramel.

"Thanks."

"Damn, *chica*, are you sick?"

Continuing into the kitchen, Molly poured herself a cup of coffee, unsuccessful at inhaling its aroma through her stuffed-up nose.

"What gave it away?" Her response was sluggish and lacked the bite she wanted to convey. Molly was not a great patient.

"Whoa, okay. So, Molly Parsons is a bit of a bitch when she's ill, huh?"

"You're a bitch all the time."

Slapping the table, Mateo let out a bark of laughter. "Hell yes, I am. I'm the Queen Bitch of this house, so you need to find your own thing."

"I never get sick," Molly grumbled into her mug.

"That's what Bessie said. I guess she was wrong and owes me twenty bucks!"

Lowering her coffee, Molly ran a hand through her unkempt hair. "What?"

"Oh yeah, we had a bet placed. I said it would take you less than a month to succumb to the rainy weather. I knew sunny California made you soft. Look, your immune system is fucked, *mija*."

"It's just allergies."

"To the rain!"

"Whatever. Where's Faith?"

"Where do you think?" Mateo grinned.

Of course, Molly knew where Faith was. Cuddled up somewhere with Nathalie. In the past four weeks, Molly had seen her niece a grand total of eight times.

"Here or at Nat's?"

"Nathalie's, I think. I know Rita is away, so I presume they're taking advantage of having the house to themselves. Rita will need to clean every surface when she gets home," Mateo chuckled. "Ah, to be young, dumb and full of—"

"Speaking of Rita," Molly interrupted nasally, not wanting Mateo to finish his thought, because...gross. "Do you think you could set up a meeting with her?"

"Sure. Thinking of getting involved with her charities?"

"Or shelters. I think I need something to occupy myself with."

Mateo gave her a sympathetic smile. "She'll be back, you know."

Molly knew he wasn't talking about Faith.

"She just needs a bit of—"

"Space, I know."

Sighing, Mateo scooted his chair closer. "Honey, she's doing this for the best reasons."

"Have you spoken to her?"

"Not for a couple of days. I don't want to crowd her. Enid's taking good care of our girl, Mol."

"She's not my girl yet, Mateo."

"But you still want her to be, right?"

Nodding, Molly dropped her head dramatically to the table. "Yeah, I do. And it's crazy. We hardly—"

"Know each other. Yeah, yeah. It makes no difference. If the feelings are there, that's all that counts."

"But...but what if after her time away, she realizes I'm not what she's looking for?"

"Molly, my sweet, sweet dumbass."

"Hey!"

"Carmen Ruiz is stubborn. She'd rather chew off her own arm than admit when she needs help. And yet, since meeting you, she has suddenly found it within herself to get help—find answers to shit that has plagued that woman since infancy. Do you understand what that means?"

Molly felt like this was a trick question. "Um..."

"It means that she wants to be a better version of herself for you!"

Molly's mind wandered back to the conversation between her and Faith the day she arrived in Seattle. Faith was adamant, that when Carmen was in a better place, mentally, she would wholly give her heart to a very lucky woman. Molly wanted to be that woman. Lord knows if that would come true, but something niggled in her gut.

Carmen was taking the initiative; dealing with her demons, all so she could start fresh. Could Molly say she'd done the same? After all these years, wasn't she still haunted by her past? Too scared to fully commit to a woman until they made her feel safe? Never sticking around long enough for them to show her they could make her feel at home. No, Molly went on a gut feeling, and every time, those women never made the cut—until Carmen.

Even before they shared a passionate night bent over an old pickup truck, Carmen's presence had been soothing. The usual need to run away never surfaced...not really. But neither Molly nor Carmen were ready for more, which is why Molly found herself in her current situation.

Like Carmen, Molly knew it was time to change; time to face up to her past. That was what Faith meant all those weeks ago. Carmen was working out a lifetime of shit to get herself ready to fully give her heart to another woman.

If Molly wanted to be that woman, she needed to be on the same page, prepared to wholeheartedly embrace everything Carmen wanted to give. And to do that, Molly had to take a page out of Carmen's handbook. She needed to work some shit out!

Tapping her fingers on the table, Molly weighed her next move. First, she wanted Carmen to know she was around if she needed to talk or something. She'd send a message—nothing too forward—just saying hi.

Leaving the lines of communication open was a good thing, right? The best option was remaining friendly while Carmen was away. Molly might be out of sight, but she wanted to remain on Carmen's mind.

Second, and the scariest part, was getting a grip on her own trauma. With Faith in her life, Molly couldn't help but reminisce...and remember. It wasn't all bad, but naturally, the shit with her brother often surfaced, causing a dull ache in her chest, not to mention pangs of anxiety as she recalled feelings of being alone and scared at such a young and vulnerable age. If Carmen was going to do the work, Molly would, too.

Faith was right: Molly needed a plan to keep Carmen Ruiz if she were lucky enough to get a chance to be with her. And a surefire way for Molly to mess up a potential relationship was her tendency to run or push people away. It was a coping mechanism that only kept her living life alone.

But where the hell did she start? Maybe therapy? Carmen and Mateo were big advocates. Talking to Faith's mom? Maureen might shed some light on…what? Why her husband was such a shitty human being to his only living relatives? No, Molly needed to go to the source. She needed to go back to Kentucky.

"Are you having a stroke?" Mateo's panicked voice cut through Molly's swirling thoughts.

Snapping her eyes to Mateo, she noticed his hand on hers. Then she noticed how sweaty she felt and how fast she was breathing. Just the thought of returning "home" after all these years, was apparently enough to induce a panic attack.

"I'm…I'm okay." Rubbing her hand over the grain of the kitchen table helped center her. Listening to the rain beating on the roof tiles, and concentrating on the smell of her coffee, was enough to bring her heart rate down.

"*Chica*, what just happened?"

"I got in my own head and freaked myself out, I guess."

"Yeah, I'm gonna need more than that, honey. You got really pale and sweaty."

Wiping away the moisture that had formed on her upper lip, Molly took several glugs of coffee.

"My time here has given me plenty of opportunity to think—overthink, sometimes. I had a clear idea how everything was going to go, and it hasn't happened that way at all. Faith told me I needed a plan to keep Carmen, and so far, I've come up with nada. All I could think about was how things were way off the imaginary track I'd laid out. But my niece is a smart cookie. While Carmen is away, I need to get right with myself. Maureen and Faith being in my life is churning up some things, that if I don't handle, will no doubt mess with any kind of relationship Carmen and I try to forge."

"Faith is a smart one."

Laughing, Molly repeated Faith's observations. "She says it's all the amazing sex she's having now."

"Maybe it is," Mateo chuckled. "But I think it's more to do with her having a good head on her shoulders. She's observant and soaks things up like a damn sponge. She'll make an excellent counselor."

"She will, I know it."

"Runs in the family, *mija*."

Molly smiled. She was so proud of Faith and couldn't wait to see her succeed in a career she was going to rock.

"Everything changed when you guys showed up at the ranch. Everything!"

"So, what's next?"

"I...I think I need to go home."

"To California?"

"No, back to Kentucky. It's been years since I visited my parents' graves. I left everything behind."

"You didn't have much of a choice, Mol."

"True, but I could have gone back over the years. Instead, I kept moving, never settling, always too scared to put down roots."

"Are you sure? Sometimes things are better left in the past."

Feeling stronger and surer than ever, Molly sat a little taller. "And some things will never stay buried. I've tried that way, Mateo, and it's gotten me a whole lotta nothing. Do you know the only time I would let myself think of my family—of my home—was on my birthday? I'd spend the day alone, reflecting on everything that happened. I'd cry for my parents, and for my brother. Every year, the same.

Alone on my birthday and mourning. I can't keep doing it. I want more. Faith deserves more from me. We're a family now, and I need to learn how to navigate that."

"And you will. But before you go gallivanting off to Kentucky, you need to sleep and eat, because I'm serious, honey, you really look like crap."

"You say the sweetest things."

"Oh, let's do a facial session. Maybe some aromatherapy."

"Aren't you meeting Daniel?"

Both Faith and Mateo had a tendency to disappear for most of the day, choosing to spend time with their significant other rather than a melancholic Molly.

"Not today, *chica*. Today, it's me and you. And some wine. Yes, this calls for wine."

"I'm down with that. Wine and flu medicine should do the trick."

"Hmm, on second thought, no wine for you. Flu medicine, yes."

Pouting, Molly agreed. Wine would only knock her out and give her a headache, to boot.

"Let me grab a shower so I'm not totally gross, and we'll get to it," she said, shuffling towards the hallway.

Molly ruffled Mateo's hair as she passed, because no one deserved to be that put together without consequences. Laughing at Mateo's string of expletives as he tried to re-coif, she darted into the bathroom.

Steam was an amazing thing. It opened pores and unclogged sinuses. Molly already felt a thousand times better by the time she made it back to Carmen's room wrapped in a towel.

Spying her phone on the bed where she'd tossed it earlier, Molly drew in a breath and pulled up the message thread between her and Carmen. It still stung she'd not received anything since Carmen left, but there was no point dwelling on it.

She must have typed out ten messages, deleting them all, before she finally settled on one. It was simple and to the point; a quick, 'Hi-hope-you're-doing-well,-just-wanted-to-check-in-and-let-you-know-everything-is-great,' kind of message.

With more confidence than she'd felt in the past four weeks, Molly hit send. It was okay if Carmen didn't reply. There would be no need to get upset. Well, that was what she repeated on a loop to herself, while all the time staring at her phone, hoping a 'ding' would ring out. And it did.

Molly's heart jumped into her throat as she saw the little notification appear on her screen. Carmen had messaged back, and fast. That was good, right?

> It's great to hear from you. Enid and I are about to leave Florida for New Mexico. I'll explain later. Maybe I could call you tonight? Carmen.

So many things to unpack. First, the fact that Carmen had replied and was being weirdly chatty. Second, New Mexico? And third, she wanted to call. They were going to hear each other's voices after weeks of silence. What did that mean? Was Carmen thinking about her as much as Molly was thinking about Carmen? So many questions!

Drama wasn't usually Molly's thing, but she tore out of Carmen's bedroom like a whirlwind, grasping Mateo by the collar of his robe the moment she was in the living room. "I messaged Carmen."

Mateo was struggling to keep a straight face. "Okay? And her reaction warranted this little performance?"

Yes, Molly had acted like she belonged in a Telenovela, and maybe that kind of drama was a little over the top for a text message.

"She asked if we could talk tonight."

"And you replied, yes, right?"

"I didn't reply! I came out here and told you. What does it mean?"

"*Dios mio*! It means she wants to talk to you. That's a good thing."

"It is, and oh, she said they're leaving Florida to go to New Mexico."

Mateo's reaction was immediate. Pushing Molly back by the shoulders, his face creased with concern. "She said they're going to New Mexico? You're sure?"

"Yes, look." Thrusting her phone screen in Mateo's face, she watched him read the message.

Mateo turned his head away from the phone, his hand coming up to stroke his chin. "She's really going there," he muttered to himself.

"Going where?"

"Her version of Kentucky."

"I'm lost." Molly knew a little about Carmen's history, but clearly there was still a lot to learn.

"I'm guessing she's trying to find her birth mom. New Mexico is where she was born and then left at a firehouse."

"Oh, wow. Okay, so she's *really* delving into the past."

Mateo lowered to the couch. His attention was somewhere else entirely. Sitting next to him, Molly waited. A few minutes must have passed before he let his eyes wander to Molly's.

"I shouldn't be surprised. I knew she was struggling with the fact that her mom had left her. But I think it's my fault she never tried to find her sooner."

Scrunching her face, Molly tried to understand where he'd gotten that idea from. "Why on Earth would you think that?"

"Because she's Carmen, Protector of Mateo," he laughed humorlessly. "After everything we went through—everything I went through—I just wanted to put it all behind me. I had no interest in searching for a biological family. What was the point? They didn't want me, and I'd made my life, and my family, with Carmen."

Molly clutched Mateo's hand as he spoke. She needed to provide some sort of comfort, because Lord knows, she couldn't take the pain—that was so visibly etched across his face—away.

"Over the years, Carmen hinted at the idea of looking into our pasts and I firmly shut the door on it, but I only meant for myself. But now, I think Carmen may have shut the door on it too, because she didn't want me to get upset. That's why she went to Florida without me. She couldn't make the decision to dig into her past, with me there."

"That's not your fault, Mateo. If Carmen had really wanted answers over the years, she would have—"

"No, she wouldn't have. That's the thing you need to understand if you ever want to be with her. Carmen will always put her family first, even to her own detriment. It's just who she is. I just wish I'd figured it out sooner. Here I am, doing well, and my sister has been suffering."

"Carmen might be your protector, but she's also her own person. People move on and work through things at their own pace. There is more to it than Carmen's wish not to hurt you, Mateo. I might not know her as well as you and Faith, but I know trauma. I know how it affects people and how it makes them act. For Carmen to survive, she had to put you first. That gave her purpose. Now she's ready to take the steps necessary to heal herself."

"Then why hasn't she told me she's going?"

"Because she's still your sister. And I'm sure this is a huge decision she's struggling to process. I have no doubt she'll tell you everything once she has it straight in her head. And she's not alone. Enid is probably the best person to be with her."

Nodding, Mateo drew Molly in for a hug. "Thank you, *mija*."

"We're all family now, right?"

"Of course. I don't give facials to just anyone."

Molly was relieved to see Mateo's signature sparkle.

"Speaking of, I'm ready to be pampered."

"First you need to reply to Carmen!"

3

Faith

The room smelled of sweat, sex, and day-old pizza. It was bliss! Nathalie lay tucked behind Faith, breathing heavily on her neck. Did life get any better? The sex certainly did. Given all the practice time they'd been putting in lately, that wasn't much of a surprise.

The little worm of guilt that had taken up residence in Faith's stomach punctured her happy place. The source of the feeling lay hidden in her sock drawer. A college application shouldn't make her feel this way, and usually it wouldn't. She would be over the moon if the aforementioned college wasn't nearly a thousand miles away from where her girlfriend lived; her girlfriend, who had no idea Rita had slipped the college application into Faith's hands two weeks ago.

Rita assured Faith her late application would be considered. If she pulled her head out of her ass, spoke to Nathalie, and applied, Faith could be on her way to California at the start of the new academic year.

Easier said than done, though. Things were so good between Faith and Nathalie. They spent all their time together, although Nathalie had to travel out of town sometimes. But even then, they talked on the phone as often as possible.

Would that be the same if Faith were busy in college? At least if she stayed nearby, they would get to see each other on weekends. There would be no chance of that if she chose California. They'd be lucky to see each other every few months.

Faith had so many decisions to make that her head swam, but saying nothing was eating her up. Hell, she hadn't even spoken to Molly or Mateo yet. She'd almost told her mother last Wednesday during their weekly phone call, but Faith couldn't get the words out.

Since Maureen left Seattle and went back to the ranch, Faith found it hard to simply let the past go. Every time they chatted over message or the phone, Faith struggled to match Maureen's enthusiasm. Her mom was trying, Faith knew she was, but she couldn't help the acid burning in her stomach every time she said goodbye and her mom said, "I love you."

Where was that love when she was trapped in her parents' house?

So far, ignoring everything had been the simplest way to cope. It was childish, but in her head, it made sense. If she didn't talk about things, they didn't exist, right? Wrong! Of course they did, and she was making life worse for herself by keeping college a secret.

Nathalie's mumbled, "G'mornin," broke Faith from her internal struggle. Gosh, Nathalie looked so beautiful in the mornings...evenings, too. Hell, she looked good any time of the day.

Faith rolled over, burying her head in Nathalie's freshly dyed hair. The new look did indescribable things to Faith in very private areas. A shorter cut than before, and now it was a deep plum color, Nathalie was a sexy punk rocker. The tongue piercing and septum ring added to her new vibe.

Faith shuddered as she took in her girlfriend. Her body always reacted so easily, especially when her mind wandered.

Nathalie propped her head on her hand. "What are you thinking about?"

"You, and how sexy you are with your new hair."

"Hmm, sexy you say?" Nathalie drew herself up and over Faith. "I think I'm the one who has the sexy girlfriend. Let me show you what you do to me."

And they were off. It was the standard now. All it took was a few words or well-placed innuendos and they ignited.

Faith gained more confidence every time they made love. She felt more comfortable asking Nathalie to do certain things. Which seemed to turn Nathalie on more.

"Fingers," Faith moaned.

"As you wish," Nathalie chuckled, slipping her hand through Faith's wetness.

"More, and faster."

"Yes, ma'am."

Hurtling towards her first orgasm of the day, Faith slammed her hand over her mouth, muffling her moans. The sound of the shower turning on meant this needed to be a quiet affair.

Having Carmen hear Faith and Nathalie once, was more than enough for a thousand lifetimes. Faith did *not* need her aunt or Mateo listening in. They probably didn't even know Faith and Nathalie were here. No way did she want them to find out because she was moaning too loudly.

As the waves of ecstasy subsided, Faith fell into what she liked to refer to as her "sex fog." Everything was calm, happy, and lovely. Nathalie's warm body gently lowering on top of her made it even better.

"That was fantastic."

Nathalie licked Faith's neck, stopping at her chin, ending it with a soft bite. "Mmm, it was."

Tapping the sides of her pillow, Faith adjusted herself. "Maybe you should hop up here and let me show you just how irresistible I find you!"

With a sly grin, Nathalie drew up to her knees and began moving up Faith's body. As soon as Nathalie was in position, Faith impatiently grabbed her girlfriend's ass, pulling her down.

The first taste was always the best, in Faith's opinion. Coupled with Nathalie's intake of breath as she felt Faith's tongue explore, it was one of her favorite positions.

It only took a couple of minutes before Nathalie was gripping the headboard, her mouth hanging open in pure joy. They really were getting good at this.

"God, you have a talented mouth," Nathalie gasped as the last vestiges of her orgasm played out.

Smiling widely, Faith gathered Nathalie up in her arms the moment she shuffled back down the bed. "I wish we could stay here all day."

"Me too, but Rita's gonna whoop my ass if I'm late again."

Faith let out a giggle. "I'm sorry for getting you in trouble."

"Yeah, you look it," Nathalie laughed.

"What time do you need to go?" Faith hated this part. Having to kiss Nathalie goodbye. How the hell would she cope in California?

"I should really get moving. I'll grab breakfast with you and then head out."

Reeling in the automatic pout that was trying to plant itself on her face, Faith nodded reluctantly and exited their warm cocoon.

They heard Molly and Mateo's muffled voices as they headed to the kitchen. Grabbing a much-needed coffee, Faith watched Nathalie for a few seconds, her mind replaying their morning activities.

"Stop it," Nathalie grinned.

"I'm not doing anything."

The exaggerated innocent eyes cracked Nathalie up. "Sure. Okay, I'm going to go. Text me later?"

They shared a sweet kiss before heading down the entry hall. It was at least five more minutes of kissing before

Molly and Mateo's smooch-mocking noises finally pulled them apart.

"Jerks," Faith shouted, laughing. Nathalie chuckled, giving her one last peck on the cheek.

Wandering through to the living room, Faith sighed dramatically. "Hey, you're doing facials. On a Tuesday!"

Mateo removed his cucumber slices. "We're having a girls' day. Care to join?"

"Oh, I was going to head over to the library."

Mateo's glare pinned her to the spot. "Wouldn't it be nice to spend some time *together*?" His eyes whipped to Molly, and his glare intensified. Faith was clearly missing something.

"Stop it, Mateo, I'm fine," Molly interjected. "If Faith wants to go out, that's okay."

"No, I can go anytime. Of course, I want to spend time with you both."

"Kiddo, seriously, go out if you want."

Mateo rolled his eyes and replaced his vegetables. Okay, so maybe Faith had been a little lax when it came to spending time with anyone who wasn't Nathalie. Looking a little closer at her aunt, Faith noticed she was pale. Also, her voice sounded a little nasal.

"Are you sick, Molly?"

"No—"

"Yes, she is," Mateo tutted.

"I'm just a little congested, that's all."

"Damn, I just lost twenty bucks," Faith muttered.

Mateo barked out a laugh. "Pay up, baby girl."

"I can't believe you were in on it, too!" Molly huffed, which quickly turned into a coughing fit.

"Settle down. Do you want some hot tea with lemon and honey?"

"Oh, yeah, I want one," Mateo chimed.

"You're not sick."

"It's preventative. Now hop to it, little one, I can feel Molly's germs invading my immune system."

"And you call me dramatic," Molly mumbled.

Smiling, Faith set about preparing them all a cup of hot tea with lemon and honey. Another pang of guilt washed over her. Not only was she keeping something from her girlfriend, but she was also keeping it from her family. Plus, since Molly's arrival in Seattle, Faith hadn't given her the time she deserved. When had she become so selfish?

"That's quite the serious frown. Everything okay?" Molly's intuition was difficult to escape sometimes.

"Yeah, um...actually there's something I'd like to talk to you about. I'd like to talk to you, Mateo, and Carmen, but..."

"You could call her. I'm sure she'd be happy to talk."

Faith could see Molly was trying to put on a brave and positive face, but she was hurting. Faith wondered if her aunt knew how deep her feelings for Carmen really went.

"Maybe, but I don't want to distract her, not when she's finally taking the time to look after herself. I know Carmen. She'd drop everything if I asked her to, and that's not what I want."

"Okay, well, I'm talking to Carmen later. How about I fill her in?"

Well, this was a revelation. Carmen had been practically radio-silent for nearly a month. Faith knew Molly's mood was partly due to the lack of communication between them. So what finally broke the silence?

"That sounds like a plan. Okay, go get comfortable and I'll bring in your drink."

Instead of enduring more of this unnecessary guilt, Faith knew she just had to unload. Talking things through with Molly and Mateo was a good idea, before broaching the subject with Nathalie. She needed to come at this rationally and not let her heart make all the decisions.

Mateo removed his cucumbers again, placing them on the coffee table. Molly wrapped the plush robe Faith presumed Mateo had given her, tighter.

"So, what's happening in the world of Faith?" Mateo asked, between sips of his steaming cup of tea.

"A few weeks ago, Rita gave me a college application form. We'd been talking about my next step and how I want to become a counselor."

"Okay, that's not surprising. Rita likes to cultivate talent and support young queers."

Faith nodded. "Exactly. Well, the college is in California. Rita knows people there or something, and she thinks I'm a shoo-in."

"Wow, that's fantastic." Molly's eyes beamed with pride.

Rubbing the back of her neck, Faith bobbed her head. "Yeah...it is."

"Ah," Mateo began. "I see what's going on. You haven't mentioned this to Nathalie yet?"

Shaking her head, Faith closed her eyes, feeling the sting of tears. "No, and I feel awful. We are so happy, but how can we carry on like that if I'm all the way in California?"

Molly promptly stood, making her way to Faith. Crouching, she took Faith's hands. "Sweetie, you need to talk to her. I don't know her well, but from what I've seen so far, that girl adores you and wants to see you shine. I think she'll be ecstatic for you."

Placing his honeyed tea next to the discarded cucumbers, Mateo joined Molly. "Your aunt is right, *chica*. Nathalie will be so happy for you, and I know she'll do everything in her power to make things easier on you both."

"But she shouldn't have to. I feel like she's constantly having to work around me and my needs."

Okay, that was slightly deeper than Faith intended to go, but it was true. Nathalie was so thoughtful and caring, it sometimes made Faith wonder what she offered in return.

"That seems like a deeper conversation you need to have with her, kiddo. I'm no expert at relationships," Molly grinned, "but I know they rely on communication. Don't presume to know what Nathalie will do or think. She's there for you. Just talk to her."

"I will. But...what do you guys think...about the whole college thing?"

Shifting to the arm of the couch, Mateo gracefully crossed one pink-robed leg over the other. "What was your first reaction to Rita handing you that application form?"

Faith thought back to the conversation. To the shock and elation that rushed over her body as she studied the packet.

"I was excited. For so long, I never thought I'd amount to anything. Sure, I could probably recite the Bible from front to back, but as far as having any actual skills I could make a career out of..."

Faith grew quiet, her mind sifting through some of her darkest days.

"But since moving here," she finally continued, "meeting the group at the ranch, and talking with Rita, I think I have something to offer. I don't know if becoming a counselor is my calling, but I feel it in here." Faith clapped her palm over her heart.

"I want to help kids like me. I want to be the light in someone's darkness. Just like Carmen and Mateo were for me. And then you, Molly. I want..." Faith hiccupped, her emotions suddenly overwhelming her.

"You've found your purpose," Molly whispered. "I'm so proud of you, Faith. So unbelievably proud, and I know Nathalie will be the same."

"I agree," Mateo commented. This was possibly the most serious Faith had ever seen him. Mateo played the drama queen, but when the chips were down, he was steady as a rock; ready to get down and dirty with his feelings.

Faith needed people like that. Years of being taught to keep her mouth shut, or face severe consequences, had her unable to communicate properly at times. Everyone had baggage, and this was Faith's.

"You're both right. I'll talk to her tonight."

"Great, now do you want a mud mask? You're looking a little dry."

Rolling her eyes, Faith batted Mateo's arm. "Way to make me feel better, dude."

"Dude? Did you really just call me dude? Do I look like a dude?"

"Does his voice always get that high when he's pitching a fit?" Molly winced.

"Oh, yeah. And what's wrong with being called dude?"

"I'm not a frat bro, Faith. I have standards."

"Carmen said you slept with a lot of frat bros so..."

"Carmen is a dirty liar."

"Speaking of. How did the talking tonight thing come about?" Faith asked, noticing Molly squirm a little. Was she turning red? Oh, she had it bad.

"I messaged her this morning. Just to check in and she replied, asking if we could talk. I think she's made some decisions."

"Decisions?"

Mateo nodded slowly, his eyes dimming. "She's heading to New Mexico. It's where she was born."

"Oh, wow, okay. So, you think she's looking for her birth family?"

"That would be my guess," Molly replied, her eyes carefully watching Mateo. Faith understood this could be a sore subject for him.

Mateo poked his toes into Molly's side. "Carmen's not the only one to have an epiphany."

"Do tell."

"I...I think I need to go back to Kentucky."

Faith wasn't expecting that, or the feeling that slammed into her chest, making her gasp for air.

"Jesus, she looks like you did," Mateo shot, his arm coming to Faith's back, rubbing soothing circles.

"It's alright, kiddo, just breathe." Molly's voice was soft and calming.

Just the thought of going back there sent panic through Faith's entire body. Her father's disgusted face swam into her mind's eye, along with the awful words he'd spewed at Molly back at the ranch.

"Why? Why would you ever want to go back?"

"Because I've been running from it for too long, sweetie. I need to put some ghosts to rest."

"Are you still hoping dad will come around? Because he won't, Molly. Look what he did to Mom. To me! He hates us—hates you."

"I'm not looking for his acceptance. But I need to do this. I took what you said seriously."

"What did I say?" Faith's anxiety was finally ebbing.

"You told me I needed to get on the same page as Carmen. When she comes back, if she's ready for more, I need to make sure I'm in a place to accept it. Unless I address my issues, Faith, I'm always going to be the one who runs from her problems."

"I don't understand how going back there will help!"

"Maybe it won't. But I've tried everything else."

Taking several sips of her tea to give herself a little time to process, Faith looked Molly in the eyes. Something had shifted in her aunt.

"I want to come with you," she blurted.

Molly's eyes went wide, reflecting Faith's own surprise.

"Can I?"

"Well…I mean," Molly looked to Mateo for help. Faith had just sat there panicking about Molly going back, and now she was suddenly jumping on the bandwagon.

"I know how I just reacted and what I said…but if you go back, I don't want you to go alone."

"You don't have to do that, sweetie."

"No, but it feels like the right thing to do. Maybe it would do me good, too."

"Well, if you're going, then so am I," Mateo chimed in.

"We can't all just swan off to Kentucky," Molly laughed.

Faith shrugged. "Why not? We did when we came looking for you!"

Coiffing his hair, Mateo stood. "That's true. Plus, all this rain is really doing a number on my hair. A little Kentucky heat is just what the doctor ordered."

"That's settled then." Faith stood next to Mateo, giving him a fist bump, which always ended up with him feigning hurt, as though Faith had battered his delicate hand.

"I'm going to talk to Nathalie tonight. And then we'll organize the trip."

"Hold on," Molly protested. "I'd literally only decided it might be an idea for me to go back, like an hour ago. And what? We're actually going to plan it and go?"

"Well, yeah. No time like the present. Carmen is away, I'm not in school, and you're still deciding on your next career move. Seems like the perfect time."

"Amen!" Mateo hollered.

Molly looked at him. "What about your store?"

"I've got staff."

"Molly, let's just do it. Rip off the Band-Aid, or, you know, twenty-year-old scab. All of us deserve some peace. If we can find that by going back there, then I'm up for it. Plus, wouldn't it be better to do it together? As a family?"

For whatever reason, Faith knew this was the answer. It would give her the clarity and help to decide what was the best thing to do. Yes, she'd talk to Nathalie, tell her about the college application. But she'd use this trip down Nightmare Lane to learn more about her family; more about herself.

That could only be a good thing, right?

4

Carmen

Six-thirty was evening time, right? Or was it early evening? Late afternoon? No, definitely evening, which meant Carmen was okay to call Molly now. Or would she look too eager?

"Are you looking for ways to watch porn on your phone?" As usual, Enid's contribution to the situation was uncomfortable, unhelpful, and highly inappropriate.

"No, I'm not!" Carmen squeaked.

"Well then, why the hell are you staring at the thing so hard? It's either lesbo porn or... I don't know what else."

Enid lay on the couch as though it were a chaise lounge and she, a French Madame...if French Madames wore neon tracksuits and enjoyed showing off a prosthetic leg with lady bits all over it.

"It's not lesbo porn, or any other kind. I said I'd call Molly this evening and I'm just deciding if it's too early."

"When the hell did this happen?"

"When you went to say goodbye to what's-his-face—the manager."

Carmen knew his name but couldn't bring herself to say it. Not after hearing Enid shouting it with such enthusiasm ten minutes into their "goodbye" drink.

"Okay, that makes sense. So..." Enid rolled her wrist like the queen she was.

Shrugging with feigned nonchalance, Carmen played with the breadcrumbs on the table courtesy of Enid, who was a self-proclaimed garbage rat. Throwing things everywhere and never cleaning up after herself was her forte.

Tonight, Carmen would clean the hotel suite from top to bottom, including the half a loaf of bread scattered on the tabletop.

"She messaged me. Just a check-in kind of thing. I mentioned we're heading to New Mexico. I figured it would be better to call her and explain."

Yeah, like that was the only reason!

"Uh-huh. You could have done that two days ago. Or called Mateo."

Busted! Yes, Carmen could have absolutely done both those things, however, she was sensitive to Mateo's potential reaction. This detour would absolutely bring up some things for him, and selfishly, Carmen wasn't in the headspace to look after herself *and* Mateo right now. Also, she'd never admit to the feeling that plunged into her stomach the second Molly's name flashed up on her phone.

Molly Parsons had been on Carmen's mind for weeks. She'd decided to take some space, knowing her mind—and other body parts—would be distracted if they communicated regularly.

But seeing Molly's message, Carmen couldn't stop herself from replying; couldn't stop the thought of wanting to hear her voice. And, really, she didn't want to stop.

This thing between them was perplexing and frustrating. Knowing Molly for only a few weeks didn't fit with the depth of feeling Carmen was experiencing, and she didn't know what to do with that.

There was only one other person—no scrap, that—two people Carmen had felt instantly close to, and they were Mateo and Faith. Okay, maybe three, because Enid grew on her pretty fast.

Molly was different, though, obviously. There was always an air of excitement between them, even when their only means of communication were text messages. It seemed their mutual attraction, or whatever it was, traveled through the airwaves. Or was this all in Carmen's head?

That was the part she was struggling with the most. Clearly, for a while, she'd not been in the best frame of mind, and that was scary. What if the connection she felt to Molly came down to that? An illusion, conjured up by her brain because she was so desperate to feel normal, to feel wanted by another human?

Or what if *those* thoughts were the ones that were misleading? Jesus, it was all so hard to decipher.

"You look like you're constipated. Christ, Carmen, it's not that difficult. Tap her number in and hit 'call.'"

"I'm going outside," Carmen grumbled.

Having Enid squawking in the background was a big no-no. The woman could drive her to distraction in one sentence, and Carmen needed all her faculties to get through this particular phone call.

Watching the ocean for a few calming minutes did wonders for the nerves. Tapping the little green icon, Carmen put the phone to her ear and waited, second-guessing herself every second the line kept ringing.

"Hey, you!" Molly's upbeat voice filtered through the speaker, causing a small shiver to run down Carmen's back.

"M-molly, hey."

"It's great to hear from you. How's Florida?"

"It's lovely, and hot. Enid is in paradise," Carmen chuckled.

"Oh, God, I dread to think how she's been. I'm imagining something like *Girls Gone Wild,* but senior-citizen style."

"Exactly!" They both laughed. "She's made friends with everyone, had her prosthetic covered in vaginas, and is sleeping with the hotel manager."

"Whoa, okay, hold up. I need all the details, and a glass of wine. One second."

Carmen listened to the rustling and clanking of Molly, presumably serving herself a glass of wine.

"Okay, I'm back and ready."

Grinning, Carmen plunged into the tales of Enid Butcher in Florida. By the time she'd finished recalling everything, Molly was belly laughing down the phone.

She was so easy to talk to. There was no awkwardness, which Carmen thought there most definitely would be. It was like no time had passed since they shared more than pleasant words at the ranch.

Joining in with Molly's laughter, Carmen felt some of the tension she'd stored in her neck muscles slowly ebb away. "So, you see, it's been a wild ride!"

"You were brave, taking her along in the first place!"

"Brave or stupid."

Their laughter died down.

"So," Molly began, causing Carmen to tense again. "New Mexico."

"New Mexico." A beat of silence passed. "Is Mateo upset with me? I take it you told him."

Carmen was aware Mateo and Molly had begun to message each other before she left for Florida. It made sense for Molly to have a point of contact that wasn't just Carmen, in case of an emergency.

"I showed him the message. I...I was happy to hear from you. I'm sorry if you didn't want him to know."

"No, it's fine, I should have called him. Hang on, what do you mean you *showed* him the message?"

"Oh," Molly laughed. Carmen picked up on the nervous tone. "Funny story. I'm in Seattle."

"What? Now?"

"Yeah, um...I arrived just after you left. Literally. I think your cab pulled out in front of mine. Instead of a flying visit, I stayed."

"But...what?"

"I needed to be closer to Faith. Plus, her mom turned up at the ranch. It was a big thing. I didn't want to wait until my scheduled visit, not with everything being so fraught and fragile."

"You're in my house?"

"Um, yeah...is that not okay?"

"Of course it is! Why didn't you call me? Why didn't Mateo?"

"We wanted to give you space, Carmen."

Space. That's what she'd needed, and now that Mateo, Molly, and Faith had afforded her that, Carmen felt more broken. Her family was keeping things from her because they thought she couldn't cope.

"How long are you staying?"

"I, um, haven't put a timeline on it. I think it's important to be here for Faith. We have so much time to catch up on, plus, I'm thinking of talking to Rita."

"She would love that! Someone with your experience is just what she looks for."

"Yeah." Another stretch of silence. Carmen had so many things going round her head, it was hard to keep her mind focused. "He's not angry. Mateo. Worried, sure, but not angry."

Kicking her toe against the railing, Carmen let Molly's words sink in. She didn't want Mateo to be worried. But, of course, he would be.

"Will you tell him I'm okay, and will call when we arrive?"

"Of course. *Are* you okay?"

"Surprisingly, yes. When we first got here, I felt a little lost. I made this snap decision to get out of town and then didn't know what to do with myself, but Enid has been great. A pain in the ass, but great."

"And the decision to go to New Mexico?"

Dropping her head to her chest, Carmen squeezed her eyes shut. Molly only knew the bare bones of her past. It was difficult enough to open up to Mateo, but she'd tried. And she needed to do that with Molly, too.

"It's the thing I can't move on from...being abandoned." As hard as she fought, Carmen lost the battle against the tears forming in her eyes. "I need to know why. Why didn't they want me?"

"Oh, Carmen." Just those two words sighed in a gentle caress through the phone helped. "We can be with you tomorrow if you want?"

"No." Carmen all but barked, regretting it immediately. "No, but thank you. I... This is going to sound horrible, but I need to do this without worrying about Mateo. Or you and Faith, for that matter."

"It's not horrible, I get it, I promise. But we are just a call away. You don't have to do *all* of it alone. Lean on Enid. And *call* me."

"O-okay," Carmen croaked through her emotions. She needed to do better with staying in contact. And she owed Mateo a phone call. "I'll message when we get there. I, I um, need to go now. Send my love to everyone."

"Look after yourself, Carmen."

Santa Fe, New Mexico: where Carmen's life began. How she wished she could recall *something*, anything, to cement the fact this was her birthplace. But there was *nothing*, not even a scrap of a memory. Child Protective Services had shipped her off long before she'd been old enough to form a cohesive thought. Santa Fe was just another city now.

"Oh, it's pretty," Enid announced, her face plastered to the cab's window.

Carmen gazed out at the Pueblo-style architecture, willing her brain to make some kind of connection.

"How far is the hotel? I'm going to piss my pants if we don't arrive soon. I think it's already coming out," Enid announced.

"Two minutes," the cab driver answered, looking suitably alarmed.

"Do *not* wet yourself," Carmen chastised, half-joking. Enid was a law unto herself.

"I'm not incontinent. Calm down, I just want the driver to get a move on," she whispered, smiling wickedly. "Oh, I'm not going to be able to hold on much longer!"

The driver pressed down on the gas pedal, hurtling them forward. Carmen simply shook her head. Only the universe could decipher Enid Butcher and her manic ways.

Carmen tipped the driver generously. Enid was costing her a fortune. Did the old woman care? Not one bit. She practically skipped into the hotel, greeting everyone with gusto. The receptionist looked alarmed at first, but Enid's overwhelming positivity and banter soon won her over.

The Rosewood Inn of The Anasazi was extraordinary. Happy to have splashed out on the five-star hotel, Carmen took it in with glee. The Rosewood was all pine beams and cozy décor. They had a room each, both with a wood fireplace beautifully molded into the wall.

Enid wasted no time settling in. The room service menu was the first thing she picked up.

"Drop off your shit and come back here. A cocktail is in order after a day of traveling."

Not even bothering to argue, Carmen followed instructions. A cocktail *did* seem like a good idea, especially when faced with tomorrow's task.

Dumping her bags, she took a few minutes to splash cold water over her face. Enid was wonderful at distraction, but the second Carmen was alone, her decision to come to Santa Fe and face her past came crashing down like a tsunami. Tomorrow she would return to the place her mother had dumped her: Fire Station No. 1.

By the time she returned to Enid's room, a tray of assorted goodies was waiting: snack foods and alcohol. Oh, and Enid in her underwear.

"Should I even ask why?"

Enid fanned her face. "It's like a fucking oven in here! I need to air myself out."

"Why did you light the fire? It's summer!"

"Because I like the ambiance. You've seen me in my undies before."

"Not by choice then, and not by choice now!"

"Lighten up. Have a drink. No, make it several. Let's get wild!"

Carmen was not getting wild. She was getting a headache. Traveling all day wiped her out, and no matter how hard she tried to put tomorrow's excursion to the back of her mind, it continued to bash against her skull. One cocktail and she was going to bed.

It was not one cocktail, but many, many cocktails, and a gummy. The weed wasn't an issue. In fact, it helped chill Carmen out after experiencing crippling anxiety, no doubt brought on by too much alcohol. The cocktails were to blame for her queasy stomach and pounding head. Enid, of course, was no worse for wear the next day. The woman had an iron constitution.

"Did you sleep at all?" Enid poured Carmen a second cup of coffee.

"A little."

"Was it just the booze, or..."

"Or. Definitely or. I just couldn't settle down."

"You don't have to do this, sweetie. There's nothing wrong with changing your mind."

"I know, and thank you for being here, Enid. I appreciate you."

"Oh, honey, I know that."

A comfortable silence descended as Carmen readied herself. The fire station was only a half mile from the hotel. For all Carmen knew, she was going to turn up and no one would be able to help. It was over thirty years, closer to forty, since she was taken there. What were the odds she would find someone who was around at the time?

Calling the station crossed her mind, but every time she picked up the phone, her throat seized and her voice vanished.

If the trip ended up being a waste, she'd pack up and go back to Seattle. Carmen's time in Florida had helped some, even if it was just to put some space between her "old" life and the one she was striving for. After this, she'd go home; back to her family, and back to therapy.

No matter what, Carmen Ruiz would change her life for the better.

"I think we should walk. Exercise some of that nervous energy you're emitting like the fucking sun," Enid commented, as they stepped out of the hotel and into blistering heat.

Carmen stood, wringing her hands. Her palms were sweaty, and her lip was gnawed within an inch of its life. Maybe a walk was a good idea.

"Yeah, okay. Will you be okay?" Carmen nodded toward Enid's leg.

"I could climb Mount Everest with this bad girl. You think a stroll up the street is gonna do me in?"

"Alright, I was just checking."

"Let's go!" Enid twirled on her real foot and set off at an Olympic pace.

They marched in silence. Well, Enid hummed that infernal Piña Colada song, which she still hadn't taken the time to learn.

"Slow down a second, Enid."

Carmen could see the fire station in the distance and her body was reacting...badly. Her chest was tight. Was it really, *really* hot all of a sudden?

Enid's soft hand gripped her shoulder tightly. "Just take a deep breath, honey. You're okay."

"I don't think I can do this. It's pointless. No one will remember. I'm just torturing myself for no reason."

"Breathe, Carmen."

Bending slightly at the waist, Carmen put her hands on her knees, drawing in deep breaths. Closing her eyes, she pictured Mateo's smiling face as he faux swished his hair, Faith giggling next to him in her worn overalls. And then she saw Molly: in those cutoff jean shorts, yellow tank top, and dark, honey blonde hair, smiling widely.

They were the reason she needed to do this, no matter what she found or didn't. Carmen had come this far. She owed it to them, and herself, to see if she could find what she'd been searching for: a missing piece of her life's puzzle that would help her heal.

Standing, pulling her shoulders back, she gently withdrew from Enid's touch and began to walk on. Yes, her legs felt shaky, and her breathing was still a little fast, but she was okay.

The large roll-up doors were open, showcasing the magnificent fire trucks; shiny and red, standing proud, ready to go at a moment's notice. Carmen could hear voices somewhere in the garage, but decided she'd better head for the reception area. Surely there were some health and safety laws stopping people from walking around the fire station freely.

Buzzing the door, Carmen and Enid stood shoulder to head, waiting patiently. Was Enid getting shorter?

"You're obnoxiously tall," Enid grunted, pulling a smile from Carmen. The old woman was a mind reader.

When the door buzzed open, Carmen jolted, her body in full flight mode. It was only by the grace of Enid smacking her ass, that she got her feet to move.

A giant of a man, who could probably bench press one of the trucks, stood with a smile as wide as his biceps. "Hi, how can I help you?"

Once again, Carmen's voice ceased to exist. She stood there looking dumbstruck at the guy, unable to move or talk.

"Well, hello there, sweet cheeks," Enid purred. "Aren't you a handsome fella?"

The "fella," also known as Drew, if his name badge could be believed, chuckled at Enid's advances. The woman was shameless.

"Handsome and married," he winked back.

"Shame, I'm sure we could start a fire of our own."

"Okay," Carmen blurted. She needed to shut this down ASAP. Poor Drew didn't deserve the full force of Enid Butcher on such a fine morning. He already had a stressful job, and Carmen knew how relentless the tiny old biddy could be when she set her eye on someone hunky.

"Enid, take a few steps back."

Enid threw a wink Drew's way, giving his arm a squeeze before stepping behind Carmen.

"Um...this might sound like a strange request," Carmen began, swallowing hard. "I was wondering if there is anyone still working here that may have been around, say, thirty-seven years ago?"

5

Molly

It was quite astonishing how quickly the Ruiz household could organize an impromptu road trip. As soon as Molly finished outlining her plans to visit Kentucky, Mateo jumped on his phone to organize the coverage for his boutique, and Faith was messaging Nathalie.

All that was left for Molly to do was to have a meeting with Rita before she left. It felt important to have something solid to return to, because one thing was for sure: Molly would return to Seattle, regardless of the romantic outcome with Carmen. She would make the city her home. It was time to stop running.

Any awkwardness about staying in Carmen's room disappeared after the phone call. Sure, Molly hadn't made it clear she was inhabiting Carmen's space, but after their talk, it didn't feel like a big deal.

It gave Molly a zing of excitement every morning to pick her clothes out of the closet, simply because she loved seeing her belongings hung up next to Carmen's. It signified possibility. That zing often turned into embarrassment over how lame she was being by getting all mushy over a damn closet space.

What the hell would Carmen think? Would it freak her out knowing Molly's thoughts? Was she turning into a bit of a creeper?

With only two days to go until they headed south, Molly had to focus on today's meeting. The thousand thoughts whizzing around her head had to be tamed, at least for a few hours. Rita deserved Molly at her best and most professional.

Unfortunately, Molly wasn't entirely sure what she was going to say. She had a vague idea that her expertise and experience could be of use to Rita, but that was as far as it went.

"Molly, your cab is here!" Faith called from the entryway.

Smoothing down her pantsuit one last time and giving her hair a fluff—which was pointless in Seattle weather—Molly headed out.

Concealer was a godsend considering Molly was still feeling rough. No doubt her eyes still had dark circles under them. Thankfully, her sinuses were clearing up, but she now had a runny nose. Her purse was stuffed full of tissues. How long would it take for her body to adjust? Goddamn rain.

The cab eventually pulled up to a lovely, rather large house. Rita had money. Molly remembered Faith describing the near-palatial building when it was decked out for Pride. According to her niece, it was the best place on the planet. Molly smiled; Faith was a ray of sunshine.

Taking one last deep breath, Molly skipped up the front steps and raised her hand to knock. The wooden door flew open before she could make contact, happening so quickly it was lucky she hadn't accidentally socked the lovely looking older woman in the mouth.

"Molly!"

"Rita, hi."

They hadn't officially met, but they'd spoken a few times over the phone, mainly in the background, as Nathalie and Faith video called each other.

"It's delightful to finally meet you. Come on in."

Molly followed Rita through to an enormous living room. The sofas looked expensive; the type that was probably made from some form of exotic material Molly had never heard of.

"Your house is beautiful."

"Thanks, I like it." Rita smiled. "Tea? Coffee?"

"Coffee would be great, thanks."

Molly stood awkwardly by the aforementioned sofas, a little worried about sitting on them, lest she make a mark or something.

"Sit, sit," Rita said, waving her hand between Molly and the furniture. "Shall we get business out of the way before getting to know each other?"

Wasn't it supposed to be the other way around?

"Sure."

"I'll be honest, Molly. My charity would be lucky to have someone with your experience join the team. I'm thrilled you reached out."

"I've heard a lot about you and your work," Molly replied truthfully.

Rita had a finger in a lot of charitable pies, but her work with young LGBTQIA2s+ people was her shining star. And it was the thing that gave Molly a good feeling in her gut.

"I'm always looking for new people. But I think I have a job suited to your experience."

Molly took a sip of coffee. "Please tell me more."

"Mateo, Carmen, and Faith have all regaled me with your work in L.A. and other cities. Mainly with shelters, correct?"

"Yes. But most recently, I worked on a ranch that housed young LGBTQIA2s+ people, offering them safe harbor and counseling."

"Indeed. And offering educational classes?"

"Yes."

Wow, the Ruizes and Faith really had been talking her up.

"Here's what I propose: I need someone who can work with all my shelters. Someone who will be based in Seattle but can travel around offering mentoring to new volunteers. Making sure the shelters are getting what they need, etc. A supervisor, if you will."

That was one hell of an offer. "Wow, that's..."

"A big offer, and a lot of work, I know. I've wanted someone in that sort of capacity for a while, but I never found the right candidate until now. Molly, you've been around the block. You've seen the shelters that need more help. It's my goal to help as many shelters as possible, even the ones not under my purview."

Molly found herself utterly captured as Rita spoke with passion.

"When we unite, we become stronger. The system is broken. I think we can all agree on that. So I want to take things into my own hands. I've never been one for rules." Rita offered Molly a wink.

"This year, I plan to organize a council of sorts. I want the heads of different charities to form a coalition. Waiting for federal funds is a joke. There are more than enough billionaires in the world for us to approach. I want to shake up the system and rebuild it."

"That's a lofty goal."

"Of course it is!" Rita laughed. "But things will never change if we continue to do the same thing over and over."

"You make it sound so easy," Molly chuckled.

"Oh, no. This will be the hardest thing I have ever set out to do. Make no mistake, I'm setting myself up for possible failure and heartache. But I have to try. We need to come together. I'm not just focusing on the LGBTQIA2s+ charities, I want to roll it out countrywide with every charity I oversee and more, but that will take time."

"And you want to start with youth shelters centered around LGBTQIA2s+ kids?"

"Yes. It's near and dear to my heart. You know, that's how I met the Ruiz siblings. It almost broke me the first few years I worked at that particular shelter. I come from money, and I know many people thought I'd run the shelter and charity from the sidelines while I sipped expensive champagne, happy to do the bare minimum, just enough to soothe my conscience. Those people were wrong. I've never taken my wealth for granted." Rita paused for a long sip of coffee. Molly was utterly entranced.

"My parents instilled it in me to share whatever we had. This house looks big and ostentatious, but it serves a greater purpose. It's HQ for many galas which bring in funding. It's also an overflow shelter for kids who miss out on beds."

"You're quite the inspiration," Molly replied. "I'd be honored to help you reach this goal."

"Good. That's what I was hoping you'd say. Are you okay with traveling?"

"Sure, it's nothing out of the ordinary. However, when I moved here, it was to be closer to Faith. How often would I be required to travel?"

"Maybe once or twice a month. Only for a day or two. Before that, though, I need you to help me set up a user manual of sorts; a guideline for shelters to work with: how and where they can get funding, mentoring and training new counselors and volunteers, etc… I don't want any shelter to struggle in their day-to-day operations."

"So, a cheat sheet."

"Yes!" Rita exclaimed. "Yes. I want to take the worry and burden down several notches for these places. We need a central bank of information where all shelters can pilfer from freely."

"The needs for different shelters will vary greatly, Rita."

"Of course. I'm working on that. I'm gathering contact information to forward to you. Now that you're employed," Rita winked again, "you'll need to liaise with them and then come up with a universal cheat sheet."

Molly wasn't convinced this massive undertaking was possible. Sorting out one charity often felt impossible. But what Rita was talking about blew that level of difficulty out of the water. She wanted to reform the system completely, which was exciting, but in Molly's mind, also out of reach.

"I see you're not wholly convinced. And that's fair. But what can it hurt, giving it a go, hm? We need to do more to support charities. The smaller ones, especially. I know there are like-minded people in the world that want to help. Hell, I have a few ready to push forward with me.

Now I need the workers who will be on the ground, actually getting this done. Do you want to be a part of it?"

Jesus, Rita should have been a motivational speaker. Molly's heart was pounding with a new sense of determination.

"Yes, I want to be a part of it," Molly found herself almost shouting in excitement.

"That's the spirit. When can you start?"

"I have a personal errand to run out of state. It will only be a few days. When I'm back, I'm all yours."

Rita cocked her eyebrow. "Don't let Carmen hear you say that."

Blushing—for no reason whatsoever—Molly stuttered. "Carmen?"

Rita wiggled her eyebrows. "Now we can move on to getting to know each other. Specifically, what your intentions are with Ms. Ruiz."

"Oh boy, you got the full Rita treatment, didn't you?"

Molly turned from her seat at the kitchen island, staring blankly at Mateo. All she could do was nod.

"From the slightly stunned face," Mateo began moving his head from side to side, squinting at Molly, "I'll say, you got the job—probably one you weren't expecting—and then Rita grilled you about Carmen." Molly nodded again, causing Mateo to grin. "You never quite know what to expect with lovely Ms. Rita."

"I... she...she offered me this huge job, and then out of nowhere asked what my intentions were towards Carmen." Molly's voice came out as a squeak.

Mateo simply rolled his eyes and took a seat. "*Chica*, that's just Rita. She's like our older-sister-slash-mom."

"But how did she know about me and Carmen?"

"That's easy. I told her."

"What?"

"Calm down," Mateo laughed. "We tell her everything. She's the one we go to when we need a sounding board."

"And you needed to sound off about me?"

"Not like that," Mateo replied, fixing Molly with a penetrative stare. "I went to Rita when I could see how affected Carmen was by you."

"Affected."

"Yes. Affected. She wasn't the same when we came back from California. I knew you guys hooked up. But it was clear there was more going on, and you know how Carmen is. She shut it all away...made some stupid decisions, and then—boom—had a mini breakdown and left for Florida. It was a lot and I needed to talk it out with Rita."

"O-okay." Molly couldn't argue with that.

"Rita was just messing with you. But, out of curiosity, what did you say? What are your intentions?"

"That's between me, Carmen, and now, Rita," Molly grinned.

"Fine, whatever. Now tell me about this amazing job offer."

So Molly did. And then repeated herself to Faith, Nathalie, and Daniel. But the only person she wanted to tell hadn't messaged today, and Molly was treading lightly with contacting Carmen at the moment.

Carmen hadn't called or texted the past two days. Molly was of two minds whether to contact Enid, but surely if there was something wrong, Enid would be the first person to contact Mateo, right?

No, Molly would leave it for a few more days. She had enough to worry about. Mainly, she worried about Faith, who looked green at the thought of flying.

They'd checked in online and were waiting in the main terminal, surrounded by stores selling overpriced crap. Mateo wasted no time going to the perfume counter. Faith sat down and stared at the departures board for an entire half hour without blinking.

"Faith, are you sure you want to do this?" Molly asked for the umpteenth time.

"I want to." Faith's replies were becoming less and less convincing.

"There's nothing to be worried about, sweetie."

"Uh-huh."

"What has you so freaked out?"

"Being stuck in a tin can with no way out!"

Well, that got dark, fast.

"Faith, look at me." Molly waited until Faith turned. "There are safety measures and protocols. You are not stuck in a tin can. Thousands of flights take off every day with no problems. You *will* be fine."

"I should've had you take a gummy before we got to the airport," Mateo said from out of nowhere.

"You're getting as bad as Enid," Molly shot.

"At least she would be relaxed, Mol."

"I wouldn't have taken one, but thanks," Faith cut in. "I think I'll be okay once we've taken off."

"I agree," Molly answered, patting Faith's knee. "Look, we can board. Let's get settled in our seats, and if you have questions, I'm sure there will be someone who will answer them for you. You're not the first person to get a little scared of flying."

"Yeah, okay." Faith rose to her feet, looking a little unsteady in Molly's opinion, but she didn't comment.

They made their way to the plane, shuffling along with everyone else. Molly knew before her heart rate picked up that she was about to have a panic attack. Walking towards the thing that would take her back, not just to her hometown, but to her broken childhood, was suddenly too much to handle.

"Hey, breathe." Mateo murmured.

Molly focused on the warm hand Mateo placed on her back, rubbing small circles.

"Molly, what's wrong?" Faith's worried voice brought her back. Mateo had maneuvered them to the side of the jetway, allowing other passengers to pass by.

"I'm fine, don't worry. Sorry." Wiping her head, Molly felt the film of perspiration already formed on her forehead.

"You're not fine. Are you having a panic attack?"

She nodded. "It happens sometimes. I just need a second."

Neither Mateo nor Faith spoke again. Molly listened to her surroundings. She gently shuffled her feet to feel the carpet beneath her shoes. Gradually, her heart slipped back into its usual rhythm.

"I'm good. Let's go."

The last thing Molly wanted was to freak her niece out even more, but as she looked at Faith stowing her luggage, the young woman's body language had completely changed. If the worried glances were anything to go by, Molly would say Faith's concern for her aunt outweighed her dislike of flying.

"Do you want to sit by the window, sweetie?"

Nodding, Faith scooted in, leaving Molly in the middle seat and Mateo by the aisle. Closing her eyes, she felt two hands grasp her own and squeeze.

"It's okay, Molly. We're here," Faith whispered.

Smiling, Molly opened her eyes and turned to Faith. "You are a wonderful person, Faith Parsons. Never forget that."

"It runs in the family," Faith replied. "Are you sure *you* want to do this?"

Molly smiled at Faith using her own words against her. "I have to, Faith. I deserve more than old scars. You deserve that, too."

"I'm not going for me," Faith began, "not really. I spent eighteen years there, knowing I needed to leave. You were pushed out. Our lives may have ended up in the same place, but we didn't take the same path to get there. You lost your parents. Mine just didn't want me the way I was."

"Maybe, but we both missed out on the loving family we deserved, no matter how you look at it."

"You have a loving family now," Mateo interjected. "It may not be the one you were given, or the one taken from you, but Carmen, Enid, and I are here. Rita too. I hope you both know that," he said, eyeing both Parsons.

The notion was starting to sink in.

6

Faith

Flying was awful. Why had she been so excited to try it, when all the plane did was bounce around? Leaving Faith praying to God that the noise she could hear wasn't a warning of engine failure?

No, Faith was a bus, train, or car kind of woman, for sure.

The only thing keeping her relatively sane was her worry for Molly. Seeing her usually strong and steady aunt become panicked and sweaty in the space of a heartbeat was unnerving.

It shouldn't have come as such a shock, though. Faith knew many of the details of Molly's less than happy past. She should have guessed going back to Kentucky would elicit such a reaction.

As the plane flew on, Faith kept an eye on Molly, looking for any signs of distress. There were none. Needing to keep her mind off the fact they were cruising at a death-defying number of feet above the ground, Faith opened her phone to look at photos of Nathalie and listen to their shared playlist. It was sappy and gag-worthy, but Faith couldn't help it. Nathalie was her world.

Nathalie was also still in the dark about Faith's college options. She'd meant to tell her by now, but things simply got in the way, like Faith's cowardice. No, they had to have a conversation, but surely it should wait until she was back home. But that could be a week from now?

Why hadn't she done what she'd told Mateo and Molly she'd do the day they decided on this little trip, and told Nathalie that night? Ugh, she was so frustrated with herself.

Her self-flagellation would have to wait as the pilot announced their descent into Cincinnati. Once they landed, all they had to do was pick up their rental car and get on the road. Faith still had plenty of time to do a little bit of wallowing.

One other thing Faith had failed to do was warn Molly about Mateo's love for Cher when driving. It was rather funny watching from the back seat as Molly sat, wide-eyed, as Mateo gave an all-out performance as he drove. Thankfully, they only had a two-and-a-half-hour journey.

"You're lucky," Faith giggled, sitting forward so Molly could hear her, "we had this for days," she finished, casting her eyes to Mateo, who was completely unaware, far too enveloped in the music.

"He's enthusiastic," Molly laughed.

"Yeah, now picture him like this and add Enid!"

Molly cackled. "I would give anything to have been a fly on the wall for that. Carmen must have been losing her mind."

Faith nodded while laughing. "She's certainly patient, although she and Mateo bickered like kids. Enid tried to play the adult at one point, but it was all a bit ridiculous."

Faith had nothing but fond memories of their road trip across the states looking for Molly.

The change in Molly's facial expression as she looked out the window was unmissable, and as Faith followed her aunt's line of sight, she understood why. The big "Welcome to Loretto" sign loomed in the distance.

"I don't know why this seems so huge," Molly muttered. "It's just a town."

"It's your first home. I get it," Faith replied, sliding her palm on to Molly's shoulder.

Mateo finally registered something other than Cher, because he turned the music down to a low hum. "Everyone okay?"

"We're good. Um...but could I make a request?"

It only just occurred to Faith there was somewhere she could take Molly, that would be sure—kind of—to offer a warm welcome.

"And what request would that be, my dear?" Mateo asked with a flare of drama, because why not?

"Could you go to this address?" Faith showed Mateo the address on Google Maps. Molly's focus was elsewhere, probably ruminating on some uncomfortable feelings if Faith had to guess. Mateo simply nodded.

A frisson of excitement coursed through Faith's body. There was one other person Faith had done a terrible job of connecting with. It was all well and good being head over heels for Nathalie, but dropping her friends and family was a steep cost, and to an extent, that's what Faith had done. Now that she was in Loretto, she could make it right.

Mateo pulled the car to a stop outside Alice Carter's house. Faith felt her eyes fill with happy tears as she laid eyes on the house that was her second home. Actually, it often felt more like a home than the one she'd shared with her parents.

Not only would Faith get to see her best friend, and beg for forgiveness for her recent absence, she hoped Molly would get the welcome home she deserved. After all, Alice's father had grown up with Alan and Molly.

Far too excited, Faith leaped out of the car, pulling Molly's door open. "Come on."

Molly looked almost stunned, but followed willingly. Both the Carter cars were in the driveway, so there was a good chance everyone was home. Bouncing up the porch steps, Faith knocked loudly and rapidly. She heard footsteps that were heavy and could only belong to Mr. Carter.

The door swung open, and to Faith's delight, Mr. Carter's face broke out in a huge grin. "Faith! My Lord!" he exclaimed before wrapping her up in a hug. "I'm so happy to see you're alright."

After a few more moments, he broke the hug, holding her at arm's length.

"Hi Mr. Carter," Faith beamed. "Is Alice home?" She laughed, remembering all the times she'd asked that very question. It was surreal.

"Sure is." And then Mr. Carter looked over her shoulder and his eyes got even wider. "Molly Parsons," he breathed.

"Buck Carter," Molly replied, smiling. Faith stepped aside, allowing Mr. Carter to pass by. He stood in front of Molly for a second before drawing her into a hug.

"I'm so sorry," Faith heard him whisper. There was history between them, and Faith just hoped it would be a comfort to her aunt, and maybe a chance to have some closure.

Leaving Molly to introduce Mateo, Faith slipped into the house and went upstairs. She could already hear music coming from Alice's room. It was the same playlist Alice listened to on repeat when she was studying.

Foregoing a knock, Faith gently opened the door and peered in. Alice, who was as tall as Faith, but with wildly curly hair, lay on her bed, head bopping along as she read something from a textbook.

"Well, hey there, pretty lady," Faith said loudly. She broke into a smile as she witnessed Alice's head snap up, and then she let out a scream of pure joy.

Rushing forward, Faith forcefully crashed into Alice. They hugged, hopping around laugh-crying. Faith couldn't believe how much she'd missed this girl.

"I'm so sorry I've been such a crappy friend," she choked.

Alice's head whipped from side to side. "No apologies. You needed to live a little. I'm just so darn happy to see you."

"What in the world is all this noise?" Faith heard Mrs. Carter say from down the hall. It took a matter of seconds for the older version of Alice to appear. Her face registered the same shock and joy at seeing Faith. More tears fell, and longer hugs ensued.

After a brief explanation, Faith and Alice followed Mrs. Carter downstairs to where Mateo, Molly, and Mr. Carter sat having coffee.

"Molly Parsons, as I live and breathe!"

Molly stood and embraced Mrs. Carter. At some point, Faith would ask for their story. Clearly, they knew each other well, and Faith wanted to hear about it, just to feel closer to Molly.

"You'll stay for a while, right?" Mrs. Carter asked. Molly looked at Faith, asking silently.

"We'd love to. I need some time with Alice."

"Yeah, we're going for a walk," Alice announced, already steering Faith to the door.

The warm breeze was a welcome reprieve from the chilly rain. If Faith missed one thing about her hometown, it was the warmer climate.

"I can't believe you're here!" Alice exclaimed, grasping Faith's hand. "How are you feeling being back?"

"Weird," Faith laughed. "I feel so very different from the girl who left."

"You sure as hell look it, too!"

"Thanks," Faith winked, twirling. She'd opted for stone-washed, cut-off overalls with a black tank top and her trusty Converse.

"So...tell me everything. How's Na-tha-lie?"

Faith rolled her eyes at Alice's over pronunciation of Nat's name. "She's great. More than great."

"Uh-oh, I know that tone, Faith Parsons. Spill it."

Scuffing her toe on the floor, Faith let her shoulders sag. Not only did she tell Alice about her college application and what that could mean, but she also unburdened herself regarding how badly she'd skipped out on everyone *but* Nathalie.

It felt good to talk to Alice; like old times. It also felt good to see how far she'd come since those days. Alice listened intently, always one to take onboard all the information before speaking her mind.

"Okay, let's start with you feeling guilty. Chill! I mean it, Faith, relax. I never felt abandoned or anything. We've both got lives now. Much better lives, and I'm so happy you found Nat. Found yourself. I wasn't lying when I said you looked good. You're glowing."

"I'm happy," Faith admitted proudly. "Happy I'm free to live my life how I want."

"And that shows. Yes, we should make more of an effort to call or whatever, but that goes both ways."

"Yeah, okay."

"And Molly was young once," Alice giggled. "She gets it. I'm sure she got swept away by a woman once or twice. You guys look so similar. It's weird."

"It's nice," Faith added, "to share a resemblance to someone who isn't the worst."

"I hear ya!"

"We're going to visit my grandparents' graves, I think."

Molly hadn't given them an itinerary or anything, but it was only logical.

"I gotta say, Faith, I'm surprised you came back."

"Me too! But Molly needs this and I need her. I have Mateo, Carmen, and Enid, but I want Molly to feel at home with us, and I want her to be happy."

"Healing takes time. Or that's what Mom says."

"Do you know their history?"

"Nope. Not at all. They obviously knew each other pretty well, though, right?"

"I'd say so. I'll ask Molly at some point."

"Okay, back to the other thing: college." They sat on the grass a few blocks away from the Carter residence. "You want to go." It wasn't a question. "From everything you've told me about Nathalie, she's going to be more upset you felt you couldn't tell her than she will be about your choice of colleges."

"But everything will change!" Faith heard the whining tone and snapped her mouth shut.

"Yeah, it will. Can I tell you what I really think is bothering you?"

"Of course."

"You're finally in a safe place. Not just literally. You have a home, family, and a good relationship. It's totally natural to want to stay wrapped up in that. Your body is craving stability, and you've finally got it. But Faith, you can't hide away forever."

"I'm not hiding!"

"Really? I think that's exactly what you'll be doing if you pass up on this. Sure, you will be with Nat, safe and sound at home, but how long will it be until you realize you need more? Faith, you've always dreamed of a bigger life—of opportunity. The only person holding you back, is you. Nathalie would be *so* pissed if you gave up California under the guise of choosing to be with her."

"It's not an—"

"It *would* be an excuse, because no one is making you choose between anything. This is you getting scared of the good things being taken away. Nat will be with you all the way. You can do long distance." Alice really didn't hold back. "Tell me, how badly do you want this?"

"I-I do."

"Then talk to your girlfriend and start planning for a future together where you can have it all."

"Whoa, okay," Faith chuckled nervously.

"I know it wasn't me who had to put up with your parents. But I saw how it affected you. Remember when we used to play make-believe? I'd imagine myself a princess, being rescued by a handsome prince. You pretended you worked in a high-rise building in the city, even though you had no clue what that meant," Alice laughed. "You've always wanted more and this is your chance to make it happen. Stop being scared. I mean, if you can come back here and face this place, you can go to college a thousand miles away from Nat and the gang. You've got this."

After what felt like an ass-whooping from Alice, Faith took a little time to digest the conversation. It had to wait until they'd had dinner with the Carters, but Molly and Mateo gave her some space when they checked into the hotel.

Molly was visibly lighter, so Faith patted herself on the back for taking her to see her old friends. Mateo was charmed, albeit wary. Faith knew him well enough to understand he never quite let his guard down. She loved him all the more for it.

Now, sitting on her hotel bed fiddling with her phone, Faith decided. Enough stalling. Molly and Mateo were out finding water and snacks for the evening, even though they were all stuffed from dinner.

Hitting the call button, Faith only had to wait a second before Nathalie picked up. "Hey, baby, you made it safe and sound?"

"Hey, yeah, we're here. Sorry it's later than expected. I asked Mateo to take us to see Alice and her family."

"Ah, cool. I'm sure she was thrilled to see you!"

"And then some," Faith laughed. "It worked out really well for Molly, too. Remember I told you Alice's dad grew up with my father?"

"Yeah."

"Well, I think they were all friends at one point. Lots of hugging and crying going on between Molly and the Carters."

"That must have been a nice surprise for Molly. I can't imagine she thought she'd get any kind of reception, let alone a nice one."

"That was my thinking when I suggested going to see Alice. I'm just happy it worked out. Thinking back, it could have blown up in my face."

"But it didn't. You're a good woman, baby."

Faith sighed. "I have something to tell you."

"Okay?"

"Rita gave me an application form to a college in California. She thinks it would be a good fit, and she knows people there."

"Uh-huh."

Faith scrunched her face. "You don't sound surprised."

"Because I'm not, babe. I asked Rita to talk to you about it."

"What?"

"Yeah. She suggested the college after I told her you were seriously looking into places to study, so I asked if she'd talk to you about it. It's not like I'm qualified to advise you. I thought it would be good to have someone who could give you the best options. Did I do something wrong?"

Faith burst out laughing. "Oh my God," she called into the silent hotel room.

"What? Are you okay?" Nathalie's voice sounded concerned.

"I've been worried for weeks about this, and it was your idea all along?"

"Worried? Why? And it wasn't my idea. I simply asked Rita to talk to you."

Shaking her head and dropping to the bed with a thump, Faith breathed easily for the first time in weeks.

"I didn't know how to tell you about the college. It's so far away, and I got scared. We're in such a great place. I see you all the time and we get to do...stuff."

Nathalie laughed. "Stuff...is that what we're calling it?"

"Yeah," Faith blushed. "If I go to California, that changes."

"Sure, but it's temporary."

"It's years."

"But it still has an end date. Unlike me and you. Unless you feel differently?"

Sucking in a breath, Faith tried to keep the tears at bay. "You always say the right things. You're just perfect, Nat."

"I'm not, baby, but I know how I feel. I want you to have everything you dream of. I'm not worried about the distance. Or how much time we'll lose together, because it's all working towards a future, for us both. College isn't for me, and that's cool. I love what I do, and Rita is awesome to work for. You want college, and it's within your reach, so take it. We'll figure out the rest."

"I'm going to miss you so much!"

"We can video chat as often as you like. Text, too."

"But what about…stuff?" Faith asked, smiling, knowing Nathalie would chuckle.

"Phone sex, honey. We're pretty good at that, too."

"Yeah, we are."

"Okay, I know that tone, missy, and we can't get into it."

"Why not?" Faith pouted.

"Because I'm guessing you'll have company soon."

Damn, Faith had totally forgotten about Molly and Mateo's imminent return.

"Crap!"

Nathalie burst out laughing. "As soon as you're back, I'll make it up to you, okay?"

As if Nathalie had anything to make up for. "I'll be the one making amends. Multiple times."

"I look forward to it. Now, what's on the schedule?"

"Molly still hasn't set one. I think she's kinda feeling the place out a little."

"Do you think she'll want to see your father?"

Rolling on to her stomach, Faith took a moment. It had played on her mind Molly might want another crack at Faith's father in a last-ditch attempt to get him to see reason. Faith truly hoped that wasn't the case. As far as she was concerned, Alan would never change. His hate was so deeply ingrained.

"I don't know. If she does, I'm not sure what I'll do."

"You'll know at the time, and if not, just call me, okay? I got you."

"You do, you know. You really have me, Nat."

That's when Faith finally understood, or could finally believe, the good things she had wouldn't go away just because she went to college in a different state. What she'd found in Seattle was far too precious to ever be lost.

7

Carmen

"You'll want to talk to Captain Perez." Drew smiled, unaware of the warring emotions raging through Carmen.

If she were being honest, she'd hedged her bets that no one would still be here, not from that far back. Maybe she'd even hoped it would be true, because then there wouldn't be anything to face.

"Oh, wow, okay." She was back to staring again, wide eyed.

Enid stepped up and saved Carmen. Again. "Is the good captain available?"

"Yeah. He's in his office. Would you like me to see if he's free to talk?"

Carmen could see Drew piecing things together. How often did they have members of the public wander in and randomly ask if there was anyone still working here from nearly four decades ago?

Enid's firm grip shook Carmen from her existential crisis. "Sweetie, do you want to talk to him?"

Yes, she wanted to talk to him. But no, she wasn't feeling ready at all.

"Um..."

"Drew, dear, be a strapping hunk of a man and see if the captain has time to see us in the next half an hour. We're just going to take five."

Enid steered Carmen back outside. Taking advantage of the fresh air, Carmen sucked in several lungfuls.

"I wasn't expecting to find anyone," she whispered.

"Maybe it's meant to be, ya know what I mean? To be fair, kiddo, I was doubtful you'd get what you were looking for when we came here, but this Captain What's-His-Face was around back then."

"What if he doesn't remember?"

"And what if he does? You lose nothing by talking to him, and possibly gain everything."

"You're a wise old bird, Enid." Carmen grinned.

"Call me 'old' again and you'll be pulling my vagina-painted leg out of your ass!"

The light banter broke the tension. Carmen pulled Enid into a quick hug and then went back inside once more. She could do this.

"The captain can see you anytime. Just knock on that door there." Drew pointed. Carmen gave him a tight smile, her pulse thundering in her ears.

"Will you come in with me?" she asked Enid over her shoulder.

Enid grinned. "I was, regardless."

Giving three sharp knocks, Carmen waited with bated breath until a deep, gruff voice shouted, "Enter."

Pushing the door open, Carmen's eyes settled on the man sitting at the desk. Captain Perez was a formidable guy. Even sitting down, it was plain to see he was tall and muscular. He had a few streaks of silver running through his thick, black hair.

"Captain Perez, thank you for taking the time to see us," Carmen stuttered out.

"My pleasure, Ms..."

"Ruiz. Carmen."

"And I'm Enid Butcher, but you can call me anything you like."

Captain Perez laughed heartily. "Enid and Carmen. Take a seat." He gestured to the two free chairs in front of his desk. "How can I help?"

Taking her time sitting, Carmen straightened out her already immaculate short-sleeved top.

"I understand you were stationed here thirty-seven years ago."

Captain Perez looked pensive for a moment. "Correct. I was just a rookie back then."

Carmen nodded. "Do you...do you, by chance, remember a baby being left here?"

They all sat in silence as Captain Perez searched Carmen's face. Slowly, he nodded his head. "Wow. I never thought...you're the little one I found, huh?"

"Y-you found me?"

What were the odds?

"I did. It was my fourth shift. I remember it like it was yesterday. Well, finding a wriggling baby isn't something you forget."

Tears stung Carmen's eyes. Finally, there was someone who had a history with her who wasn't Mateo.

"I'm a little lost for words," Carmen replied honestly.

"Do you know her mother?" Enid asked, forgoing any patience.

Captain Perez shifted in his seat. "We couldn't be sure," he began. "It's not uncommon for babies to be left at a station. However, we had an idea where you'd come from."

Carmen swallowed thickly. "Anything you can tell me would really help."

"One of my younger brothers was dating a girl. Her best friend was pregnant. The family kept it a secret, but I know a few people who were aware. My younger brother and his girlfriend being two of the people who knew. I didn't know the girl. And she was a girl—fifteen, I think. A Spanish immigrant. Anyway, it was only after you were left at the station and the young girl vanished, we put two and two together. Her best friend had no idea where she'd gone and couldn't say for sure you were hers. No one came forward, so you ended up in care. I often wondered what happened to you."

A tidal wave of emotion threatened to drown Carmen where she sat. Her mother was just a child—probably a terrified one.

"Is her family still in the area?" she asked, her voice wobbling with every word.

"I'm sorry, I don't know. But I can direct you to someone who might know more. My brother and his girlfriend didn't last, but they're still good friends. I'm positive she wouldn't mind talking to you."

"Thank you," Carmen rasped out.

This was a lot. Enid filled the silence, allowing Carmen a few precious moments to process. It was only when she heard Enid ask the captain if all firefighters had big hoses that Carmen jumped back in, thanking the captain for his time, taking the address he'd written on a scrap of paper.

Back outside in the heat, Carmen held her head to the sun, simply letting the rays soak into her now-tanned skin. No way Mateo could moan about her pallor now!

"How you feeling?" Enid asked.

"Honestly, I'm not sure. That was more than I imagined I'd find out."

"Me, too! But now that you have found out, are you ready to hit the road and see this Lena woman?"

"Is that her name?" Carmen hadn't paid attention to the name or address, far too eager to leave the captain's office.

"Yup, Lena Marina. I mean, I thought my name was fucking terrible, but that takes the cake, right?"

Shaking her head laughing, Carmen began the walk back to the hotel. "I think I need a drink first."

"Yes, now you're talking. Piña coladas on me!" Enid sped past Carmen, pumping her arms to propel herself even faster.

In the end, the visit to Lena Marina didn't happen. One piña colada turned into two, which then turned into Carmen getting blind drunk with Enid egging her on every step of the way.

They overstayed their welcome at the hotel bar, opting to carry on the night elsewhere—a decision Carmen was currently regretting with every fiber of her being.

The sun peeked through a slit in the curtains, hitting her square in the eye. Groaning and rolling over, Carmen hit a wall. Not a literal one, more like a human-shaped one which was sharing her bed. Enid must have passed out with her.

Or not.

Carmen could see honey-gold hair splayed out over the pillow. What the hell had she done?

Snapping out of the alcohol-induced fog, Carmen sat bolt upright, staring down at the very naked woman sprawled next to her.

"Shit," she hissed, causing the unknown woman to groan and then wake.

"Oh, hey."

Carmen watched her stretch her hands above her head, yawning. "Morning," she managed to stutter.

"Is there coffee?" This person didn't seem in the least bit fazed by their situation.

"Um, yeah, over there," Carmen pointed stupidly. Her brain was on a go-slow-slash-impending-implosion track and there was no 'mission abort' button.

The woman, whose name was completely erased from Carmen's memories, stared at her for a second before sitting up, the covers slipping down to reveal her rather pert breast. Carmen looked away.

"Ah, I see," the woman began. "You don't remember this," she said, waving between them. Carmen felt her face heat.

Clearing her throat, Carmen shook her head. "I'm sorry, I don't. I had a lot to drink."

"Yeah, I figured that's how it would go. Which is why I wasn't surprised when you fell asleep halfway through fucking me."

If the Earth could end in this second, it would still be too late.

"And you kept calling me Molly."

Covering her face with both hands, Carmen let out a pathetic moan. "Oh, I'm so sorry," she mumbled.

"It's fine. I wasn't exactly sober. You don't need to be embarrassed. I never hook up with people I've only just met, and yet I'm here. I think that shows neither of us were making great choices last night. Plus, your friend, the old woman, was really trying to get you laid."

"Jesus Christ, Enid."

"Yeah, that's her name. She's wild."

"You have no idea," Carmen laughed. "So, no hard feelings..."

"Amy. And no, random lady, no hard feelings." The small wink helped break the tension completely, leading to both women chuckling.

"I'm Carmen."

"Carmen, of course. You told me, I think."

"How about that coffee?"

"Can I grab a shower? I feel so gross."

"Sure, knock yourself out. I'll get the coffee and some breakfast ordered."

Carmen scooted out of bed with the sheet wrapped securely around her. Not looking in Amy's direction in case she accidentally got an eyeful, Carmen exited the bedroom, closing the door behind. As soon as she heard the latch click, she breathed out a long, deep sigh.

"Enid," she growled.

Searching the area, Carmen found her clothes scattered across the floor. Shoving them on, she set off to chew out Enid. Rapping on her door, Carmen paced as she waited. It took Enid a good two minutes to answer. Her hair was wild, and she was wearing only underwear. Again.

"Morning, sunshine," the old menace yawned.

"What the hell did you get me into last night?" Carmen almost barked.

"Er, you wanna try that again," Enid shot back, arms crossing over her chest.

"Enid, I woke up with a stranger in my bed."

"And? How is that my fault?"

"The woman literally just told me you were trying to get me laid. I can't remember a fucking thing."

"I'll have you know; it was you who took us to that bar. It was you that ordered shots, and it was you who declared to the entire bar you were going to get over Molly Parsons, if it meant fucking every lesbian in the world. I mean, I have to say, Carmen, I didn't know you had it in you. You're so much fun."

"I..." Carmen wasn't going to be able to show her face in Santa Fe ever again.

"Relax. Look, you had an emotional day. Hell, you've had an emotional thirty-seven years. You were due a blowout. Plus, it's reassuring to hear you're still smitten with Molly."

"Smitten?"

"Oh, yeah. And I hate the fucking word smitten. But you, honey, are it! No one declares to a room full of strangers what you did, and not be totally smitten. Anyway, that's neither here nor there. We've got time to work on that. Right now, I need you to go back to your room. Shower, because you reek. Give the girl some food, send her on her way, and then come back. When you've done that, we'll talk more. Bye."

Carmen stood with Enid's door firmly closed in her face. The conversation had *not* gone to plan. Trudging back to her own room, Carmen found Amy sitting on the couch with a coffee she'd made herself.

"Sorry, I didn't know if you were coming back," she smiled.

"Shit, sorry. God, I'm not an asshole, although I'm clearly giving off those vibes, huh?"

"Nah, I know you're okay. You were sweet last night."

"I'm really sorry. I can't remember our evening together."

"It's cool, really. We were both wrecks. No harm, no foul. I'm going to scoot. It was nice to meet you, Carmen," Amy began. "I hope you work it out with Molly. I don't think you're done with each other just yet."

Once Amy was gone, Carmen sunk to the floor, pulling her knees up, wrapping her arms around them. "What a mess," she whispered to the room.

Enid was dressed by the time Carmen arrived back at her room, and far less confrontational than before. Enid was right. It wasn't her fault, or her responsibility, to keep Carmen in line. Maybe she *had* needed a bit of a blowout. Lord knows it had been building inside for a while.

"You calmed your tits yet?" Enid asked, her neon tracksuit causing Carmen to squint.

"Yeah, sorry about that."

Sitting at the coffee table, Enid tapped Carmen's knee. "Forget it. Okay, on to today's mission: Lena Marina."

"I'm ready when you are."

A lie. Carmen was nowhere near ready, but she doubted she ever would be, not for something like this.

Enid gave her a knee a squeeze. "Ready to rock and roll, sweetie."

They sat silently as Carmen drove them the fifteen minutes to Lena's address. She presumed Captain Perez may have forewarned Lena she could expect visitors.

The neighborhood was lovely. The Spanish-style houses all looked perfectly kept, and the gardens were immaculately landscaped. Carmen couldn't help wondering if this would have been her life had her mother found the support she needed.

Pulling up, Enid jumped out of the car before Carmen had brought the vehicle to a full stop.

"Jesus, Enid, wait."

So much for having a few moments to gather herself. Impossible when she had to wrangle Enid, who was already in Lena's yard and heading for her door.

Scrambling out, Carmen jogged after Enid, ready to chew her out again. Her impending tirade was cut short when the front door opened and a woman Carmen presumed was Lena stepped out, her hands grasping her own chest.

"My God, you look just like her."

The declaration stopped Carmen in her tracks. Lena was coming close to mid-fifties, if Carmen had to guess. She was short, red-haired, and definitely not Spanish. For some reason, Carmen presumed she would be.

"You must be Lena Marina," Enid said, thrusting her hand forward, breaking Lena from her shock.

"Hi, yes, sorry, I'm Lena."

"I'm Enid, and this is Carmen."

"Carmen," Lena replied in wonder, her eyes zipping back to the still very frozen Carmen.

Feeling Enid take her hand, she allowed herself to be guided up the step until she stood directly in front of Lena.

"Um... hello."

"I never thought I'd meet you," Lena began. Tears welled in her eyes. The air was thick with unspoken questions. Carmen couldn't form the words. There were simply too many.

Enid stepped past Lena, entering her house. "Any chance of a drink? It's hot as balls out here."

"Enid, for God's sake," Carmen began. A hand stopped her, resting on her arm.

"It's no problem. I want you to come in. We have a lot to talk about."

Lena's house was all white walls and stylish accessories. Carmen wouldn't be surprised if Lena was an artist. Enid was nowhere to be seen, which was a slight concern, but Carmen had bigger things to worry about. She was aware of Lena watching her as she slowly perused her surroundings.

"Your home is beautiful."

"Thank you. Come out to the patio."

Following behind, Carmen finally got a look at Enid, who had not only helped herself to lemonade, but was also making a fucking sandwich.

"I'm sorry about my friend," Carmen winced.

Lena laughed. "I don't care. Really. I'm just so happy you're here."

They sat at a cast iron table. A swimming pool glistened a few feet away. Lena's backyard was an oasis. Plants of all shapes and sizes took up every inch of the border. Sandstone pavers created a winding walkway. Carmen was sure it lead through the tropical maze. She wondered if it lit up at night.

They sat quietly for a while, letting the reality of the situation settle in. Carmen was about to face the biggest part of her history that had caused the most amount of pain.

"You knew her?" she asked quietly.

"Mariana was my best friend."

Mariana. Carmen felt the lump form in her throat as she repeated her mother's name in her mind.

"What happened?" Carmen heard the crack in her voice, but she couldn't stop the emotions swarming.

Lena reached over and took Carmen's hand. "She'd only just turned fifteen when she found out she was pregnant. Mariana never disclosed who your father was. I'm sorry."

Carmen squeezed her hand, keeping silent, willing Lena to continue.

"Mariana and her parents moved here from Andalusia. Her father was a wonderful cook. He had dreams of opening a restaurant—living the American dream, but it wasn't as easy as that. They struggled. Mariana began helping out at my father's store, trying to earn some money. That's how we met. She was only twelve, but my dad knew the family needed a hand. We were a close-knit community back then."

"So, you became close?"

"Instantly," Lena smiled. "I was only a year older than her. I helped her learn English, and we quickly became best friends. Our parents got to know each other, and things were looking up."

"Then what happened?"

"I...I let her down," Lena choked. "I got a boyfriend, and all but abandoned her. I was young and in love," Lena scoffed, rolling her eyes. "If I'd been a better friend, Mariana might have come to me sooner. I found out she was pregnant, but by that time, she was hardly speaking to me."

A flash of pain shot across Lena's face, causing Carmen's chest to tighten.

"When I finally summoned up the courage to apologize and offer my help, she'd already given birth and taken you to the fire station. I only found out because my then-boyfriend told me his brother had found a kid on his shift. It didn't take a genius to figure it out. I ran over to Mariana's house, but she was gone. Her parents were distraught. They had no idea she'd given you up."

"But they knew about me?"

"Yes. Mariana had little choice. It was hard, but they wanted to support her."

"So why?" Carmen sniffed.

"Why did she give you up? I've asked myself that question for the past thirty-seven years and the only conclusion I came to, was that she was frightened of becoming a new mom so early in her life—of the strain it would cause her family when they were already struggling.

I think she wanted to give you the best chance at life, and that meant giving you up."

8

Molly

What an unexpected start to their journey. Molly couldn't quite fathom it. She was almost certain it would be a huge mistake coming back, but after a few hours with Buck and June, her opinion changed. Seeing them, feeling their embrace, reminiscing, felt like a warm bath. It encompassed her and washed away some of the pain.

Buck and Molly dated for all of five seconds when they were young. Molly ended up introducing Buck to June a week later and, as they say, the rest was history. Buck and June fit.

After Alan cast her out, Molly assumed Buck and June shared the same attitude as her brother. Wrongly so, obviously, but at the time, Buck and her brother were very close. They were each other's shadows. In her emotional turmoil, it made sense to Molly that Buck and June would turn her away with the same vitriol Alan spewed.

Molly replayed their conversation from the afternoon. It was full of regrets and apologies from all parties. Buck knew he should have done more to look out for Molly. June had cried, begging for her forgiveness.

There was nothing to forgive in Molly's mind. Alan was the one who'd ruined their family; the only family they'd had. Buck and June were young, in love, and unsure how to react. It was a hard situation for them all.

They'd shared food and stories. All the time, Mateo kept his hand on the back of Molly's chair, smiling tightly, ready to strike at any slight he perceived against her.

There were none, but Molly loved Mateo for taking on the role of defender. He'd learned from the best. Molly knew for a fact that Carmen would have reacted the same way.

Toward the end of their time together, Mateo thawed considerably, especially after June called him out for being a little frosty. Mateo didn't look abashed when he admitted he was weary of them and protective of Molly. That led to another lengthy conversation about Mateo, Carmen, and Enid.

Molly was surprised how open Mateo was with Buck and June. He had no issues recounting his own traumatic history. Some of which made Molly wince and want to wrap him up in cotton balls, protecting the little boy inside that suffered such atrocities.

Molly's respect for Carmen quadrupled, too. Mateo described some of the ways she'd looked after them both, ranging from taking beatings for him to working herself ragged trying to provide him with food. The woman was a saint in Molly's eyes.

Those thoughts were what led her to message Carmen. They were back at the hotel. Faith was fast asleep. Mateo was taking an inexplicably long shower, leaving Molly to ruminate and reflect.

Molly 10:09 p.m.

Hi. How is everything in New Mexico? I'm thinking of you.

Blowing out a puff of air, Molly grabbed a bag of chips and started munching. She was far from hungry, but waiting to hear from Carmen made her a little nuts. And Molly liked to eat her feelings sometimes.

The quiet rumble of her phone made her heart spike.

Carmen 10:11 p.m.

Can I call?

Launching herself off the bed, sending chip crumbs everywhere, Molly grabbed her jacket and slipped out of the room.

A handful of seconds passed before Carmen's name flashed on the screen. Taking a calming breath, she answered. "Hey."

"Hey, I didn't wake you, did I?" Carmen's voice sounded scratchy. Had she been crying?

"No, you didn't. Are you alright?"

The line fell silent. Molly resisted the urge to ask if she was okay again. Carmen's ragged breath came through clearly. Molly understood she was collecting herself before answering.

"Today has been a lot. I...I wish you were here. I wish Mateo and Faith were, too."

Molly's heart broke at the longing in Carmen's voice. "I can be there tomorrow. Just say the word."

Carmen sobbed through the phone, and Molly had never felt so useless.

"No, it...it's okay. You guys have stuff to deal with. I'll be fine. It's just nice to hear your voice. Is Mateo there?"

"I can get him on the line if you'd like."

"Please."

Gritting her teeth, Molly blinked back the tears forming. Opening the door, she ran into Mateo, just exiting the bathroom. He saw the anguished look on Molly's face immediately.

"What's wrong?" he whispered, trying not to wake Faith.

Molly simply handed him the phone. "Take it outside."

Mateo took the phone and looked at the caller ID. He didn't wait a second longer before slipping out of the room, just as Molly had.

Spotting Faith's tablet on the bedside table, Molly made a decision. Carmen needed them. By the time Mateo reappeared, she's booked three flights to New Mexico for the following afternoon.

"How is she?"

Mateo's lip trembled, his head dropped, and his shoulders shook. Molly drew him in and held him as tightly as she could manage. Rustling behind them was the only indication that Faith was now awake. Her hands snaked around them both.

"What's happened?" she whispered, her voice sleepy.

"We're leaving tomorrow," Molly said into the huddle. Mateo pulled back, surveying her. "She needs us."

"Who? What?" Faith looked between them with a furrowed brow.

"Carmen," Mateo answered.

"Is she okay?" Faith's voice pitched up with anxiety.

"No, she's not."

"Didn't she give you any details?" Molly asked.

Mateo shook his head. "No. She just said it had been a really hard day and that she needed to hear our voices. I've never heard her sound so—"

"Broken," Molly supplied. Mateo nodded. "I've got us on a flight tomorrow afternoon. It was the only one available."

"Thank you," Mateo replied, pulling her back into another hug. "But what about you, and this?" he asked, gesturing to the room, presumably meaning Kentucky, in general.

"I'd like to visit my parents' graves in the morning before heading to the airport."

"We can do that," Faith said.

"Let's get some rest. It's going to be a long day tomorrow," Molly supplied.

They went about their nightly rituals. Faith collapsed back into her bed and promptly fell back asleep. Her soft snores brought a sad smile to Molly's face. Mateo was quiet. His face downcast, and his mind clearly elsewhere.

"Can I sleep with you tonight?" Molly asked. Faith was starfishing the hell out of the bed Molly was supposed to share with her niece, and if she were honest, she needed Mateo's strong body to curl into.

"Come here, *chica*," Mateo said, pulling back the covers inviting her to him. They lay together, taking in the silence.

"What do you think happened?" Molly finally whispered.

"I think she found something more than she was expecting," Mateo sighed.

"Something bad?"

"Not necessarily. I doubt she really believed she'd find many answers...if any at all."

"We need to message Enid and let her know."

"Yeah. But that can wait until the morning."

Molly squeezed Mateo tighter. "Are you okay?"

"No, Mol. I'm not. I hate hearing Carmen cry. It doesn't happen often, but when it does, it fucking kills me."

"I never want to hear her sound like that ever again," Molly admitted.

"Enid will support her until we arrive. I just wish she'd never felt she had to do this alone in the first place."

"But she needed to, Mateo. This was her journey, whether we think she was right or wrong to go it alone. Enid was her compromise."

"Compromise?"

"Yes. I think Carmen knew she couldn't do it entirely alone. It would've been too hard. Enid was the safer choice. They're close, but not like you and her."

"I should be the one with her, Molly. After everything—"

"You can't see it that way, Mateo. And when it counted, she called. She needed to speak to her brother. You will be there for the most important part. She's going to need you to be strong for her, like she would be for all of us."

"I'd do anything for her. She's my only family."

"And she knows that. Let her have this. Don't hold it against her that she left you out for the first part. Just stick by her in the second."

"Always."

"Good. Now let's sleep."

"Don't go feeling me up in the night," Mateo joked. They needed to lighten the atmosphere.

"I can't help it if I snuggle. I'm a tactile person," Molly scoffed, wrapping herself around him like a koala.

"Ugh, but you're going to make me smell like a girl," Mateo huffed.

Molly snickered quietly, "Sweetie, I hate to break it to you, but you always smell like a girl. And you know it."

Mateo grinned. "I know, and I pull it off better than most women."

Smiling, Molly tapped his chest. "That you do, honey."

Molly was tired to her bones. No matter how hard she tried, she couldn't shut off her brain. It wasn't just about Carmen, although she did take up a huge amount of Molly's thoughts during the night. Her sleepless night centered around the journey she was about to take to see her parents.

Guilt was a strange emotion. Her parents were dead, Molly understood that, but her brain still conjured up a well of guilt because she hadn't visited their plots in decades. Her parents wouldn't know, but that spiritual part of Molly wondered if that was really true.

Leaving Kentucky without a final farewell was the ultimate metaphorical slap to the face. It stung more than Alan's words at times. Molly missed her mom and dad daily, but it was a little easier when she had Alan. After he threw her to the curb, there was nothing to help her heartache...no one she could lean on.

The morning atmosphere between Mateo, Faith, and Molly had been somber. They packed up their belongings with minimal chatter. The whole time, Molly had those earlier thoughts running through her mind: she'd been alone for so long. She missed her parents. She should have come back sooner.

"Stop, Molly." Faith was by her side, gently rubbing her back. "Stop punishing yourself."

Faith was an intuitive kid, or maybe she simply identified with her aunt. Giving her niece a small smile, Molly took her bags to the car.

The cemetery was a five-minute drive—just enough time for Molly to prepare herself. Mateo put the radio on low but refrained from his usual Cher antics. Letting her head rest against the window, Molly gazed upon the sun-soaked landscape.

The parking lot was empty when they arrived. The trees were a deep green, and the grounds were perfectly sculpted. Molly followed the rows upon rows of headstones.

Four rows up, three in.

She'd memorized her parents' final resting place the second they were buried. In the early days, Alan had often found Molly sitting with her parents, quietly talking to their graves. He never got angry then. In fact, he encouraged her. After a while, though, Molly was heartsick when her parents never responded. How could they? They were dead. But Molly hoped their love for her would allow them to talk to her, no matter where they were.

Wiping a stray tear from her cheek, Molly slowly walked towards their spot. Faith and Mateo followed a little further behind. Molly found their headstones in immaculate condition. A fresh bouquet lay at the base of her mother's headstone.

"Hi, guys," Molly choked. Two sets of hands enclosed her shoulders, keeping her upright and strong. She patted their hands before dropping to her knees. "I'm sorry I didn't visit. I hope you can forgive me."

A gentle breeze brushed a lock of hair across Molly's face. Smiling, she let herself believe they heard her, and that was their forgiveness. But it wasn't just her that needed it.

"Can you forgive Alan, too?" she continued. "He's lost right now. I don't know if he'll ever find himself again. I hope so. Don't hate him," she all but whispered. "Send him your love so he can find his own."

A gentle whimper from behind told her Faith had succumbed to her own emotions.

Good, she needs to let it out.

Faith had confided in Molly that Alan had never let her visit her grandparents' grave.

"This is your granddaughter, Faith," Molly smiled. She turned, taking Faith's hand, pulling her down. Faith dropped to Molly's side, leaning heavily into her.

"She's a great young woman and you would be so proud. She's just like you, Mom. But definitely has your sense of humor, Dad," Molly chuckled. "Forgive Alan for what he did to her, too."

They sat silently, letting the sun warm their faces.

"This is Mateo," Molly spoke again. "He's a wonderful man. I think he's our guardian angel, along with his sister Carmen." Another soft breeze caressed Molly's face. "Maybe you sent them to us," she remarked, smiling. "If you did, thank you."

Lifting her head to the sky once more, Molly felt it: the weight lifting, the hurt easing, and her past slipping away. She was okay. Her life had love in it. She had people on her side and it was time to embrace that, instead of running. Sitting there in front of her parents was the key. She'd needed to say goodbye. She needed them to know she was going to be just fine.

"I will be back, I promise. It might not be for a little while. I need to be there for Carmen now. I need to show her... I need to be with her."

Sitting up on her knees, Molly kissed two fingers and then placed them on her mother's headstone first, then her father's.

Standing, she took Faith's hand, helping her up. They stood for a few more moments before turning to leave. The air simmered with tension as Molly brought her eyes up from the ground.

There before her was Alan. Her heart rate picked up, slamming in her chest, and her body tensed in recognition of the man standing before them. Her natural instinct was to don armor, ready for a fight, and ready to protect.

The last person she wanted to run into was the one standing twenty yards away, staring at her with familiar eyes. Molly's emotions were raw and painful, but they were healing, too. Alan might want a fight—a confrontation—but he wasn't going to get one. Molly didn't have anything left to say.

Looking at her brother, Molly noted his disheveled state. Alan had clearly let himself go. His usually styled hair was greasy and wild. He had a short beard, and his eyes were red.

Molly waited for the moment Alan would burst into profanities, but it never happened. His eyes shifted between Faith and Molly several times, and Molly swore she saw regret.

Mateo gently took Molly's and Faith's hands and hooked them through his crooked elbows, escorting them away. In the car, the trio let out a collective puff of air.

"Are you guys okay?" Mateo asked.

"I'm fine," Faith replied, her gaze locked onto her father, still standing there looking at them.

"Molly?"

Molly kept eye contact with her brother for a few more seconds. "I'm good. Ready to go."

Mateo started the car and backed out. Molly looked back one more time. Yeah, she was ready. The trip had fulfilled its purpose. Molly would never run again, especially not from love, and it might be premature, but she was sure Carmen would be the one to offer that to her.

Her mind wandered back, as it so often did, to Faith's comments all those weeks ago. Carmen deserved the same level of commitment as she was willing to give to others. Her trip home to Loretto may have only lasted a short time, but it was all that Molly needed to set herself on the path to contentment and what she hoped would be the love of her life.

Her heart said it was right. She felt her parents giving her their support. Maybe she was just full of emotions, and she was actually talking garbage. Well, until she was proven wrong, Molly Parsons would believe Carmen Ruiz was hers to keep. Now she just had to make sure the woman herself knew that, and help her in whatever way she could.

They still had a few hours until their flight, so Mateo suggested they stop for a bite to eat. None of them had much of an appetite at breakfast, so they'd skipped it.

Airline food sucked, so they agreed to stop at a diner. Mateo and Faith led the way inside.

"I'll be there in a second. Order me a sandwich," Molly called to them.

Mateo gave a thumbs up.

Fishing out her phone, Molly did the one thing that was way overdue. She called Ruth, her ex. Ruth had been deeply in love with Molly. They'd moved in together and Molly had left, unable to give Ruth what she needed.

Now Molly understood the pain she'd caused by running. Once she left Kentucky this time around, Molly planned to leave her baggage behind. So, to be fully rid of it, she needed to make amends.

Ruth answered after the third ring. "Molly?"

"Hey, Ruth. How are you?"

"Um...okay. You?"

Molly ran her palm across her face. "I'm sorry. That's what I am."

"O-okay?"

"I ran from you, Ruth, and I know I broke your heart. I-I've been working hard to face up to some stuff."

"Where are you?"

"Loretto."

Ruth let out an audible gasp. "Wow, that's...a lot."

"Yeah. But I needed to come back."

"And how are you feeling, really?"

Molly smiled. Ruth was such a lovely woman. "Honestly, I feel better. But I need you to know how sorry I am."

Ruth huffed. "Thanks. I don't really know what to say."

"You're not required to say anything. You don't have to forgive me. That's not why I called. I just wanted you to know that I know how I treated you. And I'll live with that."

"I don't want you to. You're forgiven, okay? I-I've met someone, and she's wonderful."

Molly's smile was the first genuine one in the past twenty-four hours. "I'm so happy for you, Ruth. So very happy."

Ruth's voice lowered. "And you?"

Molly grinned. "Yeah, I've met someone."

"Is it Carmen?"

Molly was momentarily taken aback. And then she remembered Ruth had met Faith, Carmen, Enid, and Mateo. But how did Ruth know Carmen and she were...whatever they were?

"Um..."

Ruth laughed. "I thought so. I don't know why, but I could see it when she visited."

"We hadn't even met then," Molly protested, yet remained curious.

"Yeah, I know. I can't explain it. I just kinda knew she'd be the one."

Molly swallowed hard. "That's yet to be decided, but I'm working on it."

"Work hard and don't let her go, Molly. Don't run."

"I have no intentions of it," Molly stated. "None, whatsoever."

9

Faith

It felt as if Faith's life was one big contradiction. Or at least it swung from one extreme to the other. On the one hand, she felt completely settled in life, and love. But on the other, everything felt completely unstable, like her life could blow up at any moment.

How was that possible? Her personal life *was* as settled as it had ever been. She had a wonderful girlfriend, an amazing found family, and the opportunity to go to college. She had a career to work towards and an exciting future to carve out.

However, life felt chaotic because those wonderful people, the aforementioned family, were struggling. Molly had to confront her past, which was also Faith's, to some degree.

Then there was Carmen: Faith's defender, her rock, who seemed solid on the outside, but was finding things so hard on the inside, and Faith hadn't noticed...not quickly enough, anyway.

Faith was coming to understand what being a part of a loving family involved. For so long, she'd only looked out for herself, out of necessity, but now there were other people to think of—to help. And sometimes she didn't know what to do with all the feelings that reality elicited.

While Faith was getting everything she wanted and concentrating on that, her people were suffering and it made her feel like garbage. She felt like there was a constant in her own head and heart. She understood she had the right to think of herself and her needs, and her family would encourage that, but how could that be the right thing to do? Being selfish like that; it wasn't right.

So, as she sat in the back of the car while Mateo drove them to the airport, Faith promised herself and whoever else could hear: she would do better. That's the reason she wanted to be a counselor, after all—to help. And who better to start with than the people that had given her a second chance at life?

Mateo was extremely quiet during the drive and had been all day. It didn't take a genius to understand how worried he was about Carmen. Faith just wished she knew how to make him feel better. Maybe letting him sit with his feelings was the best thing, though.

Both Carmen and Mateo had told Faith, on many occasions, she should always feel her feelings. It was her body's way of coping and healing, but Faith knew just how hard doing that could be sometimes.

What they hadn't said was how it made the people watching it feel useless. Had Carmen and Mateo felt as bad watching Faith cry over her parents as she was feeling now, watching them? Had they felt as useless?

Ugh, this wasn't the time. Faith needed to be strong. She'd messaged Enid, checking in, and told her Mateo was struggling and they'd had an emotional trip to Kentucky. Maybe she shouldn't have let anything slip about their travels, but Faith hated secrets and she was sure the way to get through all of this was to lean on each other.

Molly and Carmen were similar in a way. They had to do things by themselves, although Carmen was clearly the more stubborn one. Faith wondered how well Molly would have coped if she hadn't had Mateo and Faith with her.

Carmen had Enid, but it wasn't the same as having a full wall of support. And that's what they were to each other: bricks that built a solid wall of unconditional love and understanding. It would be Faith's mission to get everyone to understand that concept, so this never happened again.

It really was a one-for-all and all-for-one kinda deal. Maybe she could get them T-shirts printed with the slogan, so they never forgot.

"We're here," Mateo called, dragging Faith's attention back to the car. She waited outside the rental office as Mateo and Molly dealt with returning the vehicle. Watching the planes take off in the distance, Faith took in a few deep breaths.

Sending a quick message to Nathalie, updating her of their whereabouts and plans, made Faith eager to get going. Flying was awful, but she'd fly to the moon if it meant she could be there for Carmen. However, that in itself was up in the air.

Enid told Faith she'd not mentioned their plans to Carmen, worried it would be even more upsetting. Carmen seemed to be determined to keep them all at arm's length. So what would happen when they got there and Carmen blew up? How could Faith offer Carmen support?

Hmm, something to ponder while flying in the metal death trap.

They'd cut it close, timing wise, when they finally made it to the correct terminal. So close, they'd almost walked straight onto the plane. Molly offered Faith the window seat again, choosing to sit in between her and Mateo.

Oddly, looking out the window seemed to help calm Faith's nerves a little. Why did staring down from thousands of feet up, help Faith feel better about being up thousands of feet? Weird. Well, whatever worked, right?

"Want some pretzels?" Mateo asked, passing over a small bag. Another bag was already open on his lap... and a bag of chips... oh, some jerky, too.

"Where did you get all that from?" The in-flight service wouldn't begin for ages. They had seven hours to get through and they hadn't even taken off yet.

"Stocked up while you guys peed. I feel like it's a carbs kind of day," Mateo answered seriously.

Yeah, he was really worried. Mateo was a stickler for low carbs. He only consumed them when feeling "a little PMS-y." Mateo claimed to emotionally sync up with Carmen and Faith. Of course, that earned the man having things thrown at him. Carmen had followed up by shouting a string of Spanish expletives at him—for nearly half an hour.

Faith wondered if Molly knew about Mateo's sensitivity to the plight of women's menstrual cycles. A laugh burst from her mouth unexpectedly, causing Molly and Mateo to raise their eyebrows at her.

"What was that for?" Molly asked, smiling.

Faith shook her head, still laughing. "Hang on," she spluttered. By the time she got herself under control, Mateo and Molly were laughing too, still unclear of what had set Faith off.

Other people were now becoming curious as the trio howled with laughter. It was only after the flight attendant asked them politely to keep it down so everyone could hear the security announcement, they calmed down.

"What *was* that?" Mateo chuckled.

"That was a release," Molly smiled. Faith also smiled and knew her aunt was right. Sure, the memory was funny, but not *that* funny. They'd needed a damn good laugh to offset some of the pressure they'd been under.

"Sorry, that was my fault," Faith grinned. "I just remembered something."

"What?" Mateo asked, stuffing a handful of pretzels into his mouth.

"The time you told Carmen and me you always synced with our cycles."

"You said what?" Molly asked, a little louder than expected. Mateo's hand paused halfway to his mouth, his eyes wide, staring at Molly.

"What? It's true. Men can have emotional cycles too!" He said nervously.

"Carmen shouted at him in Spanish for like half an hour," Faith added.

"Yeah, she did," Mateo muttered.

"What did she say?" Molly giggled.

"Something along the lines of him just being another male taking a woman's experience and making it all about him," Faith supplied, grinning.

"Oh, damn," Molly laughed.

"Thanks for sharing, Faith," Mateo grumbled, shoving more carb-filled snacks into his mouth.

"You're welcome. And you deserved it."

"I'd say so," Molly added.

"Okay, less of picking on the queen, ladies. I'm going to get some beauty sleep." Snapping the eye mask over his face, Mateo let out a little huff of indignation, making several people who'd clearly been listening in on the conversation snicker.

Faith held Molly's hand until the plane was airborne and had finished turning. "I don't know how people do this regularly," she commented, looking through the cloudless sky to the ground below.

"I suppose the more exposure you get, the easier it becomes. I haven't flown for a long time."

Faith continued to look out the little window, gathering her spinning thoughts. "It was weird seeing him." Faith knew her aunt would know who she was referring to.

"Yeah," Molly sighed. "I wasn't expecting to see him, either."

"He looked rough." Faith turned to Molly. "What do you think happened?"

"I think he lost his family, sweetie."

Faith shook her head. "That doesn't make sense. He spent most of my life doing everything in his power to show us how much he hated us."

Molly took Faith's now-trembling hand again. Seeing her father in the cemetery had shaken Faith more than she'd like to admit. His appearance had shocked her more than anything. Faith couldn't recall a time in her life when Alan Parsons looked unclean and disheveled.

"He didn't, and doesn't, hate you. He hates himself," Molly replied quietly.

"So, what? Now Mom has left, he's falling apart?"

Molly shifted in her seat. "According to the Carters, his beloved pastor is currently sitting in a jail cell awaiting trial."

Faith felt her eyes almost bug out of her head. "What for?"

"For something I can't even bring myself to repeat. Let's just say that man has torn a lot of lives apart."

"Oh, no." Faith could guess what crime Molly was alluding to. She closed her eyes tight, praying for the first time in a long time, for the victims of that evil man. Sending them love and light wasn't much, but it was all she could do.

"I think Alan's world has come crashing down, and he's finally questioning himself and the decisions he's made."

"Y-you don't think Dad was involved, do you?"

"No," Molly answered immediately. "No chance. I think he was probably just as shocked as the rest of the congregation. Probably more so, considering he took the pastor's word as law most times."

"Was it..."

"Boys," Molly whispered.

"Dear God."

"Yes, so you can imagine what that information was like for him to hear. Of course, your mom finally leaving will add to his distress, and the fact you got away and are now happy. I'd expect he's doing a lot of soul searching."

"Do you think he might come around? Want to see us again?"

Molly shrugged. "Maybe. But it's not just *his* decision. He's caused a lot of pain. He doesn't *get* to decide if he gets another chance."

"Wow, I thought you'd be the first to want to talk to him."

Molly nodded. "I spent so long hoping. But now I know it's up to him to figure his shit out and for us to figure out ours. I've spent too many years hanging onto the past. I need to move forward, and right now, that doesn't include my brother, even if he is sorry."

Faith nibbled her bottom lip. She had meant what she'd said to her parents at the ranch all those weeks ago. She didn't hate them, and the door would always be open, but Molly had a point: her father didn't get to dictate her life anymore, and she was *not* in a place to welcome him with open arms, if that might be what he even wanted at some point.

Molly tucked a piece of hair behind Faith's ear. "Get some sleep, honey. All of this will still be here in a few hours," Molly suggested.

"Yeah, okay."

Faith liked Santa Fe. Admittedly, she'd only seen it from the back of the car so far, but that didn't matter. The Spanish influence was lovely. All those beautiful buildings. And the fact Carmen was born here added an extra bit of awesomeness.

"Wow, this is one swanky hotel," Molly commented from the driver's seat.

"Our girl sure knows how to live it up, huh?" Mateo replied, looking out the window.

"Yeah. Our girl does," Molly mumbled. Faith didn't miss the blush plastered on her aunt's face. "Okay, you guys get out. I'll take the car to the parking lot."

Mateo laughed. "*Chica*, they have a private valet here."

"Oh," Molly laughed. "Cool."

Once the car was handed off, they headed into the reception area to check in. As they'd arranged, Enid was waiting for them. She gave them a wide smile.

"Hello, you lovely people. Hi, Mateo."

"Hey!" Mateo protested, while everyone else laughed. "You could hurt a girl's feelings talking like that."

"Please. You wax ninety percent of your body. You've got a thick skin."

Faith continued to laugh into the strong hug Enid gave her. "Hey sweetie," Enid whispered against her cheek.

"I've missed you," Faith admitted.

"We're all together now."

Maybe Enid would be the person to help explain that concept to the Ruizes and Molly. Staying together was always the answer.

"You know, I don't wax *everything*," Mateo supplied.

"Yes, you do. Now, shall we get this shitshow on the road?"

"What's the plan?" Molly asked. "I don't want Carmen to feel backed into a corner. Not after she told us not to come."

"I was thinking about that. Maybe just one of you going up would be best for now. The other two can go to my room and freshen up."

"Good idea," Molly began. "Faith and I will take your room."

"No," Mateo interjected.

"No?"

Faith watched in anticipation, still unsure where she fit in to helping Carmen. "No, Mol. Faith and I will take Enid's room."

"Mateo—"

"It's the right thing, Molly. I'm doing what you said. I'm looking out for her, and the best way to do that right now, is for her to see you."

"Mateo, she'll want to see her brother!"

"Maybe, but the person she *needs* to see is you. Please trust me, Molly."

Molly nodded. "Okay, then."

"Mateo, you go up. I'm going to grab a drink from the bar with Faith."

"Don't get her drunk, she's underage. I do *not* want to get thrown out of the hotel," Molly shot with a grin, knowing full well the scenario was entirely possible, because Enid would do whatever she wanted, although Faith was sensible and wouldn't put them in any danger of being evicted.

"No promises. We're two wild ladies," Enid replied. "Oh, and Mateo, don't touch my dental dams."

They all stood in silence, letting Enid's comment land.

"I-I don't even want to know," Mateo grimaced. "I'm going to take a shower. Molly, call if you need me."

"Hold on numbnuts, you need the room keys." Enid handed two keys over. "Okay, missy, let's go."

Enid practically carried Faith to the bar. "In a rush?" Faith giggled.

"Ready for a drink, love?" Enid asked, flagging down the bartender. "It's been rough."

"Is Carmen really bad?"

"No, not bad. She's in shock and not processing."

"What did you find?"

Enid puffed out her cheeks. "We went to the fire station where she was left. I don't think she really expected to find out much. Well, she did. She met the man who found her. He gave her a brief recount of what happened, and then gave her the name of a woman who was his brother's ex-girlfriend and Carmen's mom's best friend, at the time. We went to see her."

"Oh, wow, yeah, that's a lot."

"I'll let her tell you the rest. But as you can imagine, it was overwhelming. When we got back, she just sort of broke down. I'm so glad you all are here now."

"Molly will help."

"Oh, yes. But she needs you all, Faith."

"I'm not sure what I can do."

"Just being here is a start. Carmen needs her people. She needs that emotional barrier."

Faith smiled. "I thought that earlier. We're like each other's support bricks."

"Bricks?"

"Yeah. Together, we build a protective wall."

Enid cocked her head. "You're a fucking smart kid!"

"Piña colada, Enid?" the bartender—who clearly knew Enid well—asked.

"Yes, and a virgin one for the youngster."

"You're a regular," Faith laughed.

"I'm on vacation. Now, tell me about you. What's happening in your life, honey?"

Taking a long sip of her newly deposited drink, Faith savored the flavor, and the familiarity of Enid.

"I'm applying for college. In California."

She wasn't expecting the slap on the back and Enid cheering loudly.

"Fantastic!"

Hitting her chest to try and clear the piña colada making its way down her esophagus, Faith smiled. "I'm excited."

"Wanna tell that to your face?"

"I *am* excited."

"But?"

Faith rolled her eyes. "It's stupid."

"Nothing about you is stupid, so spit it out."

"How can I get excited about leaving when Carmen and Molly are going through a lot of stuff?"

"Um, because their stuff isn't for you to fix. Your love and support doesn't stop the second you leave the state."

"No, but—"

"But nothing. And let's be honest, those two are going to get each other through their crap, probably with a lot of sex added in."

Faith slammed her hands over her ears. "No, Enid! Don't say that."

"Why? It's true! Anyhow, those poor fuckers have had to put up with you and Nathalie humping like rabbits. I say it's time for some payback."

Faith's face flamed hotter than the sun. "Oh my God," she moaned into her hands.

"All that aside, I'm very proud of you, Faith."

It amazed Faith how Enid could go from one extreme to the other. One minute she was embarrassing as all hell, and a split second later she said something that made Faith choke up.

"Thank you."

"Don't thank me. Just stop pouting about your choice."

"Alright," Faith agreed. Maybe she should stop fretting. After all, Carmen and Molly would likely get together if they weren't dumb about what was happening between them. And if they did, they'd help each other out. Plus, Mateo wouldn't be far away. Nathalie was supportive of Faith's choice. There really wasn't a valid reason not to get pumped about going; only Faith's thoughts, and deep down, she knew they stemmed from insecurity.

"Oh, you want to see something cool?" Enid suddenly said, clapping her hands in delight.

"Sure," Faith laughed. That was until Enid hopped off the bar stool and dropped her pants.

"Look, I've got a vagina leg!"

10

Carmen

The sun was slowly setting, not that it made a difference. Carmen sat staring at the notepad laying on the table in front of her, full of scribbled notes detailing as much information as she could remember—which wasn't a lot. Lena's reminiscing had thrown Carmen for a loop; rendered her numb. There was only so much her brain could cope with.

It was after Lena laid a photo of a young Mariana in her palm, that Carmen mentally checked out. Her mind had been completely overwhelmed as she stared down into familiar eyes, because it was like looking in a mirror, although Mariana seemed a little shorter. Carmen had been a little more gangly at fourteen.

Only after she and Enid arrived back at the hotel did Carmen realize Lena had continued to talk, while she stared hopelessly at the picture. Lena had given as much information as possible. But it was only later that the information seeped in. That's why she'd reached for the hotel's embossed pad and started writing. She needed to make sure she got everything down.

Enid had put a glass of water on the table and left, periodically checking in with either a snack or more water. Carmen knew she was probably worrying her friend, but she couldn't stop writing. When she finally ran out of things to write down, Carmen simply laid the pad on the table and stared out over Santa Fe. Enid continued to check in every so often but allowed Carmen her space.

It was now more than twenty-four hours since Carmen learned about her mother, Mariana Hernandez. The name scrolled on a constant loop through her head. But it wasn't only her mother's name that lingered in her mind, she had the unfamiliar feeling of having a true surname. Carmen Hernandez.

Of course, her mother probably wouldn't have named her Carmen in the first place. What name would Mariana have picked? Would she want to be found? Did *Carmen* want to find her?

The only reprieve she'd had from her spiraling thoughts was the emotional phone call with Molly and Mateo. Hearing Molly's voice was the one thing that had penetrated Carmen's numbness. As soon as that soft voice filtered through the phone, Carmen cracked. All the pent-up stress, anxiety, and shock came spilling out.

She'd cried to Mateo without revealing the truth behind her tears. That would've been a step too far. Carmen had to keep some distance—some protection. If she let them in now, how would she ever stay strong for them? And that was her job, her role, in their thrown together family.

Enid had disappeared again, presumably trying to get away from the crazy woman having an existential crisis in her hotel room. No, that wasn't fair. Enid wouldn't think something like that. Carmen was just exhausted and allowing herself to get a little maudlin with her thoughts.

There was a quiet knock on the door. Carmen glanced at the time, wondering if she'd missed turndown service or something. It was early evening, so it was unlikely to be a hotel employee.

She sat quietly, hoping whoever it was would just leave, but a second knock, and then a third, told her that wasn't going to happen.

Unfolding herself from the chair, Carmen groaned as her body protested about being folded into one position for far too long. Shuffling towards the door, she quickly looked down at herself: baggy sweats and an old tank top. Mateo would be pissed. The thought caused a ghost of a smile to appear. Rubbing her eyes, Carmen opened the door and froze.

"Hi," Molly said quietly. Molly, as in Molly Parsons, was here, standing in Carmen's hotel doorway.

"M-molly, what?"

"We took an afternoon flight. Please don't be mad."

Mad? Carmen felt the wave of relief wash over her and before she could prepare either of them, her arms wrapped around Molly and tears flowed. Her body shook with sobs as she clung to her.

Two strong arms tightly held her back, adding a gentle sway as Molly whispered calming words in her ear. When Carmen pulled back, Molly cupped her face. "Let's go inside and talk."

Carmen nodded and slunk back to her chair that probably had a permanent ass print in it by now. Molly deposited her bag by the door and joined Carmen at the table. She peered quickly at the notepad but didn't comment.

"I can't believe you came," Carmen hiccupped. She must look like an utter mess.

"We had to, sweetie."

"We?"

"Yeah, Mateo and Faith are here, too. Mateo's grabbing a shower and Faith was kidnapped by Enid."

"I... But..."

"Carmen, there wasn't a scenario where we *wouldn't* come to you. Please don't ask us to leave."

Sighing, Carmen shook her head. "I won't."

"Can you talk about it yet?"

Swallowing down another round of tears that were trying to break free, Carmen closed her eyes. "I don't know why I'm reacting like this," she began. "I came here looking for answers, Molly, and now that I have some, I feel completely lost."

Molly shifted her chair closer, wrapping her hands around Carmen's clenched fists. "Tell me what answers you found."

"We found my mother's best friend. And the man who found me, Captain Perez. He was just a young rookie back then." Molly remained quiet and Carmen took a steadying breath. "We visited the best friend. Her name is Lena Marina."

"I bet Enid had an opinion on that," Molly chuckled softly, bringing a genuine smile to Carmen's face.

"Yes. Every time she spoke to the woman, she said her full name," Carmen laughed quietly.

Molly grinned. "How did Lena react to that?"

"I think she found Enid so intriguing, she was okay with it."

They smiled at each other, but Molly made no more comments.

"Lena told me a lot about my mother. She even showed me a picture. Do you want to see?"

"I'd love to."

Carmen reached into her sweatpants pocket and withdrew the picture that felt as if it had been burning a hole in the fabric since Carmen put it in there, unable to stare at Mariana any longer.

Handing the picture over, Carmen sat back and studied Molly's reaction. Slowly, Molly unfolded the photograph and looked. Her eyes crinkled with delight.

"She's beautiful. And young." Molly remarked.

"She was 14 in that picture. Lena said it was taken a few months before she found out she was pregnant."

"Fourteen," Molly gasped.

"Yeah. Fifteen when she had me."

Carmen watched Molly continue to regard the photo of her mother.

"You look just like her. Is that okay to say?"

Carmen gave a small smile. "Yeah, it's fine. Just surreal, I guess."

"Did Lena tell you what happened, you know, after?"

"After she left me?" Carmen coughed, trying to mask the break in her voice. "She disappeared. Even her parents didn't know where she'd gone. I guess she was just a scared kid. I have no idea what I would've done in her position."

"It's hard to comprehend. She was still a child. Do you know who your father is?"

Carmen shook her head. "Mariana never said. But...I might be able to find out."

"How?"

"After Lena gave me that," Carmen said, tipping her head towards the picture, "I sort of zoned out. That's why I have a notepad full of crazy writing. At the time I couldn't take in anything Lena was saying, but when we got back here, it came rushing back and I had to write it down."

"And what did you remember?"

"Mariana contacted her about six years ago."

"Oh, wow."

"Yeah. She left a forwarding address and phone number."

"And have you thought about doing something with that info?"

"It's all I've thought about," Carmen laughed.

"Sorry, that was stupid to ask, huh?"

"Nothing you say is stupid, Molly." Carmen diverted her eyes, suddenly feeling shy. "I can't believe you're here," she breathed.

"I needed to see you," Molly admitted quietly. That charge Carmen often felt around Molly, was in the air again.

Not sure how to continue, Carmen decided to change the subject. She wasn't in a good frame of mind to even contemplate what Molly's words really meant. "So, how's Seattle?"

"Oh, yeah fine, but, um…well, we didn't come from Seattle."

"You guys went away?" That stung a little.

"I decided to go back to Kentucky."

Carmen sat up straight in her chair. "You went back? Why?"

Okay, that sounded a little rude. Molly didn't owe Carmen an explanation.

"Can we talk about it later? I'm not here to talk about me."

"Are you okay? Will you just tell me that?"

"I'm better than okay. I'm finally where I'm meant to be." Molly's gaze remained focused and unwavering. Carmen felt a little heat creep up her neck.

"G-good. That's good."

A rap on the door saved both of them from any more heavy statements or intense moments. Carmen wasn't sure she could handle Molly saying something else that almost sounded like a declaration of… more.

She wasn't imagining it. Carmen felt the change in Molly. She saw the look on her face. They were heading into fresh territory, and that was fine with her.

Mateo tackled her the second the door opened. Carmen's feet left the ground as he scooped her up and squeezed tightly. She felt his silent tears on her shoulder but remained mute, just holding her brother while they reconnected.

It was going to be an emotional day, and Carmen didn't relish the idea she'd have to repeat herself several times, but she would do it anyway.

Mateo listened intently, holding her hand as she filled him in on the visit with Lena. He took it all in without offering an opinion. That would come later, Carmen knew, once he'd had time to process. They'd had a shot of bourbon after Carmen finished retelling the story, but it wasn't enough.

The hotel room was starting to feel claustrophobic, so Molly suggested they join Enid and Faith at the bar. A cloud of uncertainty lingered over the group as they got seated in the hotel restaurant. Enid needed some food to soak up her cocktails. Carmen took several minutes to hug Faith and have a quick chat with her, but it was nothing as heavy as her conversations with Mateo and Molly. That could wait for now.

They perused the menu and Faith filled Carmen in on her decision to apply to college, which Carmen was thrilled to hear. It didn't go unnoticed how the younger Parsons chose her words carefully when referring to their recent trip.

"It's lovely to have the gang back together," Enid remarked when Faith finished talking. If Carmen had to guess, Enid was on her third or fourth piña colada. The older woman wore a rosy glow on both cheeks.

"It is," Carmen agreed. "Thank you...for coming even when I—"

"Wouldn't be anywhere else," Mateo spoke, his face still buried in the menu. "I'm starving."

"Enid dropped her pants in the bar," Faith chirped.

All eyes shifted to Enid, happily munching on a wedge of pineapple, her eyes focused on a man at the bar probably twenty years her junior. After weeks with Enid, Carmen recognized the look—Enid was on the prowl.

"Enid, why did you drop your pants?"

"Hmm?" Enid replied, her eyes snapping back to the group. "Sorry, sweetie, I was just eyeing up my dessert," she grinned. Faith chuckled, Molly outright laughed, and the Ruizes rolled their eyes.

Carmen cleared her throat. "I asked why you dropped your pants in the bar."

"Oh, right! I wanted to show Faith my leg. Oh shit, I haven't shown it off to Molly or Mateo. Hold on." Enid pushed back in her chair and stood. Her fingers went to the waistband of her pants.

"No!" a collective cry rang out, causing many of the restaurant's patrons to stop eating and look towards the unruly group.

Enid huffed and sat down. "Fine, later then. It's brilliant. Carmen will agree because it's got her vagina on it."

"No! It has not!" Carmen almost shouted. "*Por favor*, stop announcing that!"

"Okay, someone needs to explain," Mateo said, his eyebrows collecting in his hairline. Molly smirked, already aware of Enid's new fashion statement.

Carmen scrubbed her face. "Enid met a woman in Florida. She was an artist or something."

"Hippie," Enid interjected.

"Yes, hippie. Anyway, they got high. A lot," Carmen punctuated. "It got all 'feminist rights' and 'down with the man.' The next thing I knew, she was sporting a vagina leg."

"When you say 'vagina leg'..." Mateo queried.

"The hippy drew a bunch of different vaginas on her prosthetic. Apparently, one represents mine. It does not! I'd like that on the record."

"Oh my God, Enid!" Molly cackled. "I *definitely* want to see the leg now."

Carmen watched Molly go beet red when she realized what she'd just insinuated. And then, to make it worse, she tried to explain herself while acting all flustered and adorable.

"I don't mean because it has your...or not yours exactly. Not that I haven't... Just the leg, because...it's funny." The last two words came out in an embarrassed whisper.

Mateo hid behind his glass of water, sniggering. Faith patted her aunt on the shoulder. Her lips rolled in, trying to stop a laugh from escaping. Of course, Enid got straight to the point. "Oh, Molly, what the fuck was that?"

Carmen couldn't hold back. The laugh she released was from deep inside. It echoed around the quiet restaurant. Soon, three other bellowing laughs joined in as Molly hid her head in both hands. Even the tips of Molly's ears were a deep red.

"You guys are assholes," Molly moaned as their laughter continued. Only when an amused-looking server approached, mini notebook in hand, did they curb the playful mockery.

"I think we need some more of these," Enid called to the server, pointing to her glass. No one argued. They placed their food orders and settled back into easy conversation.

Now and then, Carmen caught herself looking at Molly for a beat too long. It was just so good to see her. And Molly did look good. She was a little pale, but that was to be expected. Seattle wasn't exactly known for giving people a good suntan.

Carmen had so many questions. How long would Molly stay in Seattle? Would she miss California? Why did

Carmen miss California so much? She kept her questions to herself as the group ate, happy to have a reprieve from the stress and drama.

Enid was way past tipsy by the time the meal finished. When she began catcalling the guy at the bar, Carmen called it a night. "Okay, Mrs. Butcher, you're cut off."

"Pffft, I'm fine," Enid slurred.

"Sure," Carmen rebutted, taking Enid by the shoulders, stopping the woman from losing her balance due to her prosthetic.

"Er, where are we all sleeping?" Faith asked from behind the group.

Carmen peered over her shoulder. "Oh, yeah, you guys need a bed."

"Mateo and Faith are in with me!" Enid announced.

"It makes sense," Mateo interjected. "Molly's stuff is already in your room."

Carmen attempted to give her brother a subtle glare, earning a wry grin in return.

"I can sleep on the couch," Molly called. "It's big enough."

"Nonsense," Enid cut in. "Carmen needs a warm body to help her get through such troubling times."

Carmen kinda hated them all in that specific moment, because now she was picturing Molly's body, and it wasn't like Carmen didn't know what a sublime body Molly had.

Great, now she was having flashbacks to the truck. Oh, the delicious noises Molly had made...

"Hey, Carmen, head in the game. You nearly walked me into that plant," Enid shot.

Carmen blinked rapidly, coming back to the present. "Right," she coughed. "Sorry, come on, let's get to the rooms."

With Enid safe in Mateo and Faith's care, Carmen led Molly down the corridor to her room. Taking a deep breath, Carmen closed the door and went about her usual routine. Molly seemed happy enough to leave Carmen to it, opting to unload her bag and refold some clothes.

In the bathroom, Carmen showered and brushed her teeth as usual, but her body was all too aware of Molly being in the other room. Chastising herself repeatedly, she called for Molly to let her know the bathroom was now free.

Settling under the sheets, Carmen did her best to calm her thoughts. It shouldn't bother her so much that Molly was here, right? Before leaving Seattle, Carmen knew Molly was important. She was someone special, but maybe

Carmen hadn't quite admitted just how important Molly was.

Even after a tumultuous few days, Molly's mere proximity made everything seem so irrelevant. It didn't matter that Carmen knew where her mother lived or that she didn't know how to process that information, because right now, Molly Parsons was just a few feet away... Naked.

Closing her eyes, Carmen listened to Molly come out of the bathroom and close the door. She heard Molly settle on the couch, which had a blanket on the back.

And then she heard her own heart beat a little louder at the thought of sharing a bed with Molly. That was what she wanted—no, needed. Carmen *needed* Molly close. She needed Molly to make things better.

"Molly?"

"Yeah?"

"Would...would you share my bed?"

A few moments of silence descended, before Carmen heard soft padding across the carpet. She felt the sheets shift and the cool air reach her legs. She smelled Molly's shampoo and saw her outline settle on the pillow next to her.

"Just tell me what you need, Carmen."

"Will you hold me?"

Carmen rolled her back to Molly. A warm arm snaked around her waist and Molly's breath skimmed across Carmen's neck.

Yes, Molly Parsons was the most important person.

11

Molly

Molly lay with Carmen curled into her body. They fit so perfectly. Even with Carmen's taller body, everything slotted together, like they were meant to be in this very position all the time. She'd treat this precious moment for what it was—a gift. Carmen Ruiz had let down her defenses and allowed herself to be completely vulnerable. It was something Molly knew she struggled to do, even with Mateo.

Yes, Molly was taken aback when Carmen asked to share a bed, but she didn't utter a word. If the one thing she could offer Carmen was a little comfort, then that was what she'd do. It quickly became clear that Molly would do almost anything for Carmen, a thought that at one time would have caused a panic—but not now. If anything, it cemented Molly's belief that she was exactly where she was supposed to be at that moment.

The clouds of her past were clearing. A new excitement bubbled under the surface of her skin. The idea of settling down in one place and building something that would last, now outweighed her old feeling of panic. Molly's fight-or-flight mode had been switched on for so long, she often wondered if it was even possible for her to stop long enough to see the benefit of staying still.

But then Carmen Ruiz turned up and flipped the switch. It was this strong, beautiful Hispanic woman who finally got Molly to slow down and believe in the possibility of a future that included stability and trust; of planting roots, and knowing they'd grow into something beautiful and permanent.

Now Molly would return the favor. She'd show Carmen what it was like to be loved. If that had to be done as a friend while Carmen worked through her past, so be it. Molly would wait. She'd prove to be the person Carmen could trust with all of her: past, present, and future.

In her musings, Molly hadn't realized her lips had gravitated to Carmen's neck. Inhaling deeply, she breathed in Carmen's addictive scent. She was helpless to stop herself. Carmen was simply intoxicating.

Molly's only hope of getting out of this enticing, but unsure, situation, was for Carmen to have fallen asleep due to exhaustion, unaware of the light whisper of Molly's lips on her skin.

Carmen's ragged breath proved that theory unlikely, and Molly lost her damn mind. Her lips purposefully connected with Carmen's skin, giving a gentle caress with her tongue. Carmen bucked her ass backward into Molly's front.

The arm Molly had snaked around Carmen when she got in bed, the one that had simply held her, now retreated, dancing its fingertips across a tense abdomen.

Molly felt Carmen's muscles contract. She heard the sheet rustle as Carmen attempted to turn around, but Molly held her in place.

"No, stay there," she whispered. "I just want to feel you for a second."

Carmen halted her movement, reaching back to grip Molly's hip. "Molly..." Carmen almost pleaded.

Whether this was purely a need to help Carmen let go of the last few days' worth of stress, Molly didn't know. That could be discussed in the morning. Right now, she just wanted to make Carmen feel something more than lost.

Their first time together had been rushed, passionate, and rough. Tonight would still have the passion, but Molly knew a tenderness had grown between them. They'd take their time and savor this night.

Carmen's nipples were already hard when Molly brushed her fingers over them, drawing a soft moan. She gently scraped her teeth across Carmen's shoulder as she palmed each breast with fervor.

"Molly, please."

Massaging Carmen's breasts one last time, Molly let her hand slowly trail down Carmen's body. Her boxers held little resistance to Molly's probing fingers.

Slipping her hand beneath Carmen's waistband, Molly took her time brushing her fingers through Carmen's soft curls. She thought back to the night in the back of the old pickup truck. She'd had Carmen on her back, eating her pussy with an animalistic appetite, never stopping to fully take in this wonderful creature. Molly wouldn't make that mistake tonight. She'd commit every inch of Carmen to her memory.

The hand that caressed Molly's hip squeezed harder as Carmen's moans grew more desperate. Molly shut her eyes, happy to concentrate on touch alone. The wetness that greeted her fingers sent a shot of arousal to Molly's clit. Her breath hitched as she continued to traverse Carmen's pussy with delight.

Carmen shifted slightly, lifting her top leg and planting her foot on the mattress, opening herself up. Dipping two fingers into Carmen's entrance, Molly coated herself in Carmen's excitement before pulling out and trailing them back up to Carmen's clit. She bit down gently on the space between Carmen's neck and shoulder as she began drawing circles.

They both sighed out a needy groan as Carmen gently rolled her hips. Although Molly had yet to be touched, she was just as close to coming as the writhing body beneath her fingers.

"Inside," Carmen hissed.

Molly gave one last pressured circle before gently pushing two fingers back inside. Carmen sucked in a breath, exhaling with a loud moan. Molly picked up her pace. Her own need was now at the boiling point. Her hips pushed into Carmen's ass, reveling in the friction caused by their sleepwear. Heavy breaths permeated the bedroom, only drowned out by the squeak of the bed as they moved faster.

"Oh," Carmen growled. "Oh, yes... I'm coming," she sang, her back arching.

Molly ground harder and thrusted faster. A sensational wave of pleasure burst through her body, causing her own cry to escape. They rode out their orgasms, syncing their movements until both women were completely spent.

As Molly came down from her high, the reality of what she'd initiated sunk in. Lost in the haze of her feelings, she hadn't stopped to consider if what they had just done would only cause more upset for Carmen.

Flexing her hand that was still buried inside Carmen, Molly tried to think of something to say.

It didn't matter, though, because when Carmen rolled and faced Molly, their eyes connected, and Molly did her best to read Carmen's thoughts. They became crystal clear as Carmen inched forward, taking Molly's lips between her own.

The kiss was soft, yet bruising. Maybe it was the intention behind the kiss that felt hard. Parting her mouth, Molly welcomed Carmen's tongue. She welcomed its insistence, allowing Carmen to explore until they were both breathless all over again.

Carmen rolled them both until she hovered over Molly. Reaching up, Molly plucked the hair tie holding Carmen's luxurious hair in its usual topknot. As the raven locks cascaded down, cocooning them, Carmen lowered her hips and rolled. They continued kissing slowly, each basking in the other's presence.

Molly let her hands drag up and down Carmen's back, feeling almost feverish in her need to feel Carmen without clothing. Tugging at the bottom of Carmen's tank top, Molly made her intentions clear.

Breaking the kiss, Carmen leaned back on her knees, stripping off her top. Braless tanned breasts sat high on her chest. Molly licked her lips, unable to tear her eyes away. She watched Carmen discard her boxers. This was the first time Molly had the pleasure of witnessing Carmen Ruiz in all her naked glory. And it really was glorious.

"Now you," Carmen rasped.

Molly remained silent, knowing no words were needed. Carmen hooked her fingers under the band of Molly's shorts, dragging them down at an achingly slow pace. She arched her back when Carmen lifted her tank top, allowing it to be ripped off.

They were naked. And they were longing. Molly couldn't mistake the look in Carmen's eyes. It went beyond lust, and Molly wanted to ask her what it meant but worried questioning such a thing would end their night. Carmen would come to her senses, and Molly wasn't ready for that.

Not yet. If tonight was going to be all they had, Molly wanted it to be perfect.

Carmen lowered herself back down. Their already heated skin was almost burning as they touched from chest to toe. Molly's breasts were a little fuller than Carmen's, and they pillowed, causing Carmen to look down. Her nose flared, and Molly bit her lip, more than happy to have caused such a reaction.

"You're gorgeous," Carmen whispered, still looking at their touching breasts.

Molly reached down, grabbing Carmen's ass, and pulled her closer. Taking the hint, Carmen rolled her hips again. It took only seconds for that familiar feeling to stir in Molly's center. They found each other's mouths again, picking up from where they'd left off.

Honestly, Molly would have happily kissed Carmen all night long, without the need for anything else. Carmen didn't share her thoughts, though, nipping Molly's bottom lip and trailing hot, open-mouthed kisses to Molly's breasts. Her nipples were coaxed into firm peaks by Carmen's insistent tongue.

An indulgent groan escaped Carmen's throat. "I can't get enough of your boobs."

Molly chuckled, "I would never have guessed." She felt Carmen smile against her skin.

"Let me show you what else I can't get enough of," Carmen murmured, abandoning her current task.

Molly watched with bated breath as Carmen sank lower down the bed, her hands traveling to Molly's thighs, instantly pushing them apart. A tremor traversed the length of Molly's body.

Swallowing hard, Molly watched with earnest as Carmen circled her belly button with the tip of her tongue, those strong hands flexing on Molly's thighs.

When she was just about ready to push Carmen's head down to where she ached, Molly sighed with relief when Carmen went there on her own. Every lick and kiss blazed a trail that led directly to Molly's pussy.

She almost hit the ceiling when Carmen finally licked the entire length of her.

"Shit," she gasped.

Carmen's hands snaked under her thighs and up to her ass, holding Molly tightly against her greedy mouth.

Fisting the sheets, Molly's toes curled as Carmen devoured her. This wasn't the frantic fucking they'd done the first time. This was almost reverent, and Carmen seemed lost in Molly, entirely.

Molly was desperately trying to hang on to any semblance of reality. The pleasure Carmen pulled with every swipe was astounding. Molly'd had great sex...with Carmen! But this... This was something else. Was the way she felt because Molly had finally allowed all of herself to be taken? She'd held nothing back.

Three fingers plunged inside, causing Molly to hitch a breath.

Jesus Christ!

"Come for me, Molly. Come all over this bed."

As if Carmen's words were a direct command, Molly's body readily obeyed. She'd never been much of a screamer, or a gusher, but all that was about to change. Molly felt the flood, heard the scream rip from her own throat, and she felt the strain in her back as she arched into what must have been the strongest orgasm she'd ever experienced.

Molly was alone. She knew it before she even opened her eyes. Disappointment burned in her throat, threatening to choke her up. But getting upset that Carmen wasn't in bed with her would be wrong. Last night had been more than either of them expected. Rationally Molly knew that, but where matters of the heart—and if she were being completely honest, ego—were concerned, rationality rarely factored in.

With herself under a modicum of control, Molly peeled open her eyes. Her body ached and her nipples were sore, rubbing against the sheets. She turned her head to the spot Carmen should be occupying. Brushing the empty space with her hand, Molly closed her eyes again, pulling memories of last night to the front of her mind. Carmen's half of the bed was still warm, so it hadn't been too long since she'd left.

Molly wondered if Carmen would talk to her at all. Would she ignore last night? Ignore Molly? The *snick* sound, which could only be the hotel room door closing, pulled Molly up to her elbows, her eyes trained on the entrance to the bedroom. She waited patiently, listening to someone she presumed to be Carmen, putter around the suite. Footsteps got closer to the bedroom and Molly's heart rate picked up.

"Hey," Carmen whispered the second she stepped into the room, holding two coffees and a plate of pastries.

"Hey," Molly replied.

"Um, I brought breakfast. I thought we could talk."

Nodding, Molly sat up against the headboard, pulling the bedsheet with her. "Of course."

"I told Enid we wouldn't be down until later."

Great, Enid's going to be insufferable.

"Okay. Are you going to sit, or would you prefer me to get dressed and meet you in the living room?"

"Here's fine. If you're comfortable?"

"I am." Molly was impatient to know what Carmen had to say, not uncomfortable. She was turned on too, because Carmen looked good enough to eat.

Hell, she always did, but this morning, especially. Carmen wore her hair down and it almost reached her hips. Molly wanted to run her hands through it while Carmen rested her head on Molly's lap.

Taking a cup of coffee, Molly wrapped the sheet a little tighter. Carmen sat next to her, resting against the headboard too.

"So, last night." Carmen began.

"Uh-huh, last night."

"We had sex. Again."

"We did."

Neither looked at the other, opting to concentrate on their drinks. Molly didn't want to say too much until she knew where Carmen stood.

"I like you, Molly. But I think you know that."

Molly saw Carmen looking her way. Taking a breath, she met Carmen's searching eyes. "I hoped you liked me."

"Well, now you know, but..."

Ah, the "but."

"But you're not looking for anything serious?"

Carmen reached over and laid a hand on Molly's sheet-covered thigh. "It's not that, Molly. I want to be ready. I want a relationship."

"Just not with me?" Molly supplied.

"*Dios mío.* Would you let me speak?" Carmen chuckled.

Molly blushed. "Sorry."

"The reason I left Seattle was to get some perspective and some answers. I'm sure Mateo has filled in some of my history. I'm not mad if he did. You should know."

"He didn't say much."

"But you know enough, especially after yesterday."

Molly nodded, taking a sip of her coffee. "Thank you for opening up. I know it's not easy."

"No, it's not. I've never felt safe enough to open myself up like that with anyone but Mateo until you, Molly."

Another nod, because Molly didn't trust herself not to start crying.

"When we met—no, even before that, you somehow got under my skin. I couldn't explain it. Hell, I still don't think I can," Carmen grinned. "The ranch took me by surprise. I wasn't expecting to be so captivated by Faith's aunt, but I was. I am."

"It goes both ways," Molly smiled, shyly.

"And, although I left the ranch and went home, you never left here—" Carmen laid a hand on her chest, "—but it scared me, Molly. I've only lived to make sure Mateo was okay. My whole life was constructed in a way to keep the bad out. We'd suffered enough."

It was Molly's turn to lay a hand on Carmen's leg. "You've done so much, Carmen. You had to grow up far too fast. I'm in awe of your strength."

"Thank you," Carmen replied, clearing her throat. "I kept relationships short, or just physical, because that was safer. And for a long time, I was happy living that way, until...guess who came along?" Carmen smiled.

Molly blushed again. "Enid?"

They burst into laughter. "No, not Enid. Until you. I felt a connection, instantly. You felt like—"

"Home."

Carmen nodded. "Yes. But here's the thing: My heart isn't ready yet. Not until I can rid myself of the questions and the hurt that has followed me around like a damn shadow, all my life. I know if we were to start something now, I'd ruin it, and not on purpose. I'd push you away and get scared. There is this part of me that doesn't feel like I deserve love, and I know," Carmen said, a little louder to stop Molly interrupting, "I know that feeling stems from my childhood, which is why I'm here, trying to get some closure. Because, Molly Parsons, when I'm ready to give you my all, you can be damn sure I'll give you my *everything*."

Was it possible for a heart to seize due to joy? Discreetly, Molly wiped a tear forming in the corner of her eye.

"My trip to Kentucky was for the same reasons. Faith, my very astute niece, gave me some advice. She told me I needed to make sure I was on the same page as you, when you got to the point you were ready to be with me."

"She said that?"

"Oh, yes. She's got no doubts we're supposed to be together," Molly chuckled quietly. "She said when you were ready to give your heart, you'd give every inch of it, and I had to make sure I was ready to receive it. So, Carmen, I've been on my own journey, getting ready."

Their hands laced together naturally. "And how did it go?"

"It was hard, but good. I visited my parents' graves. I told them about you. I introduced Faith and Mateo. And I asked them to forgive Alan. I needed closure, too."

"Did you get it?"

"Yes," Molly nodded, "and I know you need more time, and that's okay. I'm not planning on going anywhere. I'll be here for you in whatever capacity you need me to be in."

"Are you sure?" Carmen asked. "I'm not sure how long—"

"I'm sure. I'm here."

"So...we just stay friends?"

"Yes. We get to know each other more."

"I like the sound of that." Their smiles were bright and full of hope.

"That went better than I thought," Molly admitted, still beaming. "I half expected you to have run away."

"The old me would have."

"Wow, did we just have a really honest conversation and figure it out?"

"I think we did."

"That never happens in the movies, does it? God, they make it seem really difficult." Molly grinned, knocking her shoulder into Carmen's.

"Right! We must be super evolved or something."

"Or something," Molly echoed.

12

Faith

The earth beneath Faith's feet felt suddenly unsteady, as though it may quake with any misstep. She put it down to the last few days being less than chill. A feeling of unease traveled through her stomach anytime the image of her father showing up at the cemetery came to mind. Then, seeing Carmen looking so rattled, further set Faith's nerves on edge.

Maybe it had nothing to do with her father or Carmen. Maybe it was due to the three hours' worth of sleep she'd gotten thanks to Enid kicking her every ten minutes. Or maybe the cacophony of noise the woman made every time she rolled on her back?

Sitting up, Faith raked her hands through her wild hair. Her eyes felt heavy and her body ached. Looking across the bed, she noted the absence of her favorite senior citizen.

The toilet flushed, drawing Faith's attention. Enid bounced out of the bathroom in a neon orange tracksuit. "Morning, sunshine," she sang.

Faith grunted in reply.

"Oh, boy. You look like shit warmed up, kiddo."

Charming!

"Has anyone ever suggested you visit the doctor regarding your snoring?"

Enid snorted. "I bet I sounded like a truck hauling metal spoons in the back, huh?"

"Something like that," Faith yawned.

"Tends to happen when I've had a bit too much to drink."

"Right." Flopping back down to the mattress, Faith wanted to have a few minutes, uninterrupted.

"Let's go, *chica*," Mateo shouted from the living room. "Breakfast awaits."

Grumbling every step of the way, Faith hauled herself into the bathroom and took the world's quickest shower. Mateo and Enid were chatting animatedly on the couch when Faith entered the room, still feeling unimpressed at being awake.

"I'm telling you, there's no way," Mateo said, shaking his head to punctuate his point.

"I'll bet you fifty bucks," Enid replied confidently.

"Fine, fifty bucks."

"It's early for gambling, isn't it?" Faith asked, pulling on her Converse.

"Never too early. Come on, let's get downstairs." Enid made a beeline for the door, leaving Mateo and Faith in her wake.

The hotel's restaurant was busy when they arrived. Mateo sat at the first available table for six, while Enid wandered over to the bar. Faith was so tired she could hardly tell her ass from her elbow, so she allowed Mateo to grab her and plonk her in the seat opposite him.

"You're in with Enid tonight," she grumbled.

"*Mija*, half the hotel heard Enid last night. I got about as much sleep as you!"

"You didn't have her kicking you every few minutes, though."

"I'll give you that. Okay, I'll take one for the team tonight."

The server placed a fresh carafe of orange juice on the table. Faith studied the menu. "What were you and Enid betting on?"

"Enid thinks Molly and Carmen slept together."

"As in sex?"

Mateo chuckled. "Yup."

"They did it. I'm tellin' ya," Enid supplied, sitting next to Faith.

"You really think so?"

Mateo tutted, "No way. You saw the state Carmen was in."

"Nothing that a screaming orgasm couldn't fix," Enid noted, browsing her own menu.

They were interrupted by the server coming over to take their order. Faith chose pancakes. Enid chose the same with a side of bacon, and Mateo opted for fruit.

"Shouldn't we wait for Molly and Carmen?" Faith asked, looking around the crowded dining area.

"Nope. They'll have breakfast in bed," Enid replied.

"Ha!" Mateo suddenly erupted, pointing towards the elevator. Faith and Enid looked around to see Carmen stepping out and heading their way. "Told you."

"We'll see," Enid muttered.

Waving as she approached, Carmen drew Faith into a one-arm hug. "Hey."

"Morning," Faith said, leaning her head against Carmen's side.

"You guys eat. I'm taking breakfast for Molly and me back to the room."

Faith looked away, scared to laugh out loud. Enid's smile beamed across her face, her head turning purposefully to Mateo. "Is that right? Breakfast in the room, you say..."

Subtle, Enid.

Faith looked up to see Carmen blush slightly. "Um, yeah. So I should be going."

With one last squeeze of Faith's shoulder, Carmen left. They watched her go to the bar and collect a tray. She gave them a little wave and then stepped back into the elevator.

The table remained quiet. Enid simply held her palm out to Mateo. He rolled his eyes but dutifully whipped out some bills, slapping them in Enid's hand.

"Fine, they had sex."

"Just because they're having breakfast upstairs doesn't mean they did things," Faith pointed out.

"No," Mateo said. "But that hickey on the side of Carmen's neck does."

"Oh, I missed that. So, do you think they're finally going to be together?"

The idea sent a wave of joy through Faith's chest. Carmen and Molly made such a wonderful couple. And if they ever got married, Faith would be Carmen and Mateo's actual family.

"That's a pensive look, kiddo." Enid's low voice was close to Faith's ear.

Smiling, Faith shook her head. "Just thinking."

"Care to share, *chica*?"

"Um, it's nothing."

"Well, now you have to tell us," Enid chimed in.

"Fine," Faith chuckled. "I was just thinking if Aunt Molly and Carmen became a couple, they might get married and...and then I'd be her actual family. I'd be your family."

She saw the exchanged look. Was it pity? Pity for the girl whose parents left nothing but scars?

Faith dropped her eyes to the tabletop, feeling silly for opening her mouth. A chair scraped across the floor and Faith felt someone kneel next to her.

"You are our family, Faith," Mateo said quietly. "No one needs to be married for that."

"I know," Faith muttered.

"I should have made sure you were alright," Mateo said, more to himself than to Faith. "Seeing your father upset you."

"I'm fine."

"No, you're not, and that's okay. Let's eat breakfast and go for a walk. Yeah?"

Faith nodded. "Okay."

They ate in relative silence. Enid finished eating and immediately announced her intention to look for the "hunky man" from the bar. Faith presumed it was the one she'd been leering at yesterday evening.

Following Mateo outside, they began their walk. Having no destination in mind, it was just nice to wander.

"So..." Mateo began.

Faith stopped, took a breath, and looked at the sky. "I wasn't expecting to feel this way when I saw him again. I thought I'd come to terms with not being in his life. I was happy about it, in fact. I'd escaped. But he looked so broken, Mateo, it shocked me."

"Understandable."

"And now, I feel this anger."

"Once again—understandable."

"Not towards him. Well, it is, but I'm also angry with my mom."

"Okay. Can you elaborate?"

"I want to know the reason she stayed. Why she allowed us to go through it?"

"I thought you guys had talked this all through?"

"We've talked, and I've listened to her reasons, but they're not good enough. Sure, Dad was the one who beat me, but she helped him. Not physically. But she sure as hell helped instill his warped beliefs."

"What do you want to do?"

"What *can* I do?"

Mateo remained silent for a few minutes. "The way I see it," he began, "you can either accept what she's said about the past and try to move on, or you can talk this out. Don't be afraid to get angry. I know your mom was hurt too, and because of that, I'm sure you're hesitant to show any strong emotion toward her. She's still your mom, so you don't want to upset her on purpose. But...you can't shy away from your feelings, either. They are valid. If having it out with her is the way to go, then that's okay too."

"I just want answers," Faith sighed. "I...I don't want to get to Molly's age and still have issues, you know?"

"Totally. That's why Carmen sent me to a therapist so young. I just wish she'd done for herself what she did for me."

"But she did go to a therapist," Faith replied.

"Yeah, but I don't think she put her all into it. She was too busy looking after me and making sure we were financially stable."

"You should take your own advice, then," Faith said, hoping she wasn't crossing a line. "I know you're upset with her."

"I'm not upset."

Faith cocked her eyebrow. "Really?"

"Disappointed is more accurate. I'm disappointed that she didn't feel she could come to me."

"It looks like we both have difficult conversations ahead of us then, huh?"

"We sure do, *chica*. Come on, let's get back and see what the plan is."

According to Enid, the plan was to meet Carmen in her room. Mateo and Faith had barely walked over the hotel's threshold when they were swept up by the enigmatic woman.

"Chop, chop. Things to see, people to do."

Molly opened the door to the room, looking a little sheepish, if Faith were honest. There would be time for ribbing her aunt later. "Come in."

"Enjoy breakfast, did you?" Mateo winked. Molly punched him square in the arm, causing him to cry out dramatically. "Ow, you brute."

Enid cackled, then punched him on the other arm. "Such a drama queen."

"Alright, everyone settle down. Don't make me turn this car around," Carmen announced, walking in from the bedroom. "God, it's like running a daycare with you all."

"Hey, I didn't do anything," Mateo protested.

"What did you say?" Carmen asked, raising her eyebrow.

"Nothing... I just asked if Molly enjoyed breakfast," he grinned. Carmen walked up to her brother and flicked him on the nose.

"Not the face!" he shot, hands flying to cover his nose. Faith sat down, laughing at their antics. It never got old.

"Are we going home?" Faith asked, hoping to stop Mateo from retaliating. They'd be in the room all day if someone didn't cut his drama off at the knees.

"Yes, well, um...maybe."

"Ah, nice and clear then," Enid scoffed.

Faith grinned and looked at Carmen, waiting for her answer. She watched Carmen look at Molly, and saw Molly wink in return. Yeah, they were together.

"Okay, so after some thought," Carmen began, casting another glance over at Molly. Faith suppressed a grin. They were too cute. "I-I've decided to meet my mother."

A heavy silence settled over the room. Mateo was the first to break it. "Are you sure?"

"I am. I came here for answers, and I got some, but I only feel half done. I'm not expecting anything from her. I think I just need to meet her, and hopefully, that will be enough for me to finally let go of it."

"I, for one, think it's a great idea," Enid chimed. "Where are we going?"

Faith sat on the sofa, looking between everyone. She watched Carmen shuffle in place, looking more uncomfortable by the second.

"Um, *I'm* going to San José." Carmen finally said, her eyes darting to Mateo.

"What do you mean, *you* are going?" he cut in.

"I love that you all came here. It means more than you can ever know, but you have lives. You, Mateo, need to be back at the boutique, and Faith, you need to be getting yourself ready for college, working with Rita, etcetera."

Faith found herself rising to her feet. "No," she said bluntly. "No, we're not doing this again, Carmen."

"Faith..." Mateo warned.

"I'm sorry, Mateo, but no. We sat back and let her do this before. When will you all get it through your heads that we are better together, huh?"

"Faith—"

"Carmen, would you want me doing something like this alone? No, you wouldn't, and we all know it. Stop trying to be the responsible one and let us be a family. If you don't want us in the room when you meet your mom, that's cool, but you will need us for the before and after. You know how I know that?"

Carmen silently shook her head, closing her eyes as she listened.

Faith surged on. "I know it because I'd need that. I'd need my bricks."

"Bricks?" Molly mumbled.

"Yes, bricks. We are each other's support bricks, and the only way we work is when we come together and build a wall."

"Listen to the girl," Enid interjected. "She's about the only one out of you all that speaks fucking sense."

"Thank you, Enid," Faith nodded with conviction.

Carmen huffed, running a hand through her hair, which was down at the moment. Faith had only seen it out of her topknot on a handful of occasions.

"Fine. I want you to come with me."

Enid whooped, and Molly smiled, but Faith looked at Mateo. After their heart-to-heart earlier, Faith knew Carmen's instinct to leave him behind again, would hurt.

"Speak to her now, Mateo. Don't wait. She'll need you later, and you can't be there for her if you have other feelings getting in the way," Faith said quietly, so only Mateo would hear.

Mateo cupped Faith's face and gave her a warm smile before walking over to his sister. They shared a few whispers and then left the room. Molly wandered over to Faith.

"Is everything okay there?" she asked, tipping her head toward the two Ruizes.

"They'll be fine."

"We're going out tonight," Enid sang, sashaying around the room. "We need to blow off some steam before we leave. Although, I'm sure you and Carmen let off enough steam for all of us?"

"Enid," Molly ground out.

"Aunt Molly," Faith said mockingly, "did you get laid?"

"Jesus, not you too," Molly laughed.

They joked and prodded each other until the bedroom door opened, revealing two red-eyed Ruizes.

"Allergies," Mateo announced to everyone. Faith smiled at him.

Enid began sashaying again. "I want to go out and dance."

"Yes, we've made the executive decision we need you both to teach us how to Salsa," Molly added. Faith had two left feet. She did not need to learn how to dance, but she'd go along for the ride.

"Salsa, you say?" Carmen commented, a clear twinkle in her eye. Faith thought back to the night at the ranch where Mateo and Carmen showed off their impressive Salsa skills. At the time, she didn't recognize the growing attraction between her aunt and Carmen, but looking back, she remembered the way Molly gawked at Carmen.

"Let's do it!" Mateo called, pulling Carmen toward him in an effortless move.

"Um, it's a bit early yet," Faith reminded them. "I need a nap if we're going to be dancing. And you," she said, pointing to Enid, "are banned from the room."

Several gloriously restful hours later, Faith woke from a deep sleep feeling refreshed. As usual, the first person she wanted to talk to was Nat, so she sent a message, letting her girlfriend know what she was doing. They went back and forth until Molly poked her head around the door.

"We're getting ready to go soon, honey."

"Okay, I just need ten minutes."

Molly winked. "Say hi to Nat."

Faith grinned and went back to her phone. Enid wasn't as patient as Molly and strolled into the room, whipping the phone out of Faith's hand. "Let's go. I've got some Salsa to learn."

Knowing there was zero point in arguing, Faith quickly changed her clothes and washed her face.

The group buzzed with excitement, which was a really nice change. Even Faith could admit she was kind of excited to try Salsa. She'd suck, but it would be fun.

The dance club was loud and busy. Salsa music blared into the street. Carmen was already moving her hips instinctively, and Faith saw Molly checking her out.

They paid the entry fee and headed to the bar. There were plenty of other underage people, so Faith assumed it must be some kind of special night. Kids danced together with their parents. Faith smiled, watching some fumble, and others execute the moves perfectly. She was handed a Diet Coke and led over to a table.

Mateo wasted no time taking Carmen by the hand and leading her to the middle of the dance floor. The pair were good—really good. People were stopping to watch them. As the song came to an end, a loud round of applause rang out. Carmen blushed and Mateo bowed.

Carmen strolled over. "Okay, who wants to learn first?"

Molly was out of her seat in a second, taking Carmen's hand. Faith chuckled. Enid threw herself at Mateo, leaving Faith to happily sit at the table. She was lost, watching her family, when someone came and stood next to her. Faith slid her eyes to the side, only to see a very feminine pair of legs in a very nice dress, parked right next to her chair. Swallowing, Faith looked up. Staring down at her was an extremely attractive woman with hair like chocolate and piercing black eyes.

"*Hola.*"

Faith stared a little longer before she remembered she was a functioning human and needed to reply. "H-hi."

"You're not dancing?"

"I'm too klutzy," Faith smiled, hoping her nerves weren't as obvious as she assumed they would be.

"Hmmm, I'm not sure that's true. How about you let me take you for a spin and decide?"

"Oh, um, I'm sure there's someone more qualified you'd prefer to dance with," Faith protested weakly.

The mystery woman grinned. "It's a dance, not a job interview. Please?"

Biting her lip, Faith relented. She followed the woman onto the dance floor, hoping to hell she didn't make a fool of herself.

The dance went as well as expected. Faith winced every time she stepped on her partner's foot, but the woman just laughed. By the end of it, Faith was happy to sit down and not get back up. Surprisingly, the woman sat down with her.

"I'm Sara, by the way."

"Oh, um, Faith. I'm Faith."

"A pleasure to meet you, Faith." Was Sara flirting? "I'd love to have another dance. Maybe you could give me your number and we could have some lessons."

"Er, I...I don't live here. I'm leaving tomorrow."

"Well, that's a crying shame. Could I still get your number? We could get to know each other."

"I have a girlfriend," Faith blurted.

Sara shrugged. "Okay, that's cool. Is she here?"

Faith shook her head. "No, she's at home in Seattle."

"Well, if she's not here..." Sara shrugged again.

"Oh, no," Faith said quickly. "Sorry, not going to happen."

"Well, a girl's gotta try, right?" Sara smiled, rising to her feet. "It was nice to dance with you, Faith. See ya."

"Who was that?" Carmen asked, moments later. She was sweaty but smiling.

"Um, Sara."

"Uh-huh, and who is Sara?"

"No idea. She just asked me to dance and then wanted my number."

"Check you out, lady killer," Carmen laughed.

"Oh, no. Not at all. Do you know what I realized after she asked me for my number?"

Carmen shook her head. "What did you realize?"

"I'm going to marry Nat one day."

13

Carmen

Shadows danced across the bedroom ceiling. Carmen had been tracing them for hours, unable to sleep. Their night at the club was well needed and her body was already showing signs of soreness, but it was worth it. Even though she was exhausted, her mind wouldn't quiet down.

Faith's chastising earlier in the evening played on her mind. It was a clear sign that Carmen still had some things to work on. Getting answers and letting go of the past was one thing; undoing years of learned behaviors was quite another. But if she truly wanted a clean slate, that meant she had to do everything differently. Letting people in to help was a big one.

Her other conversation with Faith at the Salsa club was also at the forefront of her mind as she stared into the night. Faith announcing, so easily, she would marry Nathalie one day was a shock.

Her thoughts had nothing to do with Carmen doubting Faith and Nathalie's relationship. It was the ease of Faith's trust in her partner and in her decisions at such a young age that made Carmen pause. The younger Parsons had really come into herself, and Carmen was in awe of the changes.

Here she was, at thirty-seven, inching ever closer to another birthday, and she was nowhere near as confident in herself as Faith. When Carmen had remained quiet after Faith's declaration, the young woman had taken it as a judgment.

"I don't mean I'm going to marry her tomorrow, or anything," Faith said, her demeanor visibly changing to something more frantic. *"We're still young, and I know everyone will say I'm not old enough to know what I want or who I want. But I know Nathalie is it for me. I know that soon after I graduate and we're in settled jobs, I'll ask her to be my wife. I know it!"*

Carmen quickly put her hand on Faith's arm, stopping any more ranting. "Mija, I'm not judging or making any kinds of assumptions. I was quiet because you astound me sometimes, Faith. Your confidence and self-awareness...it's beautiful."

"Oh!"

"Only you and Nat know your hearts. If you say you want to marry her, then I trust you. I'd be honored to be there when it finally happens. And I know both of you are lucky to have found each other so early on in your lives."

Faith's eyes had teared up and they'd shared a hug—until Enid stumbled over to drag them both back to the dance floor.

The night ended late, and now Carmen lay in bed with a fully dressed Molly, cursing herself for being so damn responsible. After their talk earlier, they both decided to leave sex out of the equation until they were in a better place mentally.

Sex complicated things, and both women were determined to make this work in the long run. Possibly fucking it up with sex before they even got started seemed like a risk neither wanted to take.

So, instead of mind-altering sex, Carmen lay wide awake, ruminating on everything, including the meeting with Mariana. Molly had been a great sounding board and helped Carmen decide that she did, in fact, want to meet the woman who'd birthed her.

Molly suggested reaching out to Lena and asking her to act as a middlewoman. There was no guarantee Mariana would want to see Carmen, and if that were the case, she'd rather Lena be the one to receive the 'no' than herself.

But Mariana hadn't rejected her. She'd set up a day and time, which was now only two days away. Their flight out of Santa Fe left the next morning. They'd have one night before the meeting to unwind, and then Carmen would see her mother.

It seemed simple when explained like that, but Carmen's feelings were anything but simple. She constantly warred with herself. That natural instinct to run away was becoming harder to ignore with each passing hour, but then she looked over to a sleeping Molly and knew running away was pointless.

If she wanted Molly—wanted a settled life—it was time to face everything. She needed to air out her demons, and maybe, just maybe, have the chance to add Mariana to the small list of people she called family.

By the time 5:30 a.m. rolled around, Carmen was far too restless to stay in that bed a second longer. Slipping silently from beneath the sheets, she tugged on a pair of running shorts and a T-shirt and hit the streets of Santa Fe.

The sun was barely a wisp over the horizon as she picked up her pace and pounded the sidewalk. With a slew of questions barreling around her mind, Carmen went all out in an effort to tire herself to the point of collapse. She just needed a few hours of calm.

By the time she made it back to the hotel room, Carmen resembled a drowned rat. Sweat dripped down her face and back.

"Jesus, are you okay?" Molly asked, her face the picture of concern as Carmen bent over at the knees trying to suck in some much-needed air.

"Y-yeah!" she panted.

"Um, okay, but you look like you're about to faint. Come here and sit down." Molly tugged Carmen by the wrist, guiding her to the couch until she was sitting down. Carmen rested her head along the back of the couch, her breaths coming a little more easily. "Water. Drink it."

Carmen chugged the bottle of water and then another. "Thanks," she finally spluttered.

"Any reason, in particular, you're trying to kill yourself through exercise?"

"Couldn't sleep. Mind wouldn't stop."

"Want to chat? We have time before we need to leave for the airport."

"Thanks, I'm good. I think I'll grab a catnap." Carmen heaved herself off the couch with a lot of effort and noise. "Jesus, I'm going to hurt."

"Uh-huh!" Molly grinned. "Grab a shower and sleep for a bit. I'll wake you when we need to go."

Not one to argue with a sensible directive, Carmen dragged herself to the shower. The hot water caused her to moan loudly. She would've been embarrassed if the heat hadn't felt so good.

The second her head hit the pillow, she was out like a light until a poking sensation on her cheek roused her. Blinking rapidly, Carmen almost fell out of bed when she was confronted with a plastic toe jamming itself up her nose.

"What the fuck?"

Enid's cackle reverberated around the bedroom. "Knew I'd get you, eventually!"

"Enid, gross!" Carmen shouted, wiping her face. "I don't know where that thing has been."

Carmen eyed Enid's vagina-painted leg with suspicion. God knows what the woman got up to, and where she may have put her limbs.

"Don't worry, the toe is clean," Enid laughed, sitting on the bed and slipping her prosthetic back on.

"How did you get in here? Where's Molly?"

"I sent her to kick Mateo in the ass. The man is incapable of showering for less than an hour. I mean, what the fuck does he do, apart from jerk off?"

"Enid! No! You know the rules."

"Right, right. No discussing Mateo's man meat. Got it."

Growling in frustration, Carmen scrubbed her face once more. "Out. I need to change. We can meet downstairs."

"Oh, you *are* a grump. I'd have thought you'd be a little more relaxed after—"

"Nope! Not discussing anything else. Out!"

Sinking back onto the bed, Carmen chuckled. There was never a dull moment, that was for sure. Her bag was already packed. All she had to do was take the elevator down to the reception area and Carmen would be moving on to the next part of her journey—and it *was* a journey. She felt so different from the woman that had left Seattle a few weeks ago. Was that a good thing?

Hopefully.

Carmen's patience had long since disappeared by the time they arrived at their hotel in San José. She'd spent the better part of the day wrangling the group, which turned out being akin to herding feral cats—and that was just Enid!

Airports were already stress-inducing hubs of chaos. Add Enid Butcher to the mix, and Carmen was ready to scream. Every time she turned around, Enid had disappeared. Carmen had instantly headed in the direction of the closest bar, which was where she found Enid ninety percent of the time, chatting up some unsuspecting guy.

Then there was Mateo. Jesus, how could Carmen have forgotten how bad her brother was in airports? The second they'd entered the waiting area, he practically ran to the closest makeup and perfume shop. That was fine, as it kept him out of Carmen's hair. The only problem was getting the man to leave the store when their flight was called.

Dragging a grown man out of a treatment chair, half his face plastered in eyeshadow and foundation, while bitching up a storm, was just too much!

Molly was absolutely zero help, clearly enjoying said chaos and throwing a wink over at Carmen now and then, while tacking on a 'thumbs up'.

And Faith, Carmen's reliable ally, had devolved into a lovesick teenager constantly plastered to her phone. Since Faith's announcement she would marry Nat one day, she'd doubled down on communicating, swooning over text messages, and becoming entirely unaware of the surrounding world.

Once on the plane, Carmen had popped in her earbuds, determined to drown out any noise. She'd slipped on an eye mask and feigned sleep, hoping she would be left alone. Of course, that hadn't happened. Mateo and Enid had acted like big children, constantly needing attention.

By the time they were in a taxi on the way to the hotel, Carmen was ready to drop from exhaustion, yet she'd still had enough energy to murder someone.

Upon arrival, Carmen had stomped over to the reception desk using the last reserves of her politeness to get them checked in. Once that was done, though, she'd felt no shame in giving them all the finger—which had caused Molly to laugh—and she'd left them to fend for themselves.

The room was a lot smaller than the suite in Santa Fe, but it was good enough. Nothing mattered but the comfy looking bed that beckoned Carmen to sink into it.

She was almost unconscious when the door opened and shuffling feet caught her attention. Knowing Molly had arrived caused a small smile to appear.

The group wanted to save money, so they'd decided to bunk together again. Carmen was happy to continue sharing a bed with Molly. Her presence was soothing, and Carmen needed all the comfort she could get.

"Are you asleep?"

"Yes," Carmen moaned.

Molly snickered from somewhere at the foot of the bed. "Okay. I'm going to take a shower and then I'll join you."

"Mmmm."

Carmen presumed Molly did what she said, because when she opened her eyes again, it was sunny, meaning she'd slept through the night. Molly wasn't in bed with her and hadn't been for some time, if the temperature of the empty space was anything to go on.

Feeling groggy, Carmen took a cool shower, which helped clear the mind fog long enough to realize today was the day she'd meet her mother.

Gripping the shower tiles as best she could, Carmen had to focus all of her energy on slowing her breathing. By the time she got herself into a calmer state, her skin was cold. Shivering, she hastily dried herself off and dressed. Coffee was needed...and lots of it.

Molly, Mateo, Enid, and Faith were already in the dining area, eating breakfast and chatting happily. Molly was the first to notice Carmen's appearance. She gave her an "Are you okay?" look, to which Carmen subtly nodded.

The thought of food turned her stomach, but Molly was quite insistent that Carmen consume something more than coffee. She'd finished a small plate of scrambled eggs when Mateo touched her shoulder.

"Are you ready to go?"

Instinctively, Carmen peered at her watch, noting the time, and yes, they needed to get going. But that hadn't been Mateo's question. *Was* she ready to go? Ready to face this gigantic part of her past? Only time would tell.

"Yeah. Okay, let's go."

The minivan taxi pulled up outside a Spanish-style villa. To say everyone was slightly stunned would have been an understatement. There was a circular driveway with two luxury cars parked close to the main entrance. Mariana had money.

"Fuck, your mom's loaded," Enid blurted. Carmen still felt a twinge of unease when Enid referred to Mariana as her 'mom'.

"Enid," Mateo hissed.

"What?"

"Just..." And Carmen knew Mateo was trying to silently signal Enid, and tell her to shut the hell up.

Without a word, Carmen stepped out of the vehicle. She needed a few seconds of fresh air, and space from Enid and Mateo's bickering. She felt Molly step out and stand close by.

"Take all the time you need. We will wait outside." Molly murmured.

"No," Carmen blurted, "I-I want you all with me. I don't think I can sit in a room with her alone. Not yet."

Molly's hand slid into Carmen's, their fingers entwining. "Okay. Not a problem."

Fortified through Molly's presence, Carmen took tentative steps toward the double oak doors. She tried to take everything in: the beautifully landscaped yard, the bird houses that were dotted all over the place, the shiny cars. But none of it registered. All Carmen could see were those doors.

Molly gently urged her to take the last few steps alone. Carmen looked back at the people who were her world. Molly gave a knowing wink. Faith, Enid, and Mateo stood, holding each other's hand, smiling softly.

You've got this, Carmen.

Wringing her hands, Carmen took several large lungfuls of air. With a shaking fist, she knocked as loudly as she could and waited. Maybe time really did stop when waiting for something huge to happen. That was certainly what it felt like.

An eternity went by before Carmen heard footsteps approach from the other side of the door. Then there was silence. Was Mariana having to compose herself, just like Carmen had?

Sucking in a breath, Carmen watched the door slowly open. Standing in front of her, a little shorter and a little older, was Carmen's carbon copy: Mariana Hernandez.

All the air left Carmen's lungs in one big whoosh. They stood, staring wide-eyed at each other. The only sounds, for what felt like an eternity, were the sweetly singing birds above them.

Carmen wanted to say something. She even opened her mouth several times, but it was no use. Her voice just wouldn't work. Thankfully, Mariana managed to speak first.

"C-carmen."

Carmen nodded, because that was the only thing her brain was letting her body do. Mariana's hand flew to her mouth as a soft sob made its way from her throat. "My God, look at you!"

Carmen felt the sting of tears. She swallowed several times. "H-hi."

"Hi," Mariana stuttered. "Will you come in?"

Carmen quickly looked over her shoulder, needing her family to give her a boost of confidence and reassurance. They all smiled at her, but remained quiet.

Turning back to Mariana, she gave a shy smile. "Um, I'd like that. But, um, could my family come in, too?"

"Of course. Please," Mariana gestured to Molly, Enid, Mateo, and Faith, "Please come in. You're all so very welcome."

Molly was the first to step forward, taking Carmen's hand once more. Carmen squeezed and tugged Molly to follow her. Mariana's house was stunning. Her style was warm and inviting, and so very Spanish. Carmen felt a frisson of warmth around her heart. Had she got her taste in decorating from Mariana?

They filed into an open-plan living room with two large L-shaped couches.

"Please sit. Would you like a drink?"

"I'd murder a lemonade," Enid answered, drifting around the room, picking up knick-knacks now and then.

"Sure, I'll be just one second."

Carmen watched Mariana leave. Her hands started shaking the second her mother was out of the room.

"Shit," she whispered.

"Hey, you're alright," Molly gently replied. "Just breathe."

A few moments passed before Mariana came back, laden with a tray of lemonade and cake.

"Here, I didn't know if you'd be hungry. Um, do any of you have allergies?"

A chorus of "no" and "thank you" echoed around the room. They sat quietly, sipping on their lemonades, until the tension became too much for Carmen.

"I should introduce you," she stuttered. "This is Molly, Faith, Enid and—"

"Mateo. Her brother." Mateo's display of… whatever the hell it was, made Carmen chuckle.

"Take it down a notch, Mateo," she whispered. Mateo didn't even look at her. His eyes were firmly on Mariana.

Mariana, in turn, looked back at Mateo, her eyes smiling. No one, especially not Mateo, expected Mariana to get up from her seat opposite the Ruizes, walk over, and take Mateo's hand.

"It's an absolute pleasure to meet you, Mateo."

"Oh, um, thanks?" Mateo's display of protectiveness vanished in a nanosecond. Mariana was charming and she exuded warmth.

"It's an honor to meet you all."

"I'm sorry for turning up with a crowd of people," Carmen began, "um, but I was nervous and—"

"You don't have to explain yourself to me, Carmen. You could have turned up with an entire football squad and I'd just be happy to be this close to you. I can't believe you're here."

"Me either."

"I want you to know that I never stopped thinking about you."

Mariana's forthrightness was refreshing. Carmen had worried she'd have to try and pry answers out of her mother.

"Why...why didn't you try to find me, then?"

It was Mariana's turn to swallow several times. "I... It didn't feel like it was my right to do that. Not after I'd left you."

"Why did you leave me?" Carmen knew the reason, but she had to hear it from Mariana.

"I was so young. Just turned fifteen. I had a one-night stand, because I felt like I had to fit in with my friends. When I found out I was pregnant, I panicked. Not for me, but for my baby—for you. How could I give you a life when I couldn't even fend for myself? My parents were poor, and although they would have helped, you would have lived in squalor. I thought if I gave you away, you'd have a richer life. I couldn't face the shame of what I'd done, so I left."

"She lived through much worse," Mateo all but growled. Carmen had never seen him like this.

"Mat. Stop."

"No. Why should I? She gave you away!" And then it hit Carmen: This was less about Mariana, and more about Mateo's own trauma.

14

Molly

Today was always going to be a tough day. Molly knew that. She'd known it from the second Carmen told her she wanted to meet Mariana. She'd tried to prepare the best she could; told herself she could cope with anything. But all the preparation in the world hadn't foreseen Mateo having a crisis. Carmen, sure, but not her brother. As much as she wanted to comfort Mateo, Molly couldn't make herself move from Carmen's side.

Molly sat on the other side of Carmen, leaning forward to look at Mateo. It was the best she could do. His face was twisted with anguish as he stared directly at Mariana. His last words had struck Carmen's mother like a knife to the chest.

"No. Why should I? She gave you away."

The room was silent and tense. Carmen was flushed; her eyes unable to meet Mariana's.

"Mateo," she said, reaching over and laying her hand on his.

The anxiety radiating off Carmen was intense, and Molly found herself feeling a little pissed off toward Mateo. She got the fact he had trauma, but this wasn't about him.

"I'm sorry, Carm, I can't be here." Mateo stood, wiping a tear from his face. Carmen looked panicked. Her chest began rising rapidly and her eyes were frenzied. Molly knew Carmen would break if Mateo left. Jesus, Molly also knew Carmen would break off all contact with Mariana if Mateo had an issue. Should she say something?

"Sit down." Enid's voice rang through the room. Molly had never heard the woman sound so commanding. And she'd also never been so pleased to hear her speak.

Mateo stared at her before slowly sitting back down. His eyes fell to his lap.

"Okay, let's get this shit cleared up." Enid moved to the middle of the room, hands on hips.

Molly stared dumbstruck. She was supposed to be providing Carmen with support but was completely in over her head.

"Mateo, my boy, this isn't about you. Mariana isn't your mother—is not your past. So be the person you came here to be: your sister's support. She needs that more than she needs your opinion." Enid gave him a pointed stare before turning to Mariana.

"Mariana, you need to know from the get-go that Mateo is Carmen's family. He's been with her every step of the way since they were kids. And I'll be frank, they had a fucking awful time of it. They've only known shit, if I'm being honest, so they stick together. That's how they survived, so please understand why Mateo is so upset."

Molly saw Mariana close her eyes, her worst fear obviously coming true. Jesus, now Molly wanted to just scoop everyone up and make things better, but she knew she couldn't. They were all going to have to ride this out.

"That being said...I doubt anyone in this room doesn't understand the situation you were in at such a vulnerable age. Now," she punctuated with a finger in the air, "today is supposed to be about answers. About healing, right?" Enid didn't wait for an answer. But there was a quiet rumble of agreement. "So start talking, ask the hard questions, and listen. That includes you, Mateo. But don't be a dick. I'm going to take a tour of your house. The light is amazing."

Every pair of eyes watched Enid sweep out of the room, quite content to go snooping around Mariana's house uninvited. Carmen was the first to make a sound.

"Um, I'm sorry about Enid, she's—"

"A law unto herself," Mateo finished, looking far more composed and a little chagrined. "Please let me apologize for my outburst. I'm not sure where that came from."

Molly caught Faith's raised eyebrows. Her niece was feeling just as on edge as she was. Deciding to support silently, Molly laid her hand on Carmen's thigh. She could almost feel the sweat collecting under Carmen's clothes.

"I'm sorry," Mariana all but whispered, her voice choked with regret. "I hoped with all my heart you'd had a good life with a family that loved you."

Carmen cleared her throat. Molly felt like her heart was about to fall out of her chest.

"I wish I could say that was true. But we got through it together." Carmen threaded her fingers with Mateo's. "Enid is right. I came here today to get answers. But I think I also hoped...that maybe we could get to know each other and build something...if that's something you'd be interested in."

Sweet Jesus.

"Yes!" Mariana exclaimed, her eyes full of unshed tears. "Please believe me when I say I want that more than anything. I know I can't suddenly become your mom. You don't need that anymore, but I want to be here—in any way you want."

Molly dared to speak, hoping she wasn't crossing a line or about to cry. "We never grow out of needing a mom."

Carmen looked her way, and surprisingly, leaned in and kissed Molly's lips gently. As much as Molly wanted to ruminate on what it meant, she wouldn't, not until later, when there wasn't a family reunion happening.

"Molly's right. We never stop needing people. Mariana, you need to know these guys come with me. We're a package deal."

Molly was happy to hear a little bit of Carmen's usual steadiness back in her voice.

Mariana's eyes crinkled with her wide smile. "It would be a pleasure to be in *all* your lives." Her eyes turned to Mateo. "And I... I'd love to be there for you too, Mateo. I...I always wanted a big family."

Holy crap, Molly thought she might explode with heart-swelling emotions. This was just too much. Mateo was outright crying, and Carmen was clenching her jaw, trying to stave off the flood of feelings Molly knew were coursing through her. Faith sat slack-jawed at the whole scenario. It was a lot.

After a slight pause, which consisted of several sniffs, and hands wiping across cheeks, Faith sat forward, hands on knees, face resting in her palms. "Did... um, did you have any more children?" Faith asked.

Apparently, this had become a group Q & A session. Molly hoped Mariana didn't mind. She was sort of thankful Enid had made herself scarce. Surely there was only so much one person could take. Adding Enid's usual line of inappropriate questioning would probably prove to be a tad too much.

Mariana shook her head, looking at Carmen. "I couldn't justify bringing another child into the world when I'd given up my first. Carlos, my husband, knew the score when we met, and was more than understanding."

"How long have you been together?" Molly asked. Carmen and Mateo still needed a few moments, by the looks of things.

"Twenty years. He has a daughter from his first marriage. She's just graduated college."

Carmen sat a little straighter. "What's her name?"

"Mia. She knows about you. Everyone in the family does."

Carmen sniffed. "You...you told people about me?"

Molly felt like she was watching the world's most emotional game of tennis. If she were honest, watching Mariana and Carmen trying to navigate through their first interaction was really bringing up some issues. She missed her mom desperately. What she wouldn't give to be able to have a conversation with her, just one more time.

"Of course I did," Mariana began. "I was ashamed of my actions, not of you. I wanted Mia to know about my baby."

Molly sat forward slightly. "What about your parents? How did that work out?"

Mariana blew out a breath. "It took me a long time to have the courage to find them. They'd moved to San José not long after I disappeared. The reunion was...difficult. They were both angry *and* joyful when I turned up at their door."

"I can imagine," Molly mumbled.

As present as she wanted to be for Carmen, Molly was struggling not to lose herself in memories, mentally playing back all the times she'd fought with her parents over dumb things.

Molly would do almost anything to travel back in time and sit down with them, allowing them to talk to her, instead of being a hot-headed teenager. She'd tell them she loved them and appreciated their advice. She'd thank them for all the love they gave her and the things they provided, even if they were only small. Molly would ensure she left her mom and dad with no doubt about how much she loved them. But that couldn't happen.

Hopefully, her parents knew all of that before the crash happened. The next time she visited their graves, Molly would make sure she said all the things she never got to say.

The weight she'd felt before visiting Kentucky had lifted, but Molly wasn't a fool. She knew there would still be times it felt painful, and that's why she'd keep her promise and continue to visit the cemetery. She'd go back to talking to them, just like she did right after the funeral, even without the hope of a reply.

Clearing her throat, Molly sucked in a quick breath. She had to focus on Carmen. "Can you tell us a little about Mia?"

It was a good thing she had snapped out of her daydream because both Carmen and Mateo were still silent.

"Mia is the spitting image of Carlos, but with less facial hair," Mariana joked, which helped ease the tension a little. "Her dream is to be a full-time writer. She's written a few short stories that have been published."

"That's really cool," Faith replied.

"She's always enjoyed writing."

"So you knew her from quite a young age?" Molly asked.

Mariana nodded. "Yes. It was...hard, at first, to be around such a young child. No matter how many years passed, I thought of you, Carmen. I tried to envision what you were like at Mia's age."

Molly's mind once again drifted off; a vision of a time that saw Carmen running around as a mischievous toddler made her smile. And then she saw herself, holding that baby, realizing the little girl belonged to her and Carmen. She was their daughter. The effect of the daydream almost stole Molly's breath away.

It did no good getting ahead of herself like that. Carmen wasn't even Molly's girlfriend yet, and here she was, picturing children. Would Carmen even want kids? It would be understandable if she didn't. Maybe she'd prefer to adopt?

God, she remembered Ruth asking about kids and Molly had wanted to throw herself out of the window. The thought of a little person depending on her felt claustrophobic. Not because she didn't like kids—she loved them—but Molly only knew how to look after herself. The look on Ruth's face when Molly blanched, stuck in her memory like a talon.

"Hey babe, so I have a question for you." Ruth sat down next to Molly, her hand immediately playing with the ends of Molly's hair. It was Ruth's go-to thing when she wanted to talk about something she thought Molly would find uncomfortable.

Molly set her laptop down. She'd been conversing with Bessie, a friend who ran a ranch in California. It looked like a wonderful place and so full of potential. Molly had been giving Bessie some ideas of how to keep the place running now that Bessie's wife was sadly no longer there to help.

"Yeah, what's on your mind?"

"I was talking to Mom earlier."

That never boded well for Molly. Ruth's mom was the quintessential matriarch who liked to butt her nose into everyone's business, wanting to know when they were getting married or popping out babies.

Molly was self-aware enough to know her issues probably stemmed from jealousy. She didn't have a mom, and it still stabbed like a shard of glass when she saw a mother/daughter relationship she would never have, even after all these years.

Molly shook her head. Those thoughts would have to wait a little longer. Her birthday wasn't for a month.

"How is she? Still hoping your dad will let her redecorate the upstairs guest bedroom?"

"Ha, something like that. But we got talking and...well, do you want kids?"

Molly felt all the color drain from her face. Her eyes grew wide, and she instinctively leaned away from her girlfriend. Ruth saw the reaction and looked devastated.

Molly's stomach ached. She didn't want to upset Ruth, but she couldn't lie either. Right now, it was a struggle just to settle into their house in Phoenix. Molly felt itchy, like she needed to move; not just in this very moment, but on a bigger scale.

Standing from the couch, Molly paced a few times, a hand running through her hair.

"Honey, you know I can't think about those things yet. I'm swamped with work. We've just moved here, and you're starting a new job."

Ruth sighed, her shoulders slumping. "I didn't ask if you wanted a baby now, Molly. I asked if you wanted kids."

What the hell could Molly say? "Yes, but I can't imagine having them with you." *Didn't seem appropriate.* "I don't know. It's not something I think about."

"I want them, Molly. I want two or three little ones, and I'd like them with you. Maybe after we're married—"

"Whoa, who's getting married all of a sudden?"

Ruth bit her lip. "Jesus, Molly. Does the thought of being with me forever make you feel that shitty?"

Molly was doing this all wrong. Ruth was a good woman who loved her. Molly cared for Ruth, but not in the same way Ruth cared for her, and she was a shitty person for allowing it to get this far.

When Ruth got the new promotion and wanted to move, Molly was more excited about the traveling than the settling-down-with-the-girlfriend aspect of the whole thing.

"Ruth, look, I'm sorry. I'm just not in the frame of mind to be thinking about these things."

And then, to really cement her standing in the shitty girlfriend hall of fame, Molly proceeded to tell Ruth about Bessie and the ranch and how the older woman needed some help.

Suffice it to say, Molly's lack of enthusiasm that day spelled the end of the relationship, for which Molly still felt awful. Even after talking to Ruth and apologizing for her behavior back then, she still felt like crap. Some things, the brain just wouldn't allow a person to forget.

Molly brought herself back to the conversation again. She hoped Mariana and Carmen would be able to look beyond their past and make this work. She also hoped that if, or when, the conversation turned towards kids again, Molly wouldn't have the same reaction. But surely, if she could sit here and think about marriage and children with Carmen, without the walls feeling like they were closing in, that meant something. It meant Molly was ready, right?

15

Faith

This was intense! Mateo and Carmen clung to each other like their lives depended on their connected hands. Molly looked lost in her own painful and emotional thoughts, and Faith, well, she was just overwhelmed by it all. She'd had some intense conversations before, but this one here? This outweighed everything.

Faith, herself, wasn't immune to the feelings being stirred up by Mariana's presence. There was no escaping the pain radiating from the woman, or the longing in Carmen's eyes. It almost felt intrusive to witness. But Carmen had wanted them all there, and Faith could do that, even if she was entirely uncomfortable.

Where the heck is Enid?

Ever since she'd opened her mouth and asked if Mariana had more children, Faith had wanted to sink into the floor. What had she been thinking, asking such a personal question?

The only reason she could come up with was simply being swept away in the moment. As Mariana spoke, Faith wanted to know everything. Although it wasn't her history, she had become invested and wanted Carmen to have the closure she deserved. Maybe not closure, but a chance to have a relationship with her mom.

Mom. That word. One that should conjure familiar, loving feelings. It occurred to Faith that everyone in this room, except Enid and Mariana, had strained or non-existent relationships with their parents, at least as far as she knew.

They were a group of lost souls looking for a connection; searching for someone to finally claim them and love them wholeheartedly, as only a parent could and should.

They had each other. That wasn't in question, but it was clear Molly had been right when she said a person never outgrows the need for a mother—or a parent. Carmen was a shining example. In Faith's opinion, Carmen Ruiz was the strongest person she knew, but under all of it lay a child needing the security of a parental figure. Someone to reassure *her* everything would be okay.

Maureen Parsons flitted into Faith's mind. Her own mother, who now lived on the ranch in California and was desperately trying to grasp at a second chance at life.

Faith was happy her mother had escaped; happy she no longer had to suffer bruises. But what about the internal bruises her mother had inflicted on Faith?

The conversation between her and Mateo played on a loop. Faith was angry. She didn't want to be, but the situations in which she kept finding herself wouldn't allow her to put the past to rest.

Gosh, was this her life now? Would she carry emotional scars for the rest of her life, and be destined to endure ongoing emotional trauma? Would she still be thinking about her childhood when she reached her forties?

Had it been naïve to think that as soon as she escaped, everything would just fall into place? Looking at her aunt, who was still glassy-eyed, absently staring into the distance as Carmen and Mariana spoke, Faith knew the answer. Like Molly, she would deal with the aftermath of her own upbringing for quite some time.

Needing a break, Faith quickly and politely excused herself, stating she needed the bathroom. Mariana broke from the conversation long enough to point Faith toward the restroom.

Clutching the phone, which sat in the front pocket of her overalls, Faith slipped into the bathroom, locked the door, and immediately called Nathalie.

"Hey, babe."

"Nat," Faith sighed.

"Whoa, are you okay?"

"Can we FaceTime?"

"Sure, one second."

Faith pressed the camera button and waited. Nathalie's face appearing on the screen had an immediate calming effect.

"Has something happened? Is Carmen okay?"

"I'm not sure anyone is okay," Faith answered honestly. "Jesus, Nat, it's intense. Enid is the only one not crying or looking like they're about to have a full meltdown."

"Okay, take it from the top. Where are you?"

"In the bathroom. I needed a break—needed to see you."

Nathalie remained silent while Faith studied her face. They smiled sweetly at each other until Faith was ready to talk. She recounted every minute of their trip to date. Nathalie blew out her cheeks, looking wide-eyed.

"Yeah, I can understand why it's all a bit much for you, baby. What can I do?"

Faith shook her head gently. "Just being on the phone with me is more than enough."

"Ugh, I wish I was with you. I want to just wrap you up in my arms."

"God, I'd love that," Faith sighed. "I'll take an extra-long hug when we get home."

"Deal," Nathalie smiled. "Any idea of when that will be?"

Shaking her head, Faith ran a hand through her hair. "No. It could be later today, or it could be a few days. I'm not sure any of us really knew what to expect."

"That's fair."

"I..." Faith began, then thought better of it. A tendril of an idea had begun to grow ever since the conversation with Mateo.

"What? Tell me."

"I...think I might go to California—to the ranch—before coming home."

"O-okay."

"I have some things I need to say to my mom. This trip has made me see what could happen if I let my feelings fester. I'm terrified I'll wake up one day in my later years and still harbor crap from before I left home. As much as I love Carmen, Mateo, and Molly, I don't want to have their issues when I'm older."

Nathalie nodded. "If that's what you need to do, honey, I support you. Will you let me know when you decide to go?"

"Of course. Now I should probably get back out there. Actually, I should find Enid. Lord knows what she's been getting up to."

"Oh boy. Yeah, go and reel her in, babe," Nathalie laughed, "but call me later, yeah?"

"Sure. I love you."

"Love you, too."

Setting the phone on the bathroom counter, Faith splashed some cold water over her face. The chill shocked her brain into focusing on the here and now. She'd talk to the others later regarding her plans. For now, she'd find Enid and get back to supporting her family.

It didn't take long to pinpoint the old girl. Faith found her leaning into the personal space of a tall Spanish man who looked utterly terrified. As much as Faith wanted to drool over the size of Mariana's kitchen, she had to take action before the guy wet himself.

"Enid, there you are!"

Enid spun on her leg. "Hello, love. Everything going okay in there?"

"Emotional. Would you come back in with me?"

"Of course. I was just getting acquainted with this handsome fellow."

The handsome fellow looked like a deer in the headlights as his gaze whipped to Faith. His eyes screamed, "Please help me!"

"Oh, hello. I'm Faith." Faith stepped in between Enid and her prey, thrusting her hand out in greeting. The man shook her hand and smiled warily, probably worried Faith was as nuts as Enid.

"Carlos," he replied, "Mariana's husband."

"Oh, wow. Hi! It's lovely to meet you. That was Enid," Faith said as she threw a thumb over her shoulder, "and all I can do is apologize." Faith smiled her best *'I'm quite sane and you don't have to worry'* smile.

Carlos raised his eyebrows, his look fixedly on something behind Faith. Faith let her shoulders drop before slowly turning around. In the time it had taken Faith to introduce herself to Carlos, saving him from Enid, the aforementioned woman had slipped out the sliding kitchen doors and disrobed. Bending slightly at the hips, wearing only her underwear, Faith watched as Enid dived, surprisingly gracefully, into the Hernandez's pool.

Wiping a hand down her face, Faith turned back to a stunned Carlos.

"There really is no explanation. I'd love to say she's senile or off her meds, but that's untrue. She's an utter law unto herself. Maybe we should go into the living room."

Faith gently led a silent Carlos into the room where conversation flowed. All eyes turned to them. Smiling, Faith looked to Carmen. "This is Carlos."

Standing, Carmen looked nervous. "Um... Hi, I'm Carmen."

Carlos seemed to shake himself out of his Enid-induced stupor, and let a broad smile stretch across his face. "It's wonderful to meet you, Carmen." Stepping forward, he shook her hand and then stepped back.

"Carlos, this is Carmen's brother, Mateo. And her..." Mariana tailed off at the end.

"Friend," Molly added, saving them all from an awkward silence. Carlos shook both their hands.

"Enid is somewhere around," Molly added.

"Oh, he's met her," Faith commented, her eyes going wide.

"Shit, what did she do?" Mateo replied. "Sorry for cursing," he quickly added, looking at Mariana, as if she might scold him, which was adorable.

Faith could already see how taken the man was with the older version of his sister. His apology earned a smirk and a poke in the ribs from Carmen. A quiet "Kiss-ass" fell from her mouth.

Mariana regarded them with a heartfelt smile. "Don't worry, I swear like a sailor at times," Mariana winked.

"So, where is Enid?" Molly asked.

"Um...in the backyard."

"Well, she could do worse," Carmen chuckled.

"Swimming in their pool in her underwear."

"Yeah, that tracks," Mateo sighed, rolling his eyes. "I'll go fish her out."

All eyes followed Mateo as he swished out of the room. Faith discreetly placed a hand over her mouth, trying in vain to stop the snort she'd been holding in for some time. It escaped anyway.

"I... I'm sorry," she laughed, her shoulders shaking with the force of her laughter. As though they were a line of dominoes, each person fell into a fit of giggles.

When they all had themselves back under control, Mariana spoke. "Where did you meet Enid? She's quite the character."

"She's my neighbor. We've actually only known each other for a short while, but the woman grows on you."

"Like fungus," Mateo supplied, re-entering the room. "She's out of the pool and drying off."

"Enid really is one of a kind," Molly smiled. "She was my neighbor before she was Carmen and Mateo's."

"Oh? So...you two aren't?" Mariana waved between Carmen and Molly.

"Um," Molly began.

"Not yet," Carmen interjected with a smile. "It's a long story."

"Well, if you're happy to share, Mariana and I would love for you to stay and tell us. I was going to put the grill on."

Carlos looked as hopeful as Mariana that they'd stay. Faith's eyes connected with Carmen, who looked a little taken aback. Hoping it was the right thing to do, Faith gave a little nod of encouragement.

"Yeah, okay, that would be nice."

Whether it was because they were all congregated outside in the fresh air, or because the tension of the first meeting had finally diminished, Faith didn't know, but she felt lighter than she had before coming to Mariana's.

Carmen was way more relaxed. She still kept shooting side looks at Mariana, but had stopped wringing her hands. Molly hadn't left Carmen's side, and now and then, they held hands. Faith could see her aunt was taking her role as Support Person Numero Uno to heart. Faith figured this was Molly showing Carmen she was all in.

Mateo was surprising everyone by helping to grill the meat. Enid, bless her soul, had passed out on the sun lounger, and Faith hovered between them all. She wanted to make sure Enid didn't burn. But also, that Mateo didn't singe off his eyebrows. All hell would break loose if that happened. He usually wasn't one for cooking. Faith could only guess he was being swept up in the domesticity of it all.

"So, you helped Faith look for her aunt," Mariana said to Carmen, smiling up at Faith as she joined the trio at the table. Mariana's backyard was as impressive as her house. Carlos was a successful lawyer and Mariana worked as a real estate agent for the biggest firm in San José.

Carmen nodded. "Yup. Faith just showed up one day, and we've been together ever since. Isn't that right, kiddo?"

Faith rolled her eyes playfully at the term. "Correct. It's safe to say Carmen and Mateo saved my life."

In a surprise move, Mariana reached over and took Carmen's hand. Carmen jerked at the touch, causing Mariana to pull back quickly.

"I'm sorry, I shouldn't have done that."

"No," Carmen began, taking a breath, "it's fine. I'm just a bag of nerves today."

Faith squeezed her hands together on her lap as she watched Carmen tentatively reach to take Mariana's hand back. Looking over to her aunt, Faith saw she had tears welling.

"I think we'll leave you two for a little while, if that's okay?" Molly asked, eyeing Carmen.

Carmen looked at Molly and then at Faith. "O-okay."

"Come on, Faith, let's take a walk."

Following her aunt, Faith caught up and linked their arms together as they strolled around the expansive garden.

"That was a lot, right?"

Molly chuckled. "Yeah. But I think it's going to be really good for everyone."

"I thought Mateo was going to lose it at one point."

Molly nodded. "They've had a lot to deal with. Emotions are funny things. I doubt Mateo thought he'd ever react like that."

"But he seems okay now. Like he seems to want to be around Mariana."

"I think they'll end up having a good relationship. Mateo needs a mom just as much as Carmen does. In fact, I think it will be the best thing that's happened to the two Ruizes in a long time."

"What do you mean?"

"We both know Carmen has been Mateo's parental figure. Taking on that role meant she put parts of herself away."

"Like looking after herself," Faith replied.

"Exactly. Mateo came first. Now, I'm hoping Mariana might take on some of the burden."

"You really think they'll get close? I'm worried Carmen will shut down."

Molly pointed to a stone bench. "Why do you say that?"

Faith sat down cross-legged. "That's what she does when there is a lot of emotion involved. When we got back from California, she retreated into herself. I know that's different to what's going on here, but I think it's still a valid concern."

"I didn't know it was that bad." Molly chewed her lip.

"Meeting you rocked her world, Mol. And I don't mean because you—"

"I get it," Molly laughed, holding up her hand to stop Faith from explaining further.

"I just don't want her to do that again, you know?"

Molly pulled Faith into a side hug. "I don't think that will happen, honey. This is the one thing that's haunted Carmen her entire life. I'd be worried if Mariana hadn't been as receptive, but it's clear they want the same thing."

"I hope so," Faith breathed. "I want her to be happy."

"Me, too."

A beat of silence passed between them, then Faith grinned, turning her body towards Molly. "So..."

Molly looked back, raising her eyebrows. "So?"

"Come on, Molly. You have to tell me what's going on between the two of you."

Molly chuckled, "You're getting as nosy as Mateo!"

"Spill. Come on, I tell you everything." Faith knew she was whining like a petulant kid, but it wouldn't matter if her tactic worked.

"Jeez," Molly laughed. "We talked."

"Talked?"

"Yes, talked."

"Is that it? Well then, Enid owes Mateo some money back," Faith muttered, completely disappointed in the lack of gossip.

Molly cleared her throat. "No, she doesn't."

Faith pumped her fists in the air. "Yes! You got it on? Are you together?"

"Calm down," Molly laughed, dragging Faith's arms back to her lap. "We're taking it slow."

"Molly, any slower and you'll be going backwards."

"Carmen needs time, okay? But after today, I'm feeling confident it's going in the right direction."

"Oh, I really hope so. You guys are so cute!" Faith clapped excitedly. "I want to be a bridesmaid!"

"Whoa, slow down."

"Okay, okay. No pressure," Faith grinned. "But seriously, Molly, I'm really happy for you both."

Molly blew out a breath. "Me, too. There's still a lot to think about. Bessie and the ranch are on my mind, and I have this job with Rita to consider."

"Are you thinking of going back to California?"

"No. But I want to make sure the ranch is okay. Bessie called the other day and I think one volunteer has left, leaving her shorthanded."

Faith tapped her chin. "Mom's still there, right?"

"Yeah. And as far as I know, she's not planning on leaving. But your mom's still learning. Bessie needs someone with more experience."

"What if I visited for a while?"

"Visited? You want to go to the ranch?" Molly mimicked Faith's cross-legged position. "When?"

Faith fiddled with the hem of her shorts. "I think I have my own stuff to sort out. As much as Mom and I have talked, and to a degree, reconciled, I'm still furious. Coming here, watching all this unfold, has made me realize I don't want to wait until I'm old to figure my crap out. I plan to go to college, be with Nathalie, and build a career. Living life to the fullest is all I want, and I'm scared my past will disrupt my life, like it has for all of you. Sorry if that sounds awful. You know I love you, Carmen, and Mateo. I just don't want to...you know." Faith was rambling.

"Hey, I get it, and I agree. I'll skip the part where you think coming up to forty is old," Molly grinned. "Don't wait to get right with yourself. Do you want me to come with you?"

Faith shrugged. "Only if you want to. I know you're supposed to start your new job when we get back."

Truthfully, Faith desperately wanted Molly to tag along. She'd read them all the riot act about sticking together and now struggled to listen to her own advice.

"Bricks, remember?" Molly stated gently, poking Faith's knee with her finger. "I'll call Rita and explain. I don't think she'll have a problem with it."

"Thanks, Molly. Maybe one day we'll just be able to get on with life."

"Oh, sweetie, I have no doubt. This is just a speed bump in all of our lives. Before you know it, you'll be neck-deep in college studies, wishing for the days when you could take an impromptu trip with your bonkers family."

Faith smiled. She couldn't wait for that day to come.

16

Carmen

Her safety net had just stood up and walked away. Carmen felt her pulse speed up as she watched Molly take Faith on a walk. Things were feeling good when there were other people around, but now, Carmen found herself alone with her mother.

If Mariana's smile was anything to go by, she, too, was feeling the sudden strain.

Come on, Carmen. The hard part is done. Just talk!

"Um...so this just got weird again, huh?"

Mariana's sweet laughter rang out. "It did, didn't it? But I hope we can get past it. I just want to know you."

Carmen sat back, willing herself to relax. "I never thought I'd be sitting here. Not in a million years."

"You and me both. I hoped...my God, I hoped I'd meet you one day. I did silly things like write you birthday cards every year. I still have them in a box under my bed."

Holy shit. It hadn't occurred to Carmen the birthday she was given as a baby wasn't her true date of birth.

"When...when is my birthday?"

Mariana swallowed down a very noticeable lump in her throat. "November. Tenth of November."

Carmen nodded her head, letting the date sink in. She'd been celebrating her birthday ten days early every year, for thirty-seven years.

"Thanks," she whispered.

"Would you like to meet your grandparents at some point? I know I might be getting ahead of myself here. I just... Oh, Carmen, I'm just so happy you're here."

Taking several sips of the lemonade that no longer had ice cubes in it, Carmen took a second.

"Maybe, um, in the future. I don't think I'm quite there yet. I... I'm not someone who deals well with change. I'll need to digest all of this...if that's okay with you?"

"This is totally in your hands, *mija*." Carmen watched Mariana pinch her eyes shut when she realized the term of endearment she'd used. "I mean..."

"It's okay. This is going to take some getting used to."

But even as she said it, Carmen knew it wouldn't take as long as she'd originally thought. Meeting Mariana had gone smoothly. Yes, she'd experienced panic and anxiety in the initial stages, but after talking to her and watching her get to know Mateo, Molly, and Faith? Carmen was already feeling comfortable.

Mariana searched Carmen's face. "Would you tell me about growing up? The truth. I'd like to know if you're comfortable telling me."

"Are you sure?" Carmen all but whispered.

"Please. I want to know everything about you. I need to know."

After a cleansing breath, Carmen told Mariana what she wanted to hear. All of it. At times, she wanted to stop, especially when she saw Mariana's face crumble and her tears begin to flow. But Carmen persisted until there were no more words.

"I'll never forgive myself. I swear it, Carmen, I only wanted the best for you, but I ruined your life."

Mariana's tears became heaving sobs, and Carmen couldn't stop herself from taking the smaller woman in her arms. She surrounded Mariana in her larger frame, their heads resting next to each other. As impossible as it was, Carmen would swear Mariana's scent felt familiar. From somewhere in the depths of her subconscious, Carmen remembered the comforting smell that was her mom.

Giving in to her own emotions, Carmen joined Mariana, crying, and allowing three decades of pain to flow into the world, finally releasing Carmen of the heavy weight of it all.

There was a lot to learn about each other, but Carmen wanted it. She wanted to get to the point where calling Mariana "Mom" didn't feel foreign. She wanted the holidays together. Hell, she wanted the stupid family fights, and to be the recipient of the overbearing worry only a parent could give.

"Okay," Carmen stuttered, moving gently away, wiping off the tears and snot that covered her face. "That's enough of that," she laughed. Mariana followed suit, chuckling through sobs.

"Everything okay over there?" Mateo called. It was a minor miracle he hadn't come rushing over to see what the problem was. Maybe it was Carlos's hand on Mateo's shoulder that kept him rooted to the spot next to the very smoky grill.

"All good, *hermano*," Carmen called. "You concentrate on keeping your eyebrows."

Mateo scoffed, "I'm a grill master now."

Carmen laughed. "The burgers are on fire!"

"Shit," Carlos hissed, turning back to the grill. Mateo stood with a pair of barbecue tongs, being of no help whatsoever.

"Those can be Enid's," Mateo shouted back.

"What are mine?" Enid's sleepy voice said from behind Carmen and Mariana.

"Mateo's cooked for us."

"Sweet Jesus," Enid grumbled, making her way into Mariana's kitchen. Carmen watched Enid make herself another drink, not having a care in the world.

Molly and Faith's laughter drew Carmen's attention. She couldn't help the little frisson of heat that shot to her core as she watched Molly approach.

The woman was gorgeous, and Carmen was done hiding her attraction, although she wasn't sure she'd done a great job of it to begin with. Their relationship had changed since New Mexico. The promise of more lit Carmen's chest like a beacon.

"Just friends, huh?" Mariana's teasing voice broke Carmen's stare. She turned back to face...her mom.

"For now."

"She's lovely."

"She's *everything*," Carmen breathed.

Carmen was still picking bits of burnt burger out of her teeth several hours later. It turned out, Carlos was about as much of a cook as Mateo, but Mariana had given up trying to teach him.

The sun had long set, and the backyard was lit with strategically placed lanterns. The air was warm, and the cicadas sang loudly, but they weren't as loud as the group that sat around the large outdoor dining area.

As soon as Molly and Faith returned from their walk, the atmosphere lightened. There had been enough tears shed and truths told. Carmen didn't need to rehash anything else. She needed time to process, but for once, she didn't feel the need to do that alone. Being surrounded by laughter and love served as a much better aide than her usual self-impressed solitude.

Enid delighted Mariana and Carlos for hours. Molly practically tackled her when she tried, once again, to take off her pants, insisting everyone should see her vagina leg one more time.

Faith discussed her college application. Mateo took Mariana through his extensive skincare routine, with Molly intensely listening too. Carmen laughed along, just happy to sit back and watch her family interact.

It was probably too early to call Mariana and Carlos family. They had a lot to learn about each other, and that would take time. Neither Carmen nor Mariana wanted to rush their relationship. They had already exchanged numbers, agreeing to start messaging and occasionally having phone calls. Mariana left the timing in Carmen's hands, which Carmen was grateful for.

By the time the day wound down and everyone had started yawning, Carmen was both emotionally spent and filled to the brim. Mariana had offered them a bed for the night, but Carmen needed to take a break. She needed to talk everything over with Molly.

Awkward hugs ensued, with Mariana clinging to Carmen for a few beats longer than normal. Carmen sank into the embrace before steeling herself. Letting go proved harder than she thought. A feeling of foreboding passed over her heart; it was the vulnerable child inside, scared Mariana would disappear once more.

"Are we heading for the bar or bed?" Mateo asked, as they pulled up to the hotel.

"Bar," Enid announced, already exiting the cab.

Following along, Carmen happily sank into a booth while Mateo, Enid, Molly, and Faith waited at the bar. Closing her eyes, she took a few fortifying breaths. It had been a good day: exhilarating, exhausting, and terrifying, but good.

"Hey, I got you a beer. Is that okay?"

Molly's soft voice wound its way through Carmen's thoughts, solidifying her good mood.

"That's great."

"So, do you want to talk, or just decompress for a while?"

"Decompress—definitely. I think I've done more soul-searching and talking in the past two days than I have in my entire life," Carmen laughed.

"Agreed," Molly chuckled. "Let's just relax then."

"So," Enid chirped, sitting down next to Carmen, "thoughts on today?"

"Nope," Molly interrupted. "We're decompressing, not debriefing. Carmen needs a break."

"Aye, aye, Captain. Down the hatch, then." Enid drained her drink in three large gulps.

"Enid, I'm not carrying your old ass up to the room. Slow down," Mateo huffed, gracefully lowering himself into the booth.

"Not it," Faith called, putting her drink on the table and settling next to Molly.

"Who's not what?" Enid asked, already looking a little bleary-eyed.

"I'm not the one sharing a bed with you tonight. Mateo's on the hook this time."

"Hey," he protested, but Faith held firm.

"No way. Never again."

"I can share with Molly and Carmen," Enid announced. Carmen must have had her panic-slash-disappointment written across her face because Enid burst out laughing. "Relax, there's no chance in hell I'm getting in the middle of you two."

Molly rolled her eyes. "Anyway, moving on, Faith and I have an announcement."

That piqued Carmen's interest.

"We've decided to visit the ranch before heading back to Seattle. So, we'll leave you guys at the airport...um, whenever that will be."

No one had a clue what the plan was now. All eyes turned to Carmen. So much for decompressing.

"Um, I hadn't really thought past today," she admitted.

"That's fine, sweetie. No rush!" Enid replied.

Carmen squinted her eyes. "Are you just saying that because you want to continue drinking cocktails at nine in the morning?"

Enid barked out a laugh. "I don't need to be on vacation to do that. Although, it is a lot warmer here."

"I'll buy you a heater for the house," Carmen grinned.

"Will you supply a hunky man to feed me grapes, too?"

"I don't know any hunky men. I could send Mateo around now and then, though."

"Hey, I'm very hunky."

"You're too smooth. I like a bit of hair on my men. I don't want to be getting all hot and heavy with a chicken breast."

"Ew," Mateo grimaced. "And who says you'd get that far, huh?"

"This is so traumatizing," Faith chuckled.

"Back to the point," Molly called. "We're not in a rush to leave if you want a few more days here. Especially if you want to see Mariana again."

Carmen let the idea wash over her. It was tempting to stay for a while longer. But she'd agreed with Mariana they should take things slow. And if she were honest, Carmen was ready to think about something else. She'd happily concentrate on someone else for a while.

"I don't need to stay. Maybe tomorrow, just to relax a little before traveling. Is there a reason you're going to California?" she asked, directing the question to Faith.

"I want to visit Mom, and Bessie could use a hand."

Carmen could see there was more to it, but wouldn't push.

"And I want to make sure the ranch is okay. I still feel guilty for leaving," Molly sighed. Carmen took Molly's hand under the table as though it was something she always did.

"Want some more company?" Carmen asked, looking at Molly and Faith. "I'd love to visit the ranch again."

"Count me in," Enid called, before wandering off to the bar again.

"I'd love to join you, but I miss Daniel," Mateo sighed dramatically. "It's gross."

"It's sweet," Molly replied. "I'm happy if you want to come along, Enid." Carmen felt Molly squeeze her hand that was still linked under the table.

"Totally," Faith agreed, her face now buried in her phone, presumably updating Nathalie.

Carmen smiled. "It'll be nice for Bessie to have Enid there."

"That's because I'm a fucking riot."

"You're something, old gal," Mateo muttered, just loud enough to earn him a pinched nipple. "Ow! Shit, Enid."

"Call me 'old gal' again and see what comes next, Ken Doll."

"Oh boy. Okay, let's drink up and head to bed. It's been a long day and I cannot summon the energy to police you two," Carmen shot, downing the rest of her beer.

"I agree," Molly said, gathering up the empty glasses, ready to leave them on the bar on the way out.

"Yeah, I'm pooped," Faith yawned.

"I suppose I could do with a little extra beauty sleep," Mateo added.

The group looked down at Enid, as she was the only one still seated.

"Whatcha all looking at? You lightweights wanna go to bed? No problem. My night is still young."

Carmen's mouth opened to argue, but then she realized Enid was a grown-ass woman, and Carmen needed sleep.

The bed in the hotel had been turned down and fresh towels left. As much as Carmen wanted to fall face-first into the soft duvet, she felt sticky from a day's worth of sun. Molly obviously felt the same, as she slipped into the bathroom ahead of Carmen with a wicked smile.

"Ladies first," she called. Carmen smiled back like an idiot.

Starfishing on top of the bed, Carmen let her eyes close. She was almost asleep when her phone buzzed, waking her up. Rolling over, she plucked it from her back pocket, hoping she hadn't accidentally smooshed it when lying down.

There were two messages. The most recent was from Mariana. Carmen smiled again. Opening it up, she let out her breath. It was so strange to be conversing with the woman that had given birth to her.

For so long, Mariana was a myth; a painful reminder of how cruel life could be. And yet, after just a few hours, Carmen found herself letting go of that anger she'd been hauling around.

Typing and sending a quick reply, saying she had also enjoyed the day and was grateful they'd met, Carmen switched to the second message. It took a moment to recognize the name: Angie—the woman from the bar in Florida. Jesus, that was a surprise! No way did Carmen think she'd hear from her again.

Just as she was about to form some sort of reply, the bathroom door opened, startling Carmen enough she threw her phone across the floor. She should have taken out insurance on it. At this rate, she would have to buy a new one.

Carmen watched Molly bend down in her almost-too-short towel, pick up the phone, and skim over the screen. Carmen knew Molly had read Angie's message because the usual spark of light in her eyes dimmed a fraction.

"Here," Molly said, her smile tight. "I don't think it's broken."

"Um, thanks."

"Sure. Well, the shower's free."

Dumbly, Carmen locked her phone and slipped into the bathroom without another word. It was only when the water hit her face that she realized how stupid she'd been. Just a quick explanation of who Angie was, and Molly wouldn't have had that look on her face anymore.

The very last thing Carmen wanted was for Molly to believe she'd been fucking someone while in Florida. Molly needed to know the only woman on Carmen's mind, then *and* now, was her.

Admonishing her slow reaction, Carmen dried off, dressed, and made her way to the bed. Molly had her back turned away, but that wasn't going to deter Carmen. Sliding under the covers, Carmen summoned her courage and moved in behind Molly. She felt Molly stiffen slightly, then relax. For once in her life, Carmen was going to communicate clearly.

"Molly?"

"Hmm."

"Will you look at me?"

"Carmen, I'm tired."

"Please?"

Finally, Molly sighed and rolled over so she was almost nestled in Carmen's arms. "What's up?"

Carmen didn't like hearing Molly sounding so cold, not towards her.

"I didn't sleep with Angie. She's someone I had a drink with at the hotel bar in Florida."

"Carmen, you don't owe me an explanation."

"Please, let me talk. I had one drink and she asked me to dinner and I declined. She asked for my number. I gave it to her, only because I felt awkward turning her down. And I didn't mind if she wanted to be friends, but that's all I was ever going to offer her. I'm really surprised she messaged, to be honest. We had like a half-hour conversation."

"You obviously left an impression."

"Molly, the only woman I've been thinking about is you! But I will be completely transparent. I got drunk in New Mexico and woke up with a woman in my bed."

Molly shuffled out of Carmen's space. "Um, you really don't need to tell me. I don't want to know."

Carmen forged on. "I woke up, with no memory of her or of what happened."

"Carmen, we're not together. It's not like you cheated. Seriously, I don't need to know."

"But I need to tell you, Molly. I fell asleep on her...and I called her by the wrong name."

"Oh, shit."

"Yeah. Apparently, I kept calling her Molly."

Instead of words, Molly snorted out a laugh. "Shit, I'm sorry. Oh, God...that must have been humiliating!"

"Well, it wasn't the best morning of my life." Carmen grinned. "The point is, you are, and have been, the only person on my mind since we met, Mol. I know we're taking things slow and staying friends...for now. But please don't be under any illusion that I am looking for, or have looked for, another woman."

Scooting back in, Molly sighed. "You know, you make it really hard, Carmen Ruiz, to stay 'just friends.'"

"Because I'm an idiot?" Carmen asked, a little confused.

Molly chuckled. "No, you dork. Because you say things like that and make me want to do things that are definitely beyond the boundaries of friendship."

Carmen swallowed hard, looking down into Molly's face. God, how easy it would be to take her; explore her body like they did before. But Carmen had to resist. She had to do some processing about today, and then see where her feelings lay.

Her feelings for Molly were quite clear and didn't need scrutiny. She had to see if her head and heart were aligned, though. Ask herself if she could give everything to Molly without the risk of self-sabotaging. And yes, right now, Carmen felt good. Meeting Mariana had done a lot to aid healing of her old wounds, but she decided it was better to let the soul-stirring day end before making a snap decision. The last thing she wanted was to hurt Molly.

As if Molly had read her mind, she tucked her head into Carmen's chest and fell silent. Carmen was more than happy to lie like that all night. Their connection was strengthening with every passing minute.

17

Molly

Waking up wet and throbbing wasn't something to worry about. Well, not when Molly was alone—which wasn't the case. Carmen had played a starring role in her dreams, and, unfortunately, she'd woken up before the grand finale.

Last night, Molly had been almost certain Carmen was going to lean down and kiss her. The lust had radiated from her body. Molly was sure her own body mirrored the feeling, but Carmen didn't kiss her, and Molly realized it wasn't going to happen, so she buried herself in Carmen's chest, hoping her libido would get the message—it didn't. The pesky thing just waited until she was sound asleep to wreak havoc.

Now, her thighs were clamped tightly shut, and her breath was a little ragged. In the night they'd moved, and Carmen was now wrapped around Molly from behind. As gently as possible, Molly wriggled her way free. Carmen didn't stir. It was no surprise. Yesterday had utterly drained her.

Taking advantage of Carmen's unconscious state, Molly slipped into the bathroom. Turning the shower on, she shed her sleepwear, stepped in, and enjoyed the warmth of the water. Her clit still pulsed and she needed to take care of it. If Molly had to stay in close proximity to Carmen for the foreseeable future, she needed to make sure she wasn't in a constant state of sexual frustration.

Gliding fingers over her skin, Molly closed her eyes and visualized Carmen. The fingers tickling delicately over Molly's pert nipples were Carmen's. The palm sliding down, slowly reaching through short curls, was that of the delectable Carmen Ruiz. A low, sensual moan escaped Molly's mouth, echoing around the shower stall.

Splitting her lower lips with two fingers, Molly had to brace herself against the wall. She was so wet, and just the whisper of a touch near her clit sent a visible shiver through her body.

"Oh," Molly gasped. God, she wanted to come, but edging herself with the image of Carmen doing delicious things to her body was a good enough reason to stretch the pleasure out a little longer.

Turning, Molly leaned back, enjoying the coolness of the tiles on her ass. No longer needing a hand to steady herself, she instantly reached for her breasts. Pinching until her nipples were a little tender, Molly then drew circles around the hood of her clit.

"Jesus, yes, just like that," she hissed to an imaginary Carmen.

The double stimulation was quickly propelling Molly towards climax. Ideally, she preferred to take as long as she wanted to tease out an orgasm. The reality was Carmen could wake up any second and hear Molly's moans through the bathroom door.

As enticing as that was, Molly didn't want to put any pressure on Carmen. The next time they had sex, Molly wanted them to be entirely clear as to where they stood as far as their relationship.

The past few days had been emotionally exhausting, but it had been for the right reasons. Ridding themselves of their respective baggage allowed Carmen *and* Molly to move forward and concentrate on laying a foundation with each other. There was no doubt in Molly's mind that Carmen was the one for her. She had to trust that feeling in her chest; the one that urged Molly to follow Carmen wherever life took her, and make her feel how Carmen made Molly feel: safe, seen, and at home.

Molly had done serious dating before. She'd stayed the required time society deemed acceptable to develop "serious feelings." But none of those relationships held a candle to the feelings she'd already developed for Carmen Ruiz.

With her mind fully back on her impending climax, Molly tipped over the edge with a few more hard circles on her clit and a tug on her nipple. Biting her lip, she did her level best to keep the noise down.

"Wow," she panted after her heart had leveled out to a normal sinus rhythm.

"Molly?"

"Shit," Molly cursed, banging her head as she almost slipped on the wet shower floor. "Get it together."

"Molly, are you okay?"

"Yeah, yep, fine. Almost finished."

"Okay, no rush. I'm going to go down to breakfast. Do you want me to order you something?"

"Please. You know what I like."

You really know what I like... damn!

"No problem, I'll see you soon."

Molly listened until she heard the door click shut. A giggle bubbled up and out of her. Shaking her head, Molly toweled herself off and headed to the bedroom.

Dressed in shorts and a tank, Molly pulled her hair up into a high ponytail, knowing the heat would have her sweating, and hair on the neck was the worst feeling in those conditions.

They planned to stay another day or so and then head to the ranch, which had Molly feeling excited. She had reservations—or more like concerns—for Faith, but the only thing she could do was follow along and be there for her niece in whatever capacity she needed.

Seeing Bessie and the kids would be the highlight of their visit. They were the reason Molly had happily signed on to Faith's extra travel plans.

A part of Molly's heart would always reside on The Sunflower Ranch. Living in Seattle was nice, because it was where the people that meant the most to her lived, but she wouldn't lie and say she didn't miss the sunflower fields and fresh air, or the relationships forged with the kids who needed a place to stay.

Happy to lose herself in memories of sun-filled days in the fields, Molly made her way down to the hotel restaurant. The rest of the group had already seated themselves and were eating. Carmen gave her a heart-stopping smile, patting the vacant seat next to her.

"Morning everyone," Molly greeted, waving.

"Hello, sweetie. Sleep well?"

"God, I think I passed out as soon as my head hit the pillow."

"Same," Faith answered, barely taking her eyes from the phone in her hand.

"I," Mateo began, "am pleased to be going home later today. If I have to spend one more night in a room with Enid and her broken sinuses, I think I might commit murder."

"You're leaving today?" Molly asked, bringing up her cup of coffee and sniffing it deeply.

"I have a flight out this evening. Daniel said he's going to pamper me when I get home."

"Meaning he's been on the phone bitching at the poor guy," Carmen added.

"Hush," Mateo chuckled.

"And when are we leaving?" Enid asked, completely unphased by Mateo's comments.

"There's a flight out in the morning," Faith replied, finally putting her phone down. "Is that too soon?" she asked Carmen.

"Nope. It's perfect. Let's just relax today so we're nice and rested."

A state of calm had descended upon the group. Maybe it was because they didn't have to listen to a hyperactive Mateo belting out Cher songs, or maybe because the thought of heading to the ranch felt soothing. Whatever the reason, Molly was happy to sit in the passenger seat as Carmen drove them towards Yolo County.

The drive would only take a couple of hours, so Molly wanted to take advantage of the quiet. It sure as shit wasn't going to be calm when they arrived. She'd already received several messages from Bessie, Lisa, and Micah. They couldn't wait to see her, and she was just as eager to catch up with them, too.

Before leaving San José, Molly called Rita to update her about their plans. As expected, Rita was more concerned that the group look after themselves and take the time needed to support one another.

During the conversation, a spark of an idea had formed. Bessie needed help on the ranch. And who better to provide that than Rita? The ranch could be one of the first shelters to become a part of Rita's vision. Molly had every intention of sitting Bessie down and having a long talk.

Molly hated the idea her old friend was struggling, and she really disliked the guilt still trapped in her belly when she thought of how leaving for Seattle had put a strain on an already struggling Bessie. Before heading back to Seattle, Molly would make sure the ranch and everyone in it were taken care of.

"Oh my God!" Faith screamed, causing Carmen to swerve in a panic.

Molly whirled round, thoroughly dislodged from her musings to check that Faith was okay. "What? What's happened?"

Faith thrust her phone into Molly's face. Leaning back an inch so she wouldn't have to read cross-eyed, Molly studied the screen. It showed a picture of Nathalie posing in front of sunflowers.

"Nathalie's at the ranch!" Faith squealed.

Molly laughed out of sheer relief. "Jesus, Faith, you nearly gave us a heart attack."

"Nearly?" Carmen barked. "Fuck, I nearly ran us off the road!"

Faith, looking suitably embarrassed and sorry, blushed. "My bad," she mumbled.

A loud snore came from Enid, who was still fast asleep. She really did sound like a truck full of loose metal. No wonder Faith and Mateo refused to share a bed with her again.

"Are we all okay?" Molly chuckled. "Do you need to stop, Carmen?"

"No, I think my heart is no longer trying to exit my body through my ass!"

Molly snorted a laugh. Turning back to a sheepish Faith, she rested her chin on her hand. "So, Nathalie's in California, huh?"

Faith nodded and a giant smile bloomed on her face. "I can't believe it. I called her yesterday to let her know. She didn't say a thing."

"It's lovely she wanted to surprise you. You've got a sweet woman."

"She's the best. Gosh, I can't wait to see her."

Molly watched her niece pick at the hem of her shorts; a sure sign she wanted to ask something she felt uncomfortable asking. Finally, Molly's waiting paid off.

"Um...do you think...would it be okay..."

"You want to share a room with Nathalie, right?" Molly had to stop herself from laughing as Faith turned a deeper shade of red.

"Yeah, I mean, is that okay? I don't know the house rules at the ranch."

"Bessie won't mind. You can share with Nathalie, and um...Carmen will be in with me."

Molly noticed Carmen's side-eye and the ghost of a grin lifting her lip.

"Which means Enid can have her own space and no one has to suffer," she finished.

"Great," Faith beamed, immediately snapping her attention back to her phone.

"So, I'm in with you, huh?" Carmen muttered.

It was Molly's turn to blush. Shrugging, she let her hand wander over to Carmen's leg. "Only if you want to be there."

A shot of satisfaction traveled up her fingers as she felt Carmen's leg tense.

"I think I'll manage." Carmen's nose flared and Molly knew exactly where her mind was at. It was the same place Molly's thoughts traveled to at any given moment.

Molly couldn't go even a few minutes without getting lost in memories of Carmen naked, caressing her and sucking on her clit. She shivered.

Good Lord.

She thought after masturbating several times, she'd at least have a small reprieve from the sexual tension that seemed to lodge itself in every cell of her body. It hadn't worked...at all.

They fell silent again until Enid finally stirred. She woke and griped, "I can't feel my ass. Oh shit, I can't feel my leg!"

Molly chuckled. "Hopefully it's the plastic leg you can't feel."

"Ha, you got me. Nothing like a bit of one-legged humor to get us all going. Now, what did I miss?"

Jesus Christ! How could Enid go from zero to sixty in less than a second?

"Nathalie's in California, and Molly and Carmen are giving each other bedroom eyes. Oh, and we're nearly at the ranch," Faith said without missing a beat.

"I wasn't giving bedroom eyes," Molly heard Carmen mutter.

Enid snorted. "So, is this happening?" she asked, waving between Carmen and Molly.

"We're friends right now, okay?" Molly replied, not wanting Carmen to feel pressured.

"Friends who smash parts?"

"Jesus, Enid," Molly chuckled.

"What?"

"We're friends who...share a room, okay?" Carmen replied, to Molly's surprise.

"Ah, got ya! Friends who will probably smash parts, but it isn't quite decided yet."

"We're here," Carmen sighed, wiping a hand across her face. Molly wanted to soothe her, but definitely not in front of Enid, who looked far too satisfied with winding Carmen up.

Instead, Molly peered out the window and absorbed the familiar fields. She looked at the ocean-colored sky and smiled. It was good to be back.

Bessie was waiting on the porch, hands on hips, smiling. Molly bounded out of the car the second it came to a halt. Scooping the smaller woman up, she squeezed hard. "Oh, it's so good to see you!"

"And you, my sweet. Although," Bessie began, pushing Molly back to look her over, "you're very pale."

"That's because Seattle doesn't know what the sun looks like," Molly laughed.

Suddenly tackled out of the way by a neon blur, Molly stumbled into the waiting arms of Carmen. Taking a deep breath, Molly righted herself and glared at Enid, who was now almost dancing with Bessie. Molly couldn't stay mad, though. It was nice to see the women reunite.

A shriek of voices pierced the air. Lisa and Courtney rushed towards them.

"You're both here?" Molly gasped. "Oh, my God. I'm so happy to see you. But how? Aren't you supposed to be in summer classes?"

Courtney, who studied in New York, nodded. "Yeah, but we have this week as a study week. I'm checking in online, so it's cool I'm here. I couldn't *not* see you, Molly."

Molly hugged them both closer. "You guys look so good. How is it, living in the Big Apple?"

Lisa beamed. "We live in a shoebox, but it's awesome. My girl is doing so well," she gushed, pulling a blushing Courtney to her side.

"It's colder, but we love it," Courtney supplied. "And you? How is Seattle treating you?"

"She got sick," Faith interjected, her eyes searching the ranch.

"Rain—am I right?" Lisa laughed. "She's waiting upstairs," Lisa added, winking at Faith. Faith didn't linger.

She shot off into the house, leaving everyone to laugh kindly at her impatience.

"Where's Micah?" Molly asked. Oh, God, it felt so good to see these guys.

"At the shelter with Maureen. They'll be home in an hour or so," Bessie called from a little further down the porch.

"I'll take our bags upstairs," Carmen said, hefting Molly's bag over her shoulder. "Which room?"

"Molly still has her old room. You can take the one down the hall if you want," Bessie replied.

"Oh, no. Those two are sharing a room nowadays," Enid grinned, wiggling her eyebrows. Bessie gasped as if she'd just heard the most salacious news ever.

"Together? In the same bed?"

"Wow," Molly muttered. "Yes, we are sharing a room. Let's move on."

"Not a chance, but I'll let you off the hook for now. But believe me, Molly Parsons, we will be talking about this later."

Molly sighed. "Sweet Jesus."

"I'll just..." Carmen grinned, nodding towards the entrance.

"Yeah, that's it, leave me alone with those two," Molly joked.

"Hey, I gotta heave your bag all the way upstairs. Fair's fair, Mol." And then Molly almost flooded her panties as Carmen sent one of those sexy winks her way.

Christ, it was hard not to act on her feelings. If she had an ounce less restraint, Molly would march Carmen upstairs and strip her bare. She'd wring every drop of pleasure out of the woman.

Gritting her teeth to the point her jaw ached, Molly took a few deep inhalations through her nose. She watched Carmen disappear through the door, eyes firmly on that luscious butt.

"Oh, wow," Lisa laughed.

"Hmm?" Molly dragged her eyes away from the spot Carmen disappeared.

"Yeah, you've got it bad, Molly," Courtney supplied, fanning herself dramatically. "Hot!"

"You have no idea," she laughed. "Okay, let's grab a drink. I want you to tell me everything that's happened since I left."

As they moved to go inside, the sound of a car coming up the lane caught everyone's attention. Micah jumped out seconds later, followed by Maureen.

"Hey, we're here! I got cover for the last hour," Micah said, rushing up to hug Molly.

"It's wonderful to see you, kiddo," Molly smiled. She turned her attention to Maureen.

Even though Molly had taken Faith's mother in when she turned up bruised and battered, there was still a rift.

"Maureen, you're looking much better."

A soft smile graced Maureen Parsons' face. "I'm doing much better. Can I hug you?"

Molly nodded and entered into the embrace a little stiffer than usual. "Faith's inside," she said when they broke apart.

Maureen nodded. "Could we talk for a second?"

"Sure." Molly walked away from the house and toward the fields. They were her safe space; the place she felt able to breathe freely.

"I wanted to properly thank you for everything you've done, not just for me and Faith, but for all these kids. Being here, doing this work, has opened my eyes. I can't tell you how ashamed I am, Molly. I'll spend my life trying to make amends—with you *and* my daughter."

"I'm glad you're moving on, Maureen."

"I'm trying. Did you hear the news?"

Molly nodded. "About the pastor?"

"Yes."

"I did, and I also saw Alan."

Maureen came to a halt, her eyebrows furrowed. "What? Where? He didn't come to Seattle again, did he?"

Molly knew Faith hadn't told her mother they were taking a trip back home.

"I went back to Loretto."

"Why?" Maureen gasped.

"Because it was time," Molly stated simply. She didn't owe Maureen an explanation. The people that needed to know why, already did.

"Okay. And you saw him?"

"I did, and he looked rough."

Maureen nodded. Molly noticed the tears pooling in her eyes. "What a mess."

"Faith is here to talk to you. I won't say more than that. But the trip home was difficult."

"I know it's going to take more than a few apologies to have her in my life again, Molly. I'm prepared to do whatever it takes. I want to be the person she needed all those years ago."

Tilting her head to the sky, Molly thought of Carmen; of the way she'd embraced the possibility of having Mariana in her life.

"It's never too late, Maureen."

18

Faith

Taking the stairs two at a time, Faith headed for the bedroom she'd occupied the last time they'd stayed at the ranch. Shoving the door open with more force than she meant to exert, she almost squealed in delight at seeing Nathalie lying casually on the bed, her back resting against the headboard and a smirk on her beautiful face.

"Hey, babe," Nathalie cooed.

Faith had pretty much ignored everyone in the pursuit of finding her girlfriend. She'd feel bad about that later, but right now, the only thing she could focus on was getting her body as close to Nathalie as possible.

"Don't you 'hey babe' me," Faith growled, launching herself on to the bed.

Nathalie laughed, scooping her up into a fiery kiss. Faith grabbed at Nathalie's shorter locks, happy to elicit a moan. Their tongues fought for dominance and Faith felt herself heat up. "Take off your clothes."

"Babe, everyone is downstairs," Nathalie mumbled against her lips, but not doing a damn thing to stop Faith's wandering hands.

"I couldn't care less. I need you now!"

Sitting back on her haunches, Faith stripped her shorts and ripped off her T-shirt, swiftly followed by her bra.

"God, yes," Nathalie breathed before drawing Faith's left nipple into her mouth. The sigh that slipped from Faith was one of relief and pleasure. Four years away from this woman was going to be excruciating. They would have to find a way to see each other as often as possible when Faith attended college.

"I need you to fuck me, Nathalie."

This was a new side to Faith that even *she* found surprising. Cursing had obviously been a big no-no in the Parsons household, unless it was her father spouting it as he pummeled his wife.

It was only since living with Carmen and Mateo that she'd become accustomed and comfortable with the words, yet she rarely cursed herself, except, it seemed, when she was horny. That was when naughty Faith came to play, and she had a mouth akin to Enid.

"I...brought something with me," Nathalie stammered, her tongue only able to separate from Faith's skin for a second before she sucked it back into her mouth. Faith was definitely going to have red marks by the end of this tryst.

Throwing her head back, Faith let herself just feel for a second. "Oh baby," she moaned, "w-what did you bring?"

"A strap."

Faith ceased her movements. Liquid pooled in her panties. They'd discussed toys, and used a bullet and ventured into vibrators, but the one accessory they were most excited, and a little apprehensive, about using was a strap-on.

Nathalie had been the one who originally brought up the idea. Although they both identified as a switch, Nathalie leaned toward being a top, now and then. She'd asked Faith if she'd be comfortable with Nathalie topping her with a strap. Faith's answer was a resounding 'yes'.

"Hang on," Faith said, dismounting Nathalie, to run over to the door that was closed but not locked. If they were going to play for a while, Faith had to ensure no one could walk in on them.

Turning back to face the bed, Faith smiled as she saw Nathalie scan her from head to toe.

"You are a vision, Faith," Nathalie groaned, her tongue wetting her bottom lip in anticipation. "So... should I put it on?"

Faith nodded. Nathalie scrambled over to her luggage. Faith sauntered over to the bed, laying down, her head propped on her hand. The sight of Nathalie undressing, nervously and excitedly fumbling with their new toy sent a shiver of delight through Faith's core. And then she had to swallow back a whimper as Nathalie stood tall and proud with their new strap-on jutting out proudly between her thighs.

"It's not too big, is it?" Nathalie asked.

"No, it looks... God, it looks amazing on you. I can't wait for you to be inside me."

"Jesus, Faith, I swear to God, you could make me come just by talking."

"How about you make me come by using that?" she said, biting her lip and pointing at the purple appendage.

"O-okay." Nathalie walked back to the bed, her eyes pools of lust. "On your back."

Faith rolled back, her legs naturally opening to welcome Nathalie. Tentatively, Nathalie crawled over Faith's body. "I trust you," Faith whispered. Nathalie was excited, but it was plain to see she was also apprehensive.

Nathalie gently lowered her body. The feel of silicone between Faith's legs made her breath hitch. She was so ready for this.

"Tell me if you don't like it, or if you want me to stop," Nathalie said softly, her mouth planting delicate kisses on Faith's neck.

Without another word spoken, Faith cupped Nathalie's ass, encouraging her hips to roll. The dildo rubbed gently through Faith's wetness.

"I-I'm going to put it in. Is that okay? Do you want lube?"

Faith closed her eyes, completely lost in the moment. "No, I'm wet enough."

She felt Nathalie shift, and then felt the tip of the head circle her clit, once, twice, and then dip lower.

"I'm ready," she whispered.

Nathalie's hair brushed across Faith's breasts as she shifted her head to look down, needing to visually line the toy up properly. Faith feathered her fingers up Nathalie's sides, her breath already ragged in anticipation. And then there was a slight pressure as Nathalie slowly slid the dildo in.

"Are you okay?"

"Yes," Faith hissed. The toy was bigger than anything they'd used, but Nathalie went slow enough that Faith had time to adjust. After a few exploratory, slow thrusts, Faith knew she was ready for more. "A little faster."

Nathalie dropped to her elbows, her hips rocking a little faster. Faith's eyes fluttered shut as she indulged in the toy's effect.

"Is that good, baby?"

"Oh, yes, perfect."

"Open your eyes, Faith. I want you to look at me."

With effort, Faith opened her eyes and stared at her girlfriend. The look of awe on Nathalie's face was almost as pleasurable as the strap.

"I love you so much," Nathalie panted, her hips rolling deeper.

Faith felt herself tighten as Nathalie continued to pump. "I... I need to touch myself," she breathed. Her orgasm felt just out of reach.

"Do it." Nathalie's breathing was labored as she relentlessly thrust.

Faith snaked two fingers between their bodies, finding her aching clit. She was so hard, it only took a few pressured circles for the floodgates to unleash.

Her unconscious must have been aware of the people downstairs, because instead of letting out the guttural scream she felt building in her throat, Faith bit down hard on Nathalie's shoulder as she rode the wave of euphoria that hijacked her entire body.

The room was silent except for their combined panting. Faith clung to Nathalie until her girlfriend shifted, pulling out and leaving Faith empty. Seconds later, the dull thud of the strap hitting the floor brought Faith back to the room.

"Oh, wow."

"Yeah?" Natalie asked from beside her. "You liked it?"

"Very much." Faith turned, burying her head in Nathalie's chest.

A soft giggle caused Faith to lean back to look Nathalie in the face. "What's funny?" she smiled.

"I just wasn't expecting us to do that, like, two minutes after you arrived."

Faith blushed. "I couldn't wait. Sorry."

"Never say sorry for wanting me like that, babe. Wow, I'm really pleased I came."

Faith pulled further back until she could push Nathalie on her back. "I don't believe you have come *yet*, baby."

Nathalie grinned. "Hmm, I suppose you're right. Want to rectify that?"

Faith straddled Nathalie's lap once more. Lowering her sensitive, yet still soaked, sex directly onto Nathalie's, she began to gently sway her hips. The result was instant. Nathalie's earlier grin vanished as she bit her lip. "Y-yes."

"Mmm, that feel good?"

Nathalie grabbed Faith's hips, pulling her even closer. Faith was already beginning to feel herself build up again.

"Perfect, Faith, keep going. I won't last long."

Digging her knees into the mattress, Faith rocked harder. She felt her excitement smear over Nathalie's skin. Bringing both hands to Nathalie's breasts, Faith massaged them as she rode, edging them ever closer to climax.

"Nat, oh, I'm going to come again."

"Yes, come, baby. Come all over me." Nathalie's voice was strained as her body began to convulse. "Fuck...yes!" she gasped.

Faith fell forward as her second orgasm ebbed away, leaving her feeling perfectly sated. "I missed you," she whispered into the room.

"I missed you, too."

"How are we going to do this, Nat? When I'm away at college, it's going to be awful." The sting of tears threatened to spoil what was a wonderful moment.

"Hey," Nathalie moved Faith's face so they could look each other in the eye. "It will be hard, but so worth it, babe. I promise it's going to be fine. I'll move heaven and earth to visit you as often as possible. Please don't cry."

Unable to trust her voice, Faith leaned down and captured Nathalie's lips in a deep, slow kiss. They stayed there together until Faith felt a chill run over her body.

"Let's grab a shower."

"Then you should probably go and say hello to everyone else," Nathalie chuckled. "I'm glad your mom is at the shelter."

"Gosh, I didn't even notice. That's bad, right?"

"Stop worrying. You're young and in love. We're supposed to be assholes at this age, anyway," Nathalie laughed.

"I guess," Faith chuckled. "But you're right. I need to see everyone. Come on, let's get clean."

"With a promise of getting dirty again later, I hope?"

Faith took Nathalie's face in both her hands. "As if you need to ask."

Giggles and playful touches came to an abrupt end the second Faith and Nathalie, wrapped in towels, stepped out of the bathroom and directly into Maureen Parsons.

"Mom!"

"F-faith, hello."

An awkward silence descended. Although Maureen had reassured Faith she was accepting of her sexuality, this was the first time her mom had seen it in real life.

There was no mistaking the fact that Faith and Nathalie had been in the shower together. Maureen was blushing, her eyes darting everywhere but at the two women in front of her. Faith's first instinct was to shy away, but that feeling was unwelcome. Faith was past hiding.

"Mom, this is Nathalie, my girlfriend. Nat, this is my mom."

"It's lovely to meet you, Mrs. Parsons." Nathalie said with a confident smile.

"Yes, it's good to meet you too, Nathalie. Faith has told me a lot about you."

Smiling from Nathalie to her mom, Faith held her towel a little tighter. They really needed to get some clothes on.

"Um, we'll just get changed and meet you downstairs."

"Right, of course. See you soon."

Faith grabbed Nathalie by the arm, steering her quickly into the bedroom. As soon as the door swung shut behind them, Faith dropped her face into her hands.

"Oh my God, that was mortifying!"

Nathalie laughed. "Why?"

"We were in towels, Nat. She obviously knew we'd showered together."

"And?" Nathalie continued to dry off, unperturbed.

"Well...it's...embarrassing."

Pulling on a pair of boy shorts, Nathalie sat on the bed and regarded Faith. "Embarrassing because?"

"She's my mom. I don't want her to know about...stuff."

Nathalie threw her head back, laughing. Faith tried to scowl, but couldn't hide her grin.

"We're back to calling sex 'stuff.' Okay. And she heard nothing. Just saw two people in towels. That's not 'stuff,' babe."

"I know," Faith sighed, dropping her towel to grab some underwear. "I guess it's just not something that's ever going to feel comfortable between us, you know."

"And that's cool. You guys are starting from scratch, right? But, baby, your mom needs to know the real you. The second you try to keep parts of yourself from her, is the second you go back into the closet. There's no shame here."

"To be fair, it would be awkward if I were straight. There were a lot of 'sex before marriage' rules, back in the day."

"I get that. But they imposed those rules on you. If your mom is still living by them, that's her deal."

Faith slipped on a fresh T-shirt. "You're right. Anyway, I'll deal with all that later. I'm going to talk to her properly at some point, but for now, I want to see Bessie, Lisa, and Courtney."

"Then let's go!"

Faith entered the kitchen with an extra skip in her step. Everyone was congregated around the table, laughing and joking. It warmed Faith to see the gang looking so happy, especially Carmen, who looked visibly lighter.

"Well, look who finally joined the party!" Bessie shouted playfully.

"They were having a party of their own," Enid remarked, following up with a wolf whistle. Nathalie sniggered as Faith rolled her eyes.

"We were just saying hello," Faith scoffed.

"Ha! Multiple times by the sounds of it," Enid cackled.

Faith's eyes went wide when she spotted her mother sitting in the corner. To her surprise, Maureen was laughing quietly.

"Ugh, you're the worst. Do you know that?" Faith muttered, poking Enid in the arm.

"You love me. Now, do you want a drink? There's fresh lemonade."

"Yes, but first I need to hug some people." Faith walked around the table, hugging her friends, and sharing smiles and heartfelt hellos.

"It sucks Mateo didn't come along," Lisa commented when the table was quieter.

"He's loved up," Carmen said with a smile.

"I bet you're gutted, huh, Micah?" Courtney grinned.

"The man does have a fabulous ass," they replied.

"Jeez, you guys are incorrigible," Molly commented, but Faith saw the love in her eyes.

"Faith, a little birdie tells me you're going to be heading our way soon?"

"Does that little birdie have a penchant for neon and a plastic vagina leg?"

Bessie sat, looking confused. "I get the neon thing but—"

"I'll show you, Bess. It's fucking epic," Enid chimed in, already dropping her pants.

Molly shook her head. "Faith, sweetie, did you really need to say that?"

Faith smiled devilishly. "Yes, I believe we should all be equally traumatized."

The group spent several minutes laughing and commenting on Enid's leg. That was, until she pointed to one particular sketch. As she went to speak, Carmen physically put her palm over Enid's mouth. "Don't say it!"

Molly burst out laughing, as did Faith.

"Molly, what do you think?" Enid asked after licking Carmen's hand, which sent her recoiling.

"Yeah, Molly, is it accurate?" Faith teased.

"Okay!" Carmen shouted. "You all suck, and I'm going for a walk."

"I do love winding her up," Enid laughed. "Anyway, back to you, Faith. Tell them about school."

"I'm applying for a college in California. Rita's helping me, and hopefully it means I can study to become a counselor."

"Oh, Faith, that's wonderful. You're going to do a fantastic job. Will you continue to work for Rita after graduation?" Bessie asked, her face bright and excited.

"Yes. Actually, I'm hoping to continue during my studies, too. There's still a lot to figure out."

"And what about you, Nathalie?" Maureen interjected. "Are you going to college?"

"No. It's not my thing. I'm getting my education directly through Rita."

Faith studied her mother, looking for any hint of disapproval. She didn't see any, which was a relief.

"Nat is Rita's protégé. She'll be head of the whole thing one day," Faith gushed. She was so proud of Nathalie.

"Maybe," Nathalie smiled. "I like what I do right now."

"And what is that?" Maureen inquired.

"A bit of everything, to be honest," Nathalie chuckled. "Rita is having me work in nearly every sector. I like the diversity in my role. I like the travel, too."

"So, you'll be able to visit when Faith is in California?" Lisa asked.

"Definitely. And there will be opportunities for me to work out this way at some point, so I'm not worried."

Faith linked her hand with Nathalie's, squeezing tightly. "And I'll travel back to Seattle as much as possible."

"I'm so excited for you both," Lisa sighed. "Don't you just love, love?"

Courtney burst out laughing. "Alright, babe, relax."

"You relax," Lisa shot back playfully. "I love sitting here surrounded by happiness."

"Well said," Molly agreed. "I'm proud of you all. Look how far you've all come." Her words were a little choked. Faith felt the same. It was astounding how many things had changed since the last time they were all together.

Her eyes wandered over to her mom, who had lost all levity. Maureen's eyes were downcast, and Faith knew she was swimming in guilt, rehashing everything that had happened, and probably a whole lot more.

Once the conversation was underway again, and everyone was preoccupied, Faith made her way over to Maureen. "Want to go for a walk?"

Maureen looked up with tears swimming in her eyes. "I'd like that."

Faith led the way, walking down the lane towards the fields. Her mind wandered back to the day she met

Molly and how they'd wandered aimlessly through the sunflowers, weaving their histories together.

Back then, Faith clung to the idea of Molly. She'd needed the safety Molly represented. Now, well, she still needed her aunt. She needed all of her family, but she wasn't dependent on them to make her feel safe anymore. They'd helped her grow and become the woman she was now. It had only been a few months, but that was all Faith had needed to blossom.

Walking through the same fields now, she was offered a new opportunity; something similar to what Faith had experienced with Molly. She had the chance of a new start with her mother and a future that wasn't stained with hurt and anger, but with love and acceptance.

Faith just had to make sure her mom was on the same page, because after today, Faith would stop looking back. She would put one foot in front of the other until she had everything she dreamed of.

19

Carmen

It felt good to stretch her legs. The past few days had been a mix of sitting in cars, planes, restaurants, and hotel rooms. Carmen's body felt restless and stiff. A long walk through expansive fields was just what the doctor ordered.

It was also a good idea to have a little space from Enid, now and then. Carmen was under no illusion the old woman would be any less mischievous at the ranch. If anything, she'd probably be worse! Teasing was one of Enid's love languages, and that was fine. Carmen just needed a little time alone to digest the past few days, thereby allowing herself to fully enjoy her time on the ranch.

Being here felt right. Even before Molly mentioned she and Faith planned to detour to California, Carmen'd had the ranch on her mind. Thinking back, this place was where it all started. It was the catalyst for Carmen's need to change, and sure, that mainly came down to meeting a certain member of the Parsons clan, but she couldn't deny the ranch itself, held sway over her feelings too.

Helping, being surrounded by good people, and lending her time to the shelter, had given Carmen a sense of purpose, in a short amount of time. All of it had given her the push to sell her companies and begin working for Rita full-time. But there was still *something* missing. So far, she'd been unable to put a finger on what 'it' was, but she knew one thing. She wasn't settled in Seattle. Carmen had kept her thoughts close to her chest, unable to verbalize them yet.

Despite the love that filled the home she shared with Mateo, she didn't experience the same level of calm as she did out here in the wide-open space and the warmth. And it wasn't just California; it was The Sunflower Ranch. Carmen felt connected to it. But what did that mean for her future? Did it mean she wanted to make a huge change? Uproot her life and move? What about Molly, Mateo, and Faith?

Mateo was well on his way to domesticated bliss. That old worry of keeping her brother safe no longer factored into her future plans. Mateo had made a life for himself with his partner. There was little doubt Daniel was the one for him, and they would have a brood of mini-Mateos, eventually.

Then there was Faith, who was getting ready to really start her life. The young woman had come such a long way over the past few months, Carmen was in awe of her. Faith had a clear path, and she was already stepping out to begin her journey.

Once again, Carmen felt in her heart, that Faith would be with Nathalie for a long time to come. She would also be in California, which meant Carmen would get to see her more often if she decided to move.

As for Molly, well, that was a little more complicated. Carmen had asked for time. But the reality was, she didn't need it. Molly had set up a home in Carmen's heart many months ago and wasn't going anywhere. For weeks, Molly had consumed Carmen's thoughts, and Carmen had done her best to run from that.

She ran because that was what she did best; what she knew. But what still needed to be done was scary, and necessary for Carmen to truly change. She needed to let Molly in, especially in times of struggle. She had to trust Molly would stand by her side through the good and bad.

But how would that translate if Carmen decided she wanted to move out of Seattle? Molly told Carmen about the job offer from Rita. It meant she'd still be able to travel, but would be based in Seattle on a more permanent basis. There were so many "ifs" and "buts" to consider.

Carmen now had her mom to consider; something she never thought would happen. Her brain felt like a hive of bees. Mariana was only a couple of hours' drive away from the ranch. They'd have more opportunities to get to know each other, which was what Carmen wanted. A part of her was still angry, and she knew fixing that would take time and more therapy to work through, but having a chance to know her mom was everything.

Sick of ruminating on those same thoughts, Carmen fished out her phone and called her therapist. Before she decided on anything, or talked to Mateo, Carmen needed to make sure she wasn't making decisions off the back of a highly emotional time.

The sun beat down as Carmen walked and talked. Dr. Christine Stark had been more than accommodating over the years, often having phone consultations at a moment's notice, just like today. Carmen filled her therapist in on all the recent events; not just about herself, but also about Faith and Molly visiting Kentucky. She explained how unsettled she had begun to feel, and how her mind was leaning toward making some big changes.

As always, Dr. Stark used leading questions, helping Carmen find her own way to conclusions, rather than providing the answers. By the end of the call, Carmen felt good, which made her chuckle. Ninety percent of the time, a session with Christine left her feeling twice as shitty as before the conversation.

One call down, one to go. Mateo picked up after three rings. "Hey, *chica*. Everything alright?"

"Good, good. Is Daniel still treating you like a queen?"

"You know it! He's a true prince." They shared a laugh. "How is everyone? Is Enid behaving?"

"Of course not, it's Enid. She's already had her pants down, showing off that fucking leg. I made a swift exit after that. I'm just walking around the fields."

"Are you okay?"

Carmen stopped and lifted her head to the sun once again. "I'm good, Mateo, really good."

"For once, I actually believe you."

"I've just had a short session with Christine."

"Wow, good. I was thinking of calling her myself. Just for a check-in."

Carmen smiled. Yes, Mateo was okay. He was strong and sensible and didn't need Carmen in the same way he had before. Maybe that should scare her, or even cause her pain, but it only made her smile and feel proud.

"Do it, I think it's sensible. I might suggest it to Molly and Faith, too."

"Yeah, no reason anyone should hold on to all that crap, huh?"

"Right! And there was something else I wanted to talk about."

Carmen heard rustling. "I'm all ears, Carm. What's up?"

"I...think I want to move to California. To the ranch."

"Oh?"

"Yeah. Since we came here to find Molly, I don't know, I've just felt a connection to the place and the people. I think it's time I tried something new."

Carmen could hear Mateo breathing. She wanted to ask what he thought—ask if he was okay—but stopped herself.

After a few moments, Mateo cleared his throat. "You know, Carmen, all I've ever wanted for you is to live your life happily and for yourself. I know you settled here to make sure I was okay and had support, but I think I'm good now. Daniel has hinted a few times about looking for a house to buy—together. And I've put him off."

Carmen smiled internally as she recalled Mateo and Daniel's long-ass courting. It was even sweeter how Daniel had taken on the role of the delivery guy, just to have a chance to see Mateo. It was only after a few drinks one evening that Daniel confessed his family owned several pizzerias around Seattle, and that he was the CFO of their entire company, that Carmen realized how smitten the guy was with her brother.

Daniel had been visiting Carmen and Mateo's regular restaurant when Mateo came in one evening to pick up a pizza. Apparently, Daniel was ga-ga the second he laid eyes on Mateo. Laughing, Daniel admitted he'd become totally unprofessional and asked the manager to call him if Mateo ever placed an order, which was nuts because the Ruizes ate pizza at least three times a week.

When Carmen pointed that out to Daniel, he just shrugged and said it was serendipity because he lived just a couple of blocks from that particular restaurant.

Mateo continued to talk, pulling her back to the conversation at hand. "If this is what you want, Carmen, I'm behind you all the way. I'll miss the shit out of you, and I'm sure I'll make Daniel's life miserable for a while until I get used to you not being here with me. But if being on the ranch is the thing that brings you joy, honey, go for it."

"You won't feel like I'm abandoning you?" Carmen asked quietly.

"I could never think that about you, *hermana*. Never! We are family, and you are the person I love more than anyone in this world. I want you to have everything you've given me. Daniel and I will visit, like all the time. I'll need to make sure you aren't living in sweatpants and tank tops."

Carmen laughed. "More like shorts and tank tops."

"Well, that's a little better, I suppose."

"Look, I haven't decided anything yet. I need to talk to Molly. That's a situation that I need to get a handle on."

"Fuck yes, you do. Stop screwing around and make the woman yours."

"She's not cattle," Carmen laughed. "I want to be with Molly, and I asked her to give me time. I don't need it. I know that now, but that doesn't mean she will just fall into my arms the second I say I'm ready. It's her life, too."

"Yeah, that's lovely and all, but stupid. Molly Parsons wants to be with you. Hell, she moved to Seattle to be close to you. I put her in your room when she arrived, and don't think I didn't see her sniffing your pillow."

"Really?" Carmen didn't know Molly had stayed in her room. She closed her eyes and imagined Molly asleep in her bed. What a wonderful thought.

"Yes. Fuck, Carm, she faced Kentucky, just to make sure she was ready for you. That woman is gaga for you, Ruiz! Stop being an asshole and claim her!"

"Okay, take it down a notch. Have you had too much ice cream again?"

"I may have finished a pint earlier, but that's not the point. Carmen, life is just waiting for you to take it by the balls. That includes love. Trust yourself, and trust Molly."

"For once, I think you're right," Carmen grinned.

"Bitch, I'm always right. Now, go walk some more, let this all sink in, and call me when you've made a decision."

"Mateo, no matter what I decide, I want you to tell that hunk of a man you're ready to look for some real estate."

"I will, I promise. I love you, Carmen."

"I love you too, *hermano*."

Crap, where am I?

Carmen had been walking and talking for so long, she hadn't kept track of her surroundings. The land belonging to the ranch was vast. She knew that much. And she also knew she was still on that land as there were still beaming yellow sunflower heads as far as the eye could see, but Carmen couldn't recall ever venturing this far away from the ranch house.

Deciding to cut across the fields had proven to be a mistake, especially when she hadn't been paying attention. Now she stood on an unfamiliar dirt track, scratching her head, trying to figure out which way to go.

Playing a quick game of eenie, meenie, miney, moe, Carmen set off in the direction that won out. Eventually, the fields ended, and a forest began.

This cannot be the way back!

Taking out her phone, Carmen groaned out loud as she saw the 'no signal' notification. Was this a sign from the universe that California had no interest in Carmen Ruiz making it her home?

Scoffing at her own idiocy, Carmen rounded a bend in the road and stopped. Her breath puffed out in sheer adoration as she stood looking at a small and slightly dilapidated cabin. Judging by the exterior, it appeared to be vacant.

Letting her curiosity take over, Carmen wandered around the building, taking in its beauty. The roof looked solid, and the foundation, strong. The windows needed replacing, and the porch was probably a health hazard.

"Fuck, you're a beauty," Carmen whispered.

The sweet sound of running water caught her attention. Forgetting she was completely lost, Carmen set off in the direction of the sound. Stepping out from the tree line, Carmen let out a bark of laughter. She'd stumbled across a fucking creek. Was this place for real?

Kicking off her sneakers, Carmen sat at the edge of the water and dipped her feet in. The cold water was heaven against her hot and sweaty skin. Leaning back on her palms, Carmen tilted her head to the blue sky and breathed in the clean air. She listened to the sweet bird song and the babble of the water.

"This is fucking heaven!"

Time slipped by unhurriedly, and for once, Carmen wasn't thinking a million things. She was just there in the moment.

"I want this," she said to the trees. The more she took in her surroundings, the more concrete her decision became. When the excitement was too much, Carmen stood, dried off her feet. After a few more minutes of daydreaming, she turned on her heel and made her way back down the lane.

It took another half an hour until she was in an area that offered a cell signal. Tapping Molly's contact, Carmen waited for it to connect.

"Hey, where are you?" Molly inquired immediately.

Blushing, Carmen admitted she'd got turned around. Describing her surroundings the best she could, Carmen waited for Molly to come and get her. The rumble of a small engine drew Carmen's attention. Standing, she smiled as Molly rounded the bend on a quad.

"Well, hey there, pretty lady. Need a ride?" Molly called in a strong Southern belle accent, tipping her straw hat.

Carmen rolled her eyes, laughing. "Why aren't you just my hero," she replied in her own, and very bad, impression of a southern accent.

"Jump on, it's quite a trek back. What are you doing all the way out here?"

"I don't even know where 'here' is!" Carmen shouted over the engine.

"You're right at the property line. Your feet must be hurting after walking all this way."

Carmen thought back to the little creek and smiled. "So does Bessie own all of this, including the forest over there?" Carmen tilted her head towards the trees and the hidden cabin.

"Yeah. But this part of the ranch doesn't really get a lot of attention apart from the sunflower field."

Carmen hummed in thought. They fell silent as Molly drove them back to the main house. All was quiet when they arrived.

"Where is everyone?"

"The youngsters went into town. Bessie is in the backyard and Enid went for a nap. I'm going to grab a shower. I need to wash off the heat." Molly leaned in and kissed Carmen on the cheek, which felt… normal; like that's what they did all the time.

Happy to watch Molly walk away with an extra sway in her hips, Carmen let out a low growl. That woman was going to be the death of her. Shaking away some very impure thoughts, Carmen headed back outside. Bessie was twenty yards away, tending to her own personal vegetable patch.

"Hey," Carmen called, "need a hand?"

"I won't say no. You can clear the weeds between the strawberries if you want."

Happy to get some dirt under her nails, Carmen lowered to her knees and began weeding. They worked quietly for a few minutes until Bessie sat up and stretched out her back. "So, wanna tell me the real reason you came out here?"

Carmen chuckled. Bessie was an astute woman. Sitting back on her heels, Carmen wiped a forearm across her sweaty brow. "I'm guessing Enid filled you in on a few things?"

"Some."

"I'm ready for a change."

"Okay. And what does that change look like for you?"

"This place," Carmen breathed, daring a quick look over at Bessie. "I can't really explain it. It's just...since coming here, I feel unsettled at home."

"How can I help, sweetie?"

"Would...um...would you be open to me staying here? I'd help out and work remotely for Rita. I can spend time at the shelter. Anything you want."

"Carmen, you're more than welcome to be here. You, Enid, Faith, and Mateo injected something into the place last time you were here, and if I'm honest, I've missed it. But...well, what about Molly? I don't need Enid to tell me there's something between you now. I could see it back then."

"I'm going to talk to her about it. I just wanted to make sure it was even possible before bringing it up. We have a lot to work out."

"Then let me put your mind at rest. Carmen, I would love for you to be here. Yes, I could do with an extra pair of hands, but I could also do with your energy and compassion. It's a difficult job to take on. I couldn't really pay you, though."

"I have a job. I don't need paying."

"Well, alright, consider yourself a new resident of The Sunflower Ranch. Or, you know, whenever you're ready to move."

"Thank you. I'll talk to Molly then."

"Faith is going to be over the moon. Enid tells me she's struggled with the decision to move away."

"I think that was more about being away from Nat," Carmen smiled.

"No, she was worried about leaving you, Molly, and Mateo. You've turned that girl's life around."

"Well, if all goes according to plan, she won't have to miss me or Molly."

Bessie groaned as she stood up. "Let's grab a drink. I can honestly say you've made my day, Carmen Ruiz."

Smiling hard, Carmen jumped to her feet. "One more thing. The cabin at the edge of your property—the one in the wooded area?"

"What about it, sweetie? It's stood empty for a long time. I wanted to have it all fixed up a long time ago, but, life happened and now it just stands there, becoming lost to time. It's a shame, really. It's such a lovely area."

Carmen nodded. "What if I wanted to fix it up? I'd pay for everything. I think it's gorgeous, and…if I didn't stay in the main house, that's another room free for someone who needs help."

Bessie stopped and regarded Carmen. Her head started nodding slowly. "Yes, yes, I can see you settling in there. A little piece of paradise for you and Molly. I couldn't want anything better for the two of you. If that's what you want, you have my blessing. Make it your own. You'll always have a home here, Carmen. So will Faith, Molly, Mateo, and Enid."

Carmen took two long strides and gathered Bessie into a hug. "Thank you. I know this is right. I can feel it. Now I just have to hope Molly wants the same."

20

Molly

She didn't mean to overhear Carmen speaking with Bessie. Molly had every intention of enjoying a long shower with some tunes playing softly in the background, but then she'd realized her phone was still in the kitchen. As she'd turned to head back upstairs, Bessie's voice traveled through the window from outside.

"Okay. And what does that change look like for you?"

Change? With curiosity overriding Molly's respect for privacy, she'd edged toward the open window and listened. She heard Carmen tell Bessie Seattle unsettled her, and she wanted to stay at the ranch!

She continued to eavesdrop as Bessie asked the question that was hurtling its way around Molly's brain.

"But...well, what about Molly?"

Exactly! What about Molly? She'd held her breath, waiting for Carmen's response.

"I'm going to talk to her about it. I just wanted to make sure it was even possible before bringing it up. We have a lot to work out."

What did that mean? Did Carmen want to involve Molly in the move, or would she prefer a long-distance relationship? Hell, if they ever even got to that! She'd tuned out of the conversation until Carmen said, *"Well, if all goes according to plan, she won't have to miss me or Molly."*

That part must have been about Faith, Molly guessed. So, if she took anything from that last comment, Carmen hoped Molly would be with her in California, right?

With a new set of questions, Molly hightailed it to the bathroom. The water helped to relax her muscles, and it was nice not to feel sticky with sweat, but the shower couldn't help settle the nerves thrumming throughout her body. In just a few sentences, Carmen had opened them up to a very serious conversation.

As far as Molly knew, they were only just getting to the point where they could move past friendship, and now Carmen was talking about moving to an entirely different state—possibly together!

Huffing out a frustrated breath, Molly turned off the water and dried herself. There was no way she could wait for answers—not when the possibility of what she thought Carmen was suggesting was tangible, and very much wanted by Molly.

Sticking her head around the bedroom door, Molly listened. Voices were in the kitchen, and one was Carmen's. Good.

"Carmen," she shouted. "Can you come here for a second?"

Hearing a chair scrape back from the table, Molly strolled over to the bed and sat on the end, one leg crossed over the other, completely naked. It was time to get some clarification.

The wooden stairs creaked as Carmen made her way up. Molly's heart gave a particularly hard *thump*. Pulling her wet hair over one shoulder, Molly straightened her back. The door opened and Carmen walked in and almost tripped over her own feet as she spotted Molly.

"M-Molly, what are you doing?" Carmen whisper-hissed.

"Shut the door, Carmen." Molly's tone left no room for argument, and by the way Carmen swallowed, she liked it. "Now, stand here." Molly pointed to the spot directly in front of her crossed legs.

Carmen only hesitated for a second. As soon as Carmen was within reach, Molly uncrossed her legs and pulled her in by the waist of her shorts.

"M-Molly?"

Molly looked up into Carmen's hooded eyes. Choosing to stay silent, she flicked the button on Carmen's shorts, then gave them a sharp tug until they pooled on the floor. Next went Carmen's boyshorts. Hooking her hand at the back of Carmen's leg, Molly lifted it, placing it on the bed next to her own hip.

Carmen was understandably stunned.

"Do you want me to stop?" Molly asked. "Or do you want me to eat your pussy?"

"Jesus," Carmen gasped. "Eat...eat me."

"My pleasure." Molly snaked her hand around Carmen's ass, pulling her closer. Taking a moment to inhale Carmen's gathering excitement, Molly swiped her tongue up Carmen's slit. She reveled in the choked gasp Carmen emitted and the hand she placed firmly on the back of Molly's head.

Lapping and sucking, Molly parted her own legs, needing to relieve some of her own eagerness.

"Are...are you touching yourself?" Carmen moaned.

"Yes," Molly answered easily, ramping up the ministrations on herself and on Carmen's clit.

"Jesus fucking Christ!" The grip on Molly's head tightened, and she loved it.

Rocking her own hips into waiting fingertips, Molly consumed Carmen's pleasure before taking her clit between her teeth, giving a gentle nip. "Shit, Mol, I need to come, oh..."

"Come, Carmen. Let me feel it running down my chin."

"Molly...oh, oh yes. I'm—"

Molly sucked hard on Carmen's rigid bud, squeezing her ass. Her own fingers raced to tip herself over the edge. As Carmen's body tightened, Molly's started to tremble.

As their orgasms subsided, Molly let her head drop forward to rest on Carmen's stomach. Carmen's body sagged, both women breathing hard. Finally, Molly pulled back and looked up. Carmen stared back with a mix of awe and surprise, which had been exactly how Molly felt while she processed Carmen's earlier words with Bessie.

Rising from the bed, she gently pushed Carmen back a step. Turning, Molly mounted the bed on her knees. Looking over her shoulder, she crooked a finger, beckoning Carmen forward.

As Carmen settled in behind her, Molly reached back, taking one of Carmen's hands, guiding it to her breast. Carmen immediately rolled her nipple—just what Molly wanted.

Reaching back again, Molly guided Carmen's free hand over her ass and between her legs.

"Fuck me," she purred.

The bite on her shoulder conveyed Carmen's thoughts on that particular command. Widening her stance, Molly reveled in Carmen's fingers playing with one nipple and then the other, as other fingertips made their way between her legs.

It wasn't a surprise Carmen needed only one pass through Molly's wetness before she was ready to enter her. Two fingers pushed in slow and deep. Arching her back, Molly reached back around Carmen's neck, finding the hair tie that held up those delicious dark locks. With a bit of force, Molly pulled, and was rewarded with a growl and an extra sharp tug on her left nipple, as she scraped her fingernails over Carmen's scalp.

A sharp cry left Molly's lips as Carmen added a third finger, thrusting harder and faster. Craning her neck, Molly searched for Carmen's mouth. The kiss was messy and frantic. Molly's whole body writhed as Carmen played, extracting every drop of pleasure.

"Yes, don't stop," Molly moaned, her voice getting louder.

"I won't stop, Mol, not until you beg me to."

That was all it took. Molly grabbed Carmen's head, her own thrown back as a howl echoed around the room. Her conscious body was replaced with unadulterated exultation.

Slumping, Molly allowed Carmen's strong arms to hold her up, her head laying back on Carmen's shoulder. "That...was...out...of this...world."

"I'll say," Carmen replied, planting kisses up Molly's neck. "Want to tell me what inspired it?"

Giving one last stroke of Carmen's hair, Molly drew away, allowing herself room to turn around on the bed. Facing Carmen, Molly smiled. Leaning forward, Molly kissed her slowly before pulling back a little to rub her nose against Carmen's. "Are we more than friends now? Are we an *us*?"

Carmen took another kiss before answering. "We've always been more than friends, Molly. I'm sorry it took me so long to say it. I know I asked for time, but I don't need it. I need you. I want you; I always have."

"Then ask me to move here with you and I will. I'm in this, Carmen, all the way if you're ready."

Pulling back, Molly watched Carmen's confused expression. "How?—"

"I heard you talking to Bessie. I just needed to know we were moving forward. I can't do long distance, Carmen—not with you. And if the ranch is where you feel at home, I want to be here with you."

"Don't you think that's fast, though? We'll be practically living together. We haven't even had a date."

"So, ask me out." Molly wasn't going to let socially acceptable timings stop her from being with Carmen. It had taken her long enough to find the woman, and even longer to get to this point.

"Now?"

"Have you got something better to do?" Molly grinned.

Carmen's face stretched into a smile that, honest to God, warmed Molly through to her soul. "Molly, would you like to go out with me? On a date?"

"Hmmm, I'll have to think about it," she replied, laughing when Carmen furrowed her eyebrows before pinning her to the bed. Looking up at Carmen, who now rested over Molly on her elbows, she leaned up and nipped the end of Carmen's nose. "What took you so long, Ruiz?"

"I have no fucking idea."

Molly Parsons had never been so thoroughly fucked in her entire life!

She and Carmen had confirmed their new relationship status, verbally and physically—many, many times. It was as if giving each other permission to truly show how they felt had finally unleashed a caged animal, a.k.a. their utter need to devour one another for hours on end.

They'd missed dinner. Muted conversations downstairs made them vaguely aware they weren't the only two people in the universe, but not for long and not when Carmen would put her talented tongue on Molly...or graze those wonderful fingers up and down her back...or bend her over and ravish her pussy until she was a noodle of a human being.

No, Molly had never experienced anything quite like this. Even more surprising was the way she felt as the sunlight lit up their room the following morning. The change between her and Carmen was palpable. There was no fear she'd find herself alone in bed. The second Molly's brain became conscious of the waking world, it purred in contentment at the warmth surrounding her body.

Carmen was there, snuggled into her back, gentle puffs of air rolling over Molly's neck causing bumps to rise. The room smelled of sex and promise. Not only had they debauched each other within an inch of their lives, they'd spoken in hushed whispers.

Both finally having had the nerve to open up, they'd spilled their true feelings, and at points, it had been intense. Both women knew whatever was happening between them was strong, possibly fast, but ultimately what they wanted.

Molly listened to Carmen express her disquiet about living in Seattle. Carmen admitted she'd never properly allowed exploring what a future would look like for herself. Her life had been about making sure Mateo was safe, and then helping Faith.

But now, Molly understood that Carmen had shed that burden—the one she'd put on herself—and was ready to let her family live their lives. She was ready to demand more of herself, too, and that ultimately led to Carmen wanting to live at the ranch.

Molly had voiced her own thoughts. She was excited about the possibility of coming back to the only place that had felt like home since being ousted from Loretto.

She'd been sure to tell Carmen her job with Rita meant the world to her, and somehow, she needed both the new job and living on the ranch with Carmen to be happy. Carmen didn't miss a beat. She wanted Molly to have everything, and for once, Molly believed the sentiment to be true. She knew Carmen wouldn't be upset if Molly needed to travel. She understood Molly had a bit of wanderlust but would always come home.

It was well into the early hours by the time sheer exhaustion forced them to sleep. Now, in the light of the day, Molly had some calls to make. It was all well and good deciding these things with Carmen, but if Rita had a problem with coming to a new arrangement, their plans would have to be rethought. More likely, Molly would have to decide if she would be happy letting Carmen move back to California without her.

They also needed to talk to Faith, Enid, and Mateo. Carmen had apparently spoken to her brother, but Molly insisted, if they were serious about upending their lives, a family meeting was in order.

Rolling over, Molly brushed a few strands of hair from Carmen's beautiful face.

"Morning." Carmen croaked.

Molly smiled. "Morning. How did you sleep?"

"You mean for the four hours I got?" Carmen smiled, her eyes still closed.

Molly leaned forward, planting a soft kiss on Carmen's nose. "Well, were they a good four hours?"

"They were. Why are we awake?"

Molly giggled. "Because we have things to do."

"Is that a euphemism? Because I gotta be honest, Mol, I think you broke my body."

Tutting playfully, Molly jabbed a finger into Carmen's exposed shoulder. "Head out of the gutter, Ruiz. I need to talk to Bessie and Rita. We also need to organize a flight home or get Mateo out here to have that family meeting we discussed."

Carmen's pout was adorable. She still refused to open her eyes. "But it's warm and lovely in bed. We could just Zoom them all, right from here."

"You want to have a family Zoom meeting naked?"

"I'll pull the covers up."

Laughing, Molly rolled herself until she was atop Carmen, who now fluttered her eyelids, taking a second to adjust to the light.

"Well, hello," Carmen murmured, instantly settling lips on Molly's neck.

"Do I have your full attention now?"

"You had that a long time ago," Carmen said, nuzzling into Molly's hair, her hands wandering to Molly's ass.

Slipping a leg between Carmen's, Molly rocked gently. The hands on her ass gripped harder. "I don't think I broke your body."

"I think you're insatiable, and we might die of dehydration, but I'm okay with that," Carmen replied, biting Molly's shoulder.

Molly worked her hips until she felt Carmen's slick enjoyment coat her thigh. Their breaths became more labored as both women moved, taking what they needed. Their orgasms were fast and strong, leaving both women boneless.

"We really should grab some water or something." Molly's voice sounded hoarse. That was what multiple orgasms did to a girl's throat.

She felt Carmen's body shake with quiet laughter. "Shower and then food? I can't have you dying on me. We've only just got this thing up and running."

"Yes, leaving the bed might help us get some other things done today. Let's go!"

The shower was quick by design. Molly couldn't promise not to whisk Carmen back to bed if things got heated in the bathroom. Carmen's surprise and pout at Molly's efficiency and lack of anything sexy, was too cute.

In the kitchen, Enid was dancing her way between a pan of sizzling bacon and the table. There was a veritable feast laid out, causing Molly to worry she'd missed something.

"Morning, my little buttercup," Enid all but shouted over the Salsa music. "Sit and eat."

"Morning. Where is everyone?"

"Bessie is in the garden. Faith is still in bed with Nat. Maureen is at the shelter. The other kiddos went into town again—something to do with a market… I don't know. And I presume you know exactly where Carmen is."

Molly rolled her eyes. "I do. She'll be down in a moment."

Enid sat in the chair opposite Molly, her eyes boring a hole in her skull. "So?"

"So?"

"Hey, Enid," Carmen called, walking into the kitchen, straight over to Molly, leaning down, and planting a kiss squarely on her lips.

"Well, that answers that, then," Enid clapped. "It's about damn time. I mean, shit, you two are the anti-U-Haul of all lesbian kind. I was starting to think I'd need to take drastic action."

"I'm scared to know what you think drastic action is," Carmen replied, walking over to the Bluetooth speaker, lowering the music volume so they could all communicate without raised voices.

Molly stared at Carmen's ass. "No drastic action needed," Molly confirmed, swiping a piece of bacon. Jesus, she was starving.

"So, are you officially a couple? Can we stop farting around and actually acknowledge you two are boning like nuns?"

"Boning like nuns?" Molly choked.

"Listen, if you think those ladies are all locked up together and not touching puss, you need your head looked at!"

"Sweet Jesus," Carmen groaned.

"That's what they said," Enid shot back, laughing hysterically at her own joke. "Anyway, so?" She gestured between Molly and Carmen.

"Yeah, we're together," Carmen answered, shooting a wink in Molly's direction. Molly heated from the crotch up.

"Actually, we need to talk to you about something. We need to talk to Faith and Mateo too."

"I'm all ears, honey."

"I'll call Mateo and see if he wants to come out for the weekend. We can all talk then," Carmen suggested.

"Can you wait, Enid?"

"Sure, I'm not going anywhere. I'm going to try out the tractor later. Wanna come and watch?" she asked Molly.

"Have you ever ridden a tractor, Enid?" Molly could already see a thousand possible scenarios that all ended badly.

"Pfft. If I can ride a mechanical bull with a sombrero full of nachos and guac, while holding a penis glass, I can ride a tractor."

Molly had so many questions, as did Carmen, by the way her eyebrows reached her hairline. "Um...okay."

Enid clapped again. "Great. Carmen, you can help Bess with the heavy lifting. You need to keep in shape, build up some stamina, if you want to keep up with Molly. She's a firecracker in the sack."

"And how might you know that?" Molly retorted.

"I shared a wall with you, Mol. You don't think I heard you wear those batteries out several times a day? At one point, I was scared for your safety. That's one healthy sexual appetite!"

Molly sat stock-still, staring. "I... Why am I friends with you?"

"Why is a man smeared with whipped cream while playing golf, the sexiest thing on the planet? It's just the way of the world, Molly."

Scratching her head, Molly turned to Carmen. "I mean, how can you argue with that visual delight?"

21

Faith

Faith laid buried in Nathalie; her head nestled in the space that seemed to be made just for her, under Nathalie's head, between her neck and shoulder. Exactly where she loved to be.

Yesterday was tough. She'd hoped to have at least a couple of days to relax and show Nathalie around the ranch before wading into deep waters with her mom. But as everyone had laughed and joked in the kitchen, Faith watched Maureen's face drop and her guilt shine through. Faith knew their talk had to be then and there.

The walk they'd taken went on for miles. As soon as Faith had opened up, she hadn't been able to hold back. The conversation replayed in real time in Faith's mind.

"I need to say some things, Mom," she began. Maureen nodded but kept silent. "I'm angry and I don't enjoy feeling this way. I feel like I have this ball of hatred lodged in my stomach, and no matter what I do, right now, I can't get rid of it."

"I...I think that's probably normal, Faith, after...after everything."

Faith came to a sudden stop, unable to walk and talk any more. "Why? I just don't understand. Molly has told me how you were before I was born—before she was ejected from her home. I've gone through all the reasons you gave me when we talked in Seattle, and I just can't..." Faith was struggling to find the words.

"I can't justify the way you behaved!" she finally managed. "The times we were alone, you could have loved me. You could have spoken to me, but you didn't. You acted just like him, with hatred in your heart." Tears threatened to clog her throat.

"And now, what? You're suddenly different? After all those years? It was *you* who refused to teach me about the outside world, as much as it was him! There were times you could have gotten us away from him, but you didn't, and I think that was because, for the most part, you agreed with him!" Anger radiated over Faith.

Shaking her head, Maureen looked over the fields. "I'm not sure how to explain, Faith. I did have hate in my heart, about many things, for a long time. But I think, looking back, I used your father's new beliefs as an excuse. I was angry and miserable. Our lives blew up after your grandparents were killed. Your father pulled away and there was nothing I could do. In the beginning, I listened to his ranting and raving because it was the only way to stay close to him, but I grew bitter."

Faith didn't need her mom to tell her that. She'd seen the bitterness firsthand.

"By the time you came along, I hated myself. I hated life. We were both carefree young kids, excited to travel and see the world. But it all changed in one single day. The man I loved was broken beyond repair, and I resented the world for it."

Realizing the course of so many lives had changed the night her grandparents died, sat heavy on Faith's chest.

"Raising you became my sole focus. I knew I had to keep you in line, otherwise I'd lose you and that was unacceptable. I was bound to your father by law, and his word was gospel. He was all I'd ever known, and the thought of leaving him terrified me more than his fists. Sick, isn't it? That I preferred to take his beatings; preferred you to take them instead of being the woman I should have been—the one I was before?"

Faith swallowed hard, finding it hard to remain quiet. But she needed to hear what her mother had to say.

"I never hit you, but I know I did my fair share of damage, Faith. I will live with it until the day I die. When you ran away, I was distraught, not angry. My worst fear came true: I lost you—the one ray of light in my life."

Faith hiccupped. "You tried to snuff that light out, Mom."

Sniffing, Maureen nodded again solemnly. "I wanted you... Gosh, I don't know what I wanted. I was so lost in darkness, Faith. I vowed to make it right if we found you. But then you wouldn't come home with us. I saw how Carmen, Mateo, and Molly rallied around you, being the people I should have been for you instead of giving in to pain—instead of piling my misery onto you."

"They were the first people to make me feel safe," Faith replied through gritted teeth.

"Do you need me to leave? Take myself out of your life? I don't want to cause you any more pain, Faith. I'll do whatever you need me to."

Running a hand through her hair, Faith paced. "I don't know, Mom, really, I don't. I've wanted so badly to just forgive you and move on. Everyone deserves a second chance. I'm just angry with you, though, and I don't know how to build something fresh when I hold that in me."

"Would...would you maybe consider going to therapy with me?"

"Ugh, I don't know. Maybe...in the future."

"I...I can turn myself in, if that would help?"

Faith furrowed her brows. "Turn yourself in? What do you mean?"

Wiping both eyes, Maureen bit her lip, trying to control its tremble. "What... The way I... How I treated you was abuse, Faith. I can see that now. I...should be held accountable."

"Jesus," Faith replied. "I...I don't want you to go to the police!"

"If...if you change your mind, I will. I'll do anything, I swear it!"

Faith studied her mom's face for a few silent minutes. "I want you to go to therapy, regardless of whether we do it together. I'll do the same because I've got too much to live for, to be stuck in the past. I want to say we'll be okay, but I can't promise you that right now, Mom."

"Understood. Shall I vacate the ranch?"

"No, this is your home now. Maybe just give me some space. I think I need to talk to someone before I'm in the right frame of mind to..."

"I get it, I do. I'll do the work, Faith. Being here, surrounded by these wonderful people, makes me want to be a better person and be someone they deserve in their lives. The mom *you* deserve."

Breathing in deep, Faith gave her mom's hand a squeeze. "Okay. Um...I'm going to go back now."

"Alright, sweetie. And...for what it's worth, I think Nathalie is a lovely young woman. It's clear she deeply cares for you."

"I love her. She's everything."

"Then that's all I could ever ask for you, my love. Look after each other."

That was where Faith left the conversation, needing to take some space, and some comfort from her girlfriend.

She'd found Nathalie waiting for her on the porch and they'd escaped to the bedroom, where Faith cried until there were no more tears.

When Lisa knocked on the door asking if they wanted to go into town, Faith made the decision to buck up. She'd said what needed to be said and she was done wallowing. She'd follow in Carmen's footsteps and get things sorted in her own head. But then and there, all Faith wanted to do was spend some time with her friends, showing Nathalie the sights.

They'd arrived back late, but none of them mistook the sounds coming from Molly's room. It took five minutes of giggling before they all made their way to bed.

Nathalie had held her close all night, and Faith woke in the same position. She allowed herself a few minutes of rumination before preparing herself for a new day.

The new day would involve having a detailed discussion with her aunt. Molly and Carmen were clearly sleeping together, and Faith hoped it meant they were finally, *finally*, owning up to the fact they were definitely a couple.

Blindly grasping for her phone, Faith drew the small screen to her sleep-heavy eyes. "Crap!"

"Hmm, what?" Nathalie murmured, burying herself deeper into the bed.

"Babe, it's nearly lunchtime."

"And?"

"And I think we need to get up!"

"Why?"

"Babe, come on," Faith moaned. "Bessie will be halfway through her chores by now, and I wanted to help. She needs more help."

Nathalie rolled on her back, took a deep breath before launching herself to her feet. "I'm up, let's do this!"

Faith regarded her girlfriend with amusement. Nathalie stood with her tank top half tucked into her sleep shorts and her hair sticking up all over the place.

"Sure you don't need a minute there, babe?"

Nathalie scrubbed her face, shook out her limbs, and jumped in place a few times. "Nope, I'm pumped. Let's make these chores our bitch!"

There were exactly zero chores to be made a bitch. By the time they got downstairs, only a sweaty Carmen could be found.

"Well, hello there, young ones. Late night?"

"Not as late as some," Nathalie remarked, grinning.

"Ah, you're just jealous!"

"A lil' bit," Nat laughed.

"Hey," Faith shot laughing. "You get plenty."

"Eww, I don't want to know," Carmen mock gagged. "You're like my kid-sisters-slash-actual-kids. I claim parental or sibling rights—or whatever—to never have to hear about you two bumping uglies."

"Do you think we talk about sex too much?" Faith mused.

Nathalie scoffed. "Never. It's healthy to do it and just as healthy to talk about it."

Enid burst through the door, covered in dust and grease. "Hear, hear."

"Did you *fight* the tractor?" Carmen asked, genuinely wondering.

"The little asshole tried to die on me!"

"It did not," Molly called from the porch. "You ran over three wooden planters. The tractor was pissed and full of wood!"

"Ha, that's what she said," Enid cackled.

Faith laughed, because when Enid got going, her laugh became infectious. "Did you deal with the wood?" she managed to ask after a few seconds.

"Of course. Let it be noted that Enid Butcher could out-butch the lot of you!"

"Out-butch?" Nathalie chuckled.

"Yeah. I just need a tool belt and I'd be a pussy magnet. More than I am now."

"That's my cue to change the subject," Molly interjected, steering Enid toward the downstairs washroom. "You get washed up and changed. I don't want to be cleaning up grease all over the house."

"So bossy! Are you into that, Carmen? Does she get your motor running by—"

"Leave immediately," Molly commanded, physically shoving her through the door and closing it.

"Well played," Carmen winked.

"Okay, so this is happening, yeah?" Faith asked, pointing between them. "Like, it's not something we're all pretending isn't a thing now, right?"

"Why is everyone so interested?" Molly huffed.

"Don't huff at me, Molly Parsons. I'm the one who had to see you all maudlin and pining!"

"Pining?" Carmen asked, her face full of amusement. "Sweetie, did you pine for me?"

Faith giggled, "Oh, she pined...hard!"

"Hey," Molly shot, squinting her eyes in an effort to throw metaphorical daggers Faith's way. "And, as for you," she said, turning her eyes back to Carmen, "you bet your sweet ass I pined."

Faith wanted to jump up and down and squeal with how cute Molly and Carmen were being.

"Oh my gosh, this is everything," she said, pulling her aunt and Carmen in for a hug. "I'm so unbelievably happy for you both."

"Thanks, honey," Molly beamed.

"Hey, why are you hugging without me?" Enid asked, standing in the doorway, hands on hips.

"I just found out they're together!" Faith called from the middle of the hug.

"Ah, yes, I think we should have a cocktail to celebrate," Enid announced, skipping to the liquor cabinet.

"I wondered how long you'd be able to go without a piña colada," Carmen laughed.

"It's been one day too many," Enid called back, already mixing a drink. "I'm seventy. I'm allowed to do all the naughty things now."

"As if anything stopped you before," Molly added.

"Ha, it's like you guys know me. Anyway, come on, let's get some lunch and have a drink. We've got plenty to celebrate, don't ya think?"

Faith's mind momentarily flitted to her mom and their fractured relationship. Her face must have portrayed her feelings, because Nathalie was suddenly beside her, wrapping an arm around her waist.

"Are you okay?" she asked quietly. Faith nodded.

"Hey, Faith, fancy helping me a second?" Carmen asked, beckoning her to follow. Trailing behind, Faith tried to school her features. Carmen led them outside to the picnic bench. "Let's move this into some shade so we can eat outside."

More than happy to help, Faith grunted as she heaved the heavy table. "Gosh, that's heavy."

"So are the thoughts you're mulling over, too, I'm guessing?"

Faith planted her palms on the tabletop, dropping her head. "Ugh, I'm so sick of having upsetting thoughts. I just want to be here and enjoying myself."

Carmen straddled the bench, patting it for Faith to join her. "Wanna unload?"

"I want to forget all the crap," Faith huffed. "I spoke to Mom yesterday, and it was a lot. I've asked for space."

"Fair. You don't owe her your forgiveness, Faith."

"I know, but I want to give it to her. Not for her, but for me. I don't want to carry these feelings around anymore."

Carmen nodded. "That's a good reason. But I take it you're not quite ready to build a relationship."

"When she came to see me in Seattle, I really thought I could just move on. But after visiting Loretto, and then coming to see you, I just find myself angry."

"You know, your body is an amazing thing. It protects you when you're vulnerable. When you left home, your brain went into survival mode. It put all the hurt and pain you suffered into a secure box. When you arrived in Seattle, and then traveled around looking for Molly, you were still in survival mode."

"So, what? I'm not in that mode anymore?"

"I'd guess not. You're settled and safe. Your body is telling you you're in a safe place to deal with the aftermath of your parents' behavior. That's why it's constantly at the forefront of your mind."

"So I just have to put up with it?" Faith's shoulders sagged.

"No, you deal with it. Faith, you've already taken the most important step. Recognizing and embracing what you're feeling."

"I just want to move on, Carmen."

Faith sniffed as Carmen laid a hand on her knee. "And you are. This is temporary. You will feel better, and the negative thoughts will become fewer and fewer...but only if you deal with them head on."

Faith nodded. "I think I need to speak to someone."

"Do you want my therapist's number? She's amazing and has years of experience helping people like us."

Wiping her face, Faith gave a small smile. "Yeah, I think that's a good idea. Thank you, Carmen, for being my rock. I...I love you...like you're my mom, or sister," she chuckled, remembering Carmen's words from earlier.

Pulling her close, Carmen cupped Faith's face. "I love you too, kid. I'm always here, no matter what, okay?"

"Okay."

"Hey guys, everything alright?" Molly's soft voice pulled Faith and Carmen apart.

"Yeah, all good, Mol, just taking a few minutes," Carmen answered easily.

"I can leave you alone for a bit longer if you want?" Molly asked Faith.

Shaking her head, Faith stood up. "No, I'm fine, I promise. Does anything need doing in the kitchen?"

"Avoid the kitchen," Molly began. "Actually, go and rescue your girlfriend, and then avoid it."

"Oh, no, what is she doing?"

"It involved vegetables and...never mind, just go and get her."

Faith made it to the back porch before Nathalie came running outside, her eyes wide. "I think I'd like to stay out here."

"What happened?"

"Nothing. Enid was just telling me a story, and she had visual aids. Um...that's all I want to say. Shall we go join the lovebirds?" Nathalie gestured her head toward the table. Faith turned and smiled. Molly was sitting across Carmen's lap, running a hand through her hair.

"They were made for each other. I just know it," Faith sighed happily.

"They look happy. I'm really pleased too," Nathalie began. "Carmen has always had this air of heaviness to her, you know what I mean?"

"Yeah, I saw it, too. Like she was smiling, and laughing, but there was something under the surface."

"She's been like that since I can remember. I recall a couple of the women she tried to get serious with, but it never stuck. I think this time is the winner."

Faith watched her aunt and Carmen laugh at something. "Yeah?"

"Yeah. Rita thinks so, too. I texted her earlier and let her know they finally made it official. She's over the moon. I know there were times she worried about Carmen."

"Meeting Mariana has done a lot of good, I think."

Nathalie curled her arms around Faith's middle, resting her head on Faith's shoulder, and steering them to fully face Molly and Carmen. "Meeting you and Molly has done the most good."

"Meeting Carmen has done the most good for me, too."

"Yeah, I'd say it has. Are you okay?"

Faith sucked in a large lungful of air. "I will be."

22

Carmen

The past few days had been utter bliss. They'd been so good, Carmen felt herself waiting for the other shoe to drop. It was a default feeling for her, one that hopefully, someday, she wouldn't automatically feel, but after this morning's events, it was possible her sixth sense was right to stay wary.

Molly and Carmen had offered to take the morning shift at the shelter in town. They'd spent nearly three days wrapped up in each other and felt it was time to emerge and help out. Maureen had an appointment out of town and needed her shift covered. It was a no-brainer that Carmen and Molly would step in.

All the youngsters who had luckily secured a bed the previous night had received breakfast. Carmen had enjoyed chatting with them, as always. It was coming up to the end of their shift when all hell broke loose.

Shouting pulled everyone's attention to the entrance. A man the size of a fucking building stormed in, his face red with fiery anger. Carmen's first thought was Molly. She looked around, only to find the woman storming over to the irate man. Carmen's heart dropped to the floor. What the hell was Molly thinking?

The guy continued to scream a name. Out of the corner of her eye, Carmen saw a young girl shrink back, almost climbing under the table, her face ashen.

Molly continued towards the man, but he saw the person he had come for. With a single push, he shoved Molly to the ground. Carmen heard the crack as her head hit the floor. A white noise enveloped Carmen and she saw red. Long dormant instincts resurfaced in the blink of an eye. She and Mateo hadn't survived by themselves on luck alone. Carmen knew how to defend herself.

Today, though, she was on the offensive. Jumping over the table she'd been sitting at, Carmen launched herself at the raging man. He'd been so focused on getting to the girl, Carmen's sudden appearance, her knee to his junk, followed swiftly with another knee to his face, came as a shock. He only saw the knockout blow through bleary, tear-soaked eyes.

"Call the police!" Carmen screamed, as she ensured the stranger wouldn't be getting back up. Certain he was out for the count, Carmen raced over to Molly, who was sitting up, clutching her head. Visceral panic seared through Carmen's chest. Her brain screamed she was about to lose another person. Molly was going to leave her. Only when a hand cupped Carmen's face did she realize her panic had left her completely immobilized at Molly's side.

"I'm okay. Carmen, I'm okay."

Blurred vision and shaking overtook Carmen's body. "M-Molly?"

"Just breathe, baby. In through the nose, out through the mouth."

Scrunching her eyes shut, Carmen reached for Molly, needing to feel her. Molly scooted forward, pulling Carmen in closer. Inhaling Molly's scent, Carmen felt herself calming. And then she felt anger. It was irrational, but it was there. Molly had purposefully endangered herself by approaching what seemed to be a raving lunatic, four times her size.

Pulling back, Carmen scowled. "What the fuck was that?" she cried.

Molly, seemingly taken aback, furrowed her eyebrows. "Carmen, calm down!"

"No, don't tell me to calm down. I just watched you take on a guy you had absolutely no right going near. He could have killed you!"

"Carmen, I couldn't just let him start tearing the place apart."

"You could have and *should* have!" Carmen raised her voice, knowing she was probably scaring people, but her brain was trying to process the fact she had watched the woman she was in love with—and yes, that needed to be addressed—get pummeled.

Her skin felt itchy and her heart raced. Standing, Carmen looked for something to do. Being close to Molly felt dangerous now. In one terrifying moment, Carmen understood this woman could absolutely wreck her heart.

Thankfully, paramedics arrived and whisked Molly to the back of an ambulance. The police were quick to apprehend the guy, who had started to stir. Other shelter volunteers arrived, allowing Carmen to leave. Outside, she called Bessie, asking her to come to town. There was no way she could drive.

The paramedics were insistent that Molly should be taken to the hospital as a precaution. Carmen sat a few yards away, unable to get any closer. Her heart was still thumping through her chest as she replayed the vision of Molly getting tossed to the floor like a rag doll.

Hands clasped her shoulders, which made her jump. Faith's eyes, so similar to Molly's, looked down at Carmen with concern. "Hey, we need to go. The ambulance has just left."

Turning her head, Carmen tried to take in her surroundings, but she felt out of it. "Where's... where's Molly?"

Faith kneeled down, so they were face to face. "On the way to the hospital. Carmen, did you get hurt?"

Shaking her head, Carmen pushed up from the floor. "Is she okay? Is Molly okay?"

"She's fine. I promise. Come on, we can go and see her."

She let Faith guide her to Bessie's car. She saw the concerned looks being passed between Faith and Bessie, but there was no way to figure out what that meant. Molly, *her* Molly, had been hurt, and Carmen hadn't been able to stop it. She hadn't protected her.

Bessie led her through the hospital waiting room, depositing Carmen on a plastic seat. Carmen felt herself shaking again.

"I need to see her," she suddenly blurted. A wave of nausea swept through her stomach. The need to be close to Molly was utterly overwhelming. "I need to see Molly!"

"Hey, hey," Faith began, "Bessie is finding out where she is, and then we'll go. Okay? Just sit down for a few more minutes."

The second Bessie spoke Molly's room number, Carmen bolted. She feverishly scanned the room numbers until she found the right one. Standing at the door, Carmen froze. Bile rose in her throat. She'd failed to protect Molly and then shouted at her.

Footsteps close behind finally pulled Carmen out of her daze, but the bile was still rising. Looking around, she spotted a bag for medical waste. Hurtling towards it, Carmen reached the bag just in time to unload her stomach contents.

"Carmen, are you sure you didn't get hurt?" Faith inquired, her face a mask of concern.

"No, I didn't, I promise. You go in and see Molly. I'll just be a second."

"I don't want to leave you like this."

"Really, I'll be fine. Go and see your aunt."

Faith left reluctantly, allowing Carmen a second to succumb to the tears pricking her eyes. Wiping her face and mouth, Carmen went in search of a bathroom. Once inside, she washed her face and rinsed out her mouth. The mirror above the sink reflected her haggard state. Carmen's eyes still simmered with anxiety.

"Go and see her. Just apologize." She muttered to her reflection.

Everything in Carmen's body wanted her to run away; to hide in shame, but she had to see Molly. Returning to the room, Carmen inched her way to the partially opened door. Faith and Bessie were on either side of Molly, who looked rather pissed off.

"I don't need to be here. This is ridiculous. It's just a bump."

"The doctor wants to keep you overnight to make sure you haven't got a concussion."

"You guys can check on me at the ranch. This is dumb."

"You're dumb," Faith shot, smiling. "Molly, just stay. It's one night and then you can come home. Please? For me?"

"Wow, those are some serious puppy eyes. Fine. Ugh, where's Carmen?"

Carmen was spying from behind the door, too nervous to go into the room and face Molly's ire.

"She's just outside. I'm not convinced she's okay, Mol. Did the guy hit her, too?"

"No, I don't think so."

"She vomited and seems out of it," Bessie supplied.

Molly's eyes traveled to the door. Carmen held her breath as their gazes locked.

"Carmen?" Molly muttered. All eyes swiveled to the door. Steeling herself, Carmen pushed through the doorway and into the room. Her legs felt like jelly, and then...she broke down. Seeing Molly hurt was just too much.

"M-Molly, I'm so sorry. I'm so, so sorry," she sobbed.

"Whoa," Faith gasped, jumping from the chair. Carmen felt arms surround her, keeping her upright.

Carmen's ears buzzed, but she heard Molly's voice say, "Bring her here, Faith."

Another set of arms joined Faith's, helping move Carmen to Molly's bed.

"Carmen, look at me." Molly pleaded.

She'd failed. Molly was hurt.

"Carmen!"

Molly's sharp tone pulled her eyes up from the bed to the blue-jeweled irises of the woman she was completely gone over.

"Can you leave us for a minute, please?" Molly asked Bessie and Faith, never taking her eyes off Carmen. When they were gone, Molly said, "Listen to me, Carmen Ruiz. It is not your fault. I shouldn't have approached him, not with how angry he was. I'm sorry, I didn't think."

Carmen shook her head. "No, I should have protected you. I should have got there first."

"No. It was a split-second decision on my part, and I faced the consequences of that choice. And you did protect me. You protected that girl, too, by stopping him. The police told me what you did. That guy isn't going to be walking straight for a long while."

Molly's attempt at levity wasn't lost on her, but Carmen still had a gut-wrenching feeling tearing through her body.

"M-Molly... I can't...I can't lose you."

"Oh baby, you aren't. I'm okay."

Shaking her head again, Carmen gripped Molly's hands. "When I saw you hit the floor, I thought... Fuck, I was so scared, Molly. You have the ability to completely destroy me. If you left me, I'd be alone again... I don't know what I'd do."

"I'm not leaving, Carmen. I've only just found you."

Lifting a shaking hand, Carmen caressed Molly's cheek. "I love you, Molly Parsons. I know it's fast, and all kinds of backward, considering how scared I've been to start something with you, but this morning gave me some startling clarity: I'm yours. I think I fell in love with you even before we met. I can't tell you how much I want to run away right now and hide...but I won't...I won't hide from you, Molly. But, if you feel the same, I need you to promise me you'll never do anything like that again. Please. I can't see you get hurt...not again."

Carmen watched Molly's eyes well with tears. "I promise. I'll never do anything like that again. And of course, I feel the same. I love you, and it's scary, because I *don't* want to run away. That need-to-run feeling isn't there. I want to stay still with you. I want to build a home with you, and I've never felt that way before. Just promise me you will keep talking to me, okay? No shutting me out."

"No shutting you out," Carmen echoed, leaning in. Their lips met, and Carmen felt her anxiety melt away as it always did when Molly touched her.

Carmen spent the best part of two days alternating between fussing over Molly—who did not appreciate it in the slightest—and calling Dr. Stark for impromptu therapy sessions. Saying those three little words had done a number on Carmen, and she needed help to process.

Thankfully, Dr. Stark was damn good at her job and knew Carmen well enough by now to help her out through only a few short phone calls. It turned out, allowing herself to trust another person with her heart was a tiny bit stress-inducing for Carmen. Who knew!

"Carmen, honey, if you ask me one more time if I'm feeling okay, I'm going to drown myself in the bath!"

"Jesus, Aunt Mol, that's extreme," Faith laughed.

"Desperate times, Faith. Carmen, you're driving me nuts."

"We don't have a bath," Carmen replied.

"I'll find a fucking puddle, then. Please, babe, just relax."

Huffing, Carmen sat down next to Molly on the picnic bench. "Fine, I'll stop."

"What time is Mateo getting here?" Faith asked.

"Anytime," Carmen answered, searching the dirt road for any sign of Mateo's car.

Faith picked at the sandwich on her plate. "And you still won't tell me what this family meeting is about?"

"You're going to find out when Mateo gets here."

"It's all a little Godfather-y, don't ya think?" Enid supplied from across the yard.

"It's nothing of the sort," Molly laughed. "No horse's heads to be found."

"But why the secrecy?" Faith pushed.

"Ha, he's here!" Carmen sprang to her feet. Mateo's car skidded to a halt. The door flew open, and in pure Mateo style, he announced himself loudly, flouncing over to Carmen with a wide smile and perfectly coiffed hair. "*Hermana.*"

Carmen ran into his arms. Anyone would think they'd spent a year apart, not a week. "Hey, bro, you look soooo gay," Carmen laughed. Mateo wore a sparkly rainbow top and short shorts.

"I said that, too," Daniel laughed, as he left the vehicle in a calmer manner.

Leaving Mateo, Carmen hugged Daniel. "Daniel! Oh my God, I'm so glad you came along."

"Jesus Christ, Mateo," Enid exclaimed. "Those shorts are obscene!"

"Says the woman with lady gardens all over her leg!"

"My vajay-jays are beautiful. I swear to God, if you pop a ball out of those things, I'm coming at it with a shovel!"

"It's fantastic to see you, too," Mateo laughed, hauling the old woman off her feet.

"Let's go and eat," Molly called. Carmen hooked her arm around her girlfriend's waist, needing to keep her close. She was being emotional and needy, and yes, she knew it was irritating Molly, but since the hospital stay, Carmen just needed that extra bit of closeness and reassurance.

Sitting down at the table for dinner, the conversation came alive. Daniel was introduced to Bessie, Micah, Lisa, and Courtney. Micah still had a thing for Mateo's butt, which made everyone laugh, especially when they had no qualms about admitting it. Funnier still, Daniel high-fived them, and Mateo flicked his imaginary hair over his shoulder, quite happy to be the center of attention.

Once the food was consumed, Bessie instructed Micah, Lisa, and Courtney to help her tidy up, leaving Carmen to start the family meeting.

"Okay," she began, garnering everyone's attention. "So...um."

"Carmen and I," Molly interjected, sending a wink of support Carmen's way, "have something to talk to you all about."

"You're not getting married, are you?" Faith shot her eyes wide.

"No, but thanks for the support," Carmen laughed.

"No, no. I'd totally be okay with it, but, like, I need time to organize things," Faith answered.

"Babe," Nathalie laughed, "how about we just let them tell us what they wanted to, and we can come back to the whole marriage thing another time?"

"Sure," Faith smiled.

"Anyway," Carmen grinned, "I think we can all agree it's been a whirlwind of a summer."

"Fucking Cat-5 tornado, more like," Enid barked.

"Yeah, that's about right," Mateo nodded.

"Will you lot let me speak? Fuck!"

Enid tutted, "Alright, no need to get your boxers in a bunch."

"Babe," Carmen whined to Molly, who laughed.

"Shut up and listen."

"Bossy," Enid muttered. Molly rolled her eyes.

"A lot has changed in a short amount of time for all of us at this table. We've gained a family, and it's been tough, emotional, and scary. And that's just how *I've* felt," Carmen laughed. "We've all been through the wringer a little, but I think it's safe to say, we're finally out the other side and happier."

"Totally," Faith beamed.

"I want to thank you all for coming to California." Carmen stumbled over her words a little. She wasn't used to being open and vulnerable; not willingly, anyway. "You all helped in ways I can't express, and I'm forever grateful."

"Oh, Carmen," Mateo sighed, his eyes moist, "we just wanted to see you happy, sweetie."

"And now, thanks to you, my family, I am. I'm working through my shit."

"We're proud of you," Faith added. "I'm proud of us all."

"Yes," Carmen continued. "I'm proud of all of us, too! I think we're all going to be okay, you know?"

"We know," Molly supplied, kissing Carmen gently on her cheek.

"I... We," Carmen breathed, looking at Molly for support. "Molly and I have decided to make the ranch our home."

"What?" Faith gasped. "You're moving?"

"If that's okay with everyone."

Only Faith really looked surprised. Mateo was obviously in the know, and Carmen presumed he'd told Daniel. Enid just sat smiling, and Nathalie gave Carmen a thumbs up.

"Um, are you okay with that, Faith?"

Jumping up, Faith ran around the table and circled Carmen's body from behind. "Of course I am. We'll be close by when I'm at college. I can come and visit you here. Does Bessie know?"

"I spoke to her first."

"And, Molly, you want to move, too?"

Nodding, Molly took Carmen's hand. "It's going to take a bit of organizing, but I think it's possible. We've scheduled a meeting with Rita to talk about logistics and ideas, for the end of next week. But I want to be where Carmen is, and the ranch feels like a good place for her, so I'm completely on board. We just wanted to make sure everyone was happy with the decision. I know it's a lot to pile onto an already overloaded wagon. It's been an emotional few months."

"But this is the best kind of emotion, right?" Faith clapped, squeezing herself in between Molly and Carmen.

"We think so," Carmen chuckled. Faith was almost bouncing with excitement.

Mateo tapped his water glass. "And, well, we might as well tell you all that Daniel and I have found a house."

"You have?" Carmen asked. "Where?"

"Not too far away from our place."

"It'll need some decorating," Daniel smirked, and, for some odd reason, winked at Enid.

"Pish, pineapples are cool," Enid scoffed.

"What is happening?" Molly, just like Carmen, Faith, and Nathalie, was playing conversational tennis, with no clue as to what was going on.

Enid cleared her throat. "Okay, so I may have overheard a few conversations, and by that, I mean, I snuck around and purposefully listened in."

"About right," Faith nodded.

"I knew you were planning to move here, and that Mateo and Daniel were looking for a place to buy. And well... I know Carmen couldn't possibly live without me now, so I offered to sell my place to Mateo and Daniel and invest in the ranch."

23

Molly

Trust Enid to one-up everyone with her own spectacular news. Molly searched the faces sitting around the table. Mateo and Daniel were the only ones not slack-jawed. Molly should have known; nothing got past Enid Butcher, for heaven's sake.

"Whoa, back the fuck up," Carmen finally said.

Molly's curiosity grew. Wondering how her girlfriend, which still felt totally weird and exhilarating to say, would handle Enid's news.

"I absolutely *can* live without you. I got dressed all by myself and everything, this morning." The grin Carmen doled out was a real panty-slayer.

Molly chuckled, "Babe, I had to tell you to put your top on the right way. And you forgot...never mind."

Carmen shot her a look of betrayal, causing Enid to bark out a laugh. "See, fucking useless! And I trained Molly, so by de facto, it was me dressing you this morning."

Carmen screwed up her face. "One, I'm not sure that's the right way to use 'de facto' and two, you are in no way the one who dressed me this morning. If we're going to be living in the same place, we need better boundaries, old girl!"

Enid squinted her eyes and leaned forward. "Do you remember what I said I'd do if you ever called me 'old' again?"

Carmen rolled her lips inward, sitting back in her chair. "Something to do with a prosthetic and one of my orifices, wasn't it?"

"It was, so do you want to bend over here, or..." Enid replied, tapping the tabletop.

"Let's all get back to the topic at hand, huh?" Faith called out. "You can shove your foot up her butt later." The group snickered.

"Deal," Enid replied, giving Carmen the stink eye.

"What do you mean, you've invested in the ranch?" Molly asked, happy to help her niece keep everyone in line.

"It means the money I'm going to squeeze out of these two queens for my house is going to help build another small cabin I can stay in. I have money from my jackass of a husband that will help start the build on another, slightly bigger, cabin. Bessie, and I suppose you guys too, can fill it up with kids who need a place to stay, but also might want to learn sunflower farming. Bessie and I agree we could add a work program to help the kiddos learn some skills that will help them build a résumé if and when they're ready to go out alone."

Molly was floored. When the hell had Bessie and Enid decided all this?

"That's, wow, that would be amazing!" Molly turned her head toward the house. She wanted Bessie to come over and share in the news.

"Enid, what about, like, retirement and things?" Carmen was leaning forward, her elbows on the table.

"Bessie and I have a deal. We're going to grow old disgracefully and depend on you cretins to look after us."

"Ha! You've thought it all through then," Molly laughed.

"Listen, I'm about to drop some Enid on your asses."

"What the fuck is 'drop some Enid'?" Carmen cackled, shaking her head. Molly loved to see her so carefree. Apart from the whole 'getting hit in the head' fiasco a few days ago, which caused Carmen to lose her shit a little, their time together had been an oasis of calm and sex.

Every day, Carmen seemed to relax into herself a little more, and Molly reveled in it. Carmen's entire body seemed to light up now, and if it were possible, Molly fell for her even more.

"Oh, I know what that means," Molly interjected, raising her hand as though she were in school.

Mateo sniggered and muttered, "Nerd."

"It means Enid is about to get serious. So y'all better listen up, because she won't repeat herself, and she'll probably throw something at you, like her leg, if you don't pay attention."

"Thank you, Molly," Enid nodded, her nose in the air. "Quite right—shut the fuck up and listen."

"Always the wordsmith," Nathalie murmured, causing a few low chuckles.

"You lot, for all my sins, are my only family. I don't have kids or siblings, so I've been on my own for a while, which, I may state, I don't mind. I'm a fucking delight and happy in my own company."

Molly shook her head, laughing quietly. How did she get so lucky as to have this bonkers woman in her life?

"That being said, these past few months that I've had the pleasure of spending with you all, getting to know you, have been truly happy for me. It's been a privilege watching you face your fears head on, coming out the other side stronger, and forming this wonderful patchwork family."

A grin spread across Molly's face as she looked around at her 'patchwork family', who were hanging on Enid's every word.

"I like to think I've been able to contribute something, even if that was just a few laughs. I love you all, and I'd like to spend my sparkly years having adventures with all of you. And yes, I know the proper term is 'golden years', but I refuse to be associated with a phrase that means 'old and waiting to die.' Mateo, you'll need to visit, because once I'm in the sun, permanently, I'm never leaving, FYI."

"Jesus, Enid," Mateo spluttered.

"Yeah, warn a person, will ya?" Carmen added, wiping her eyes. "We love you too, you know. I couldn't have gotten through the last few weeks without you."

"I know," Enid sighed. "Like I said, you need me to survive."

Carmen shook her head, smiling. "So, what's next?"

"We can only stay for a couple of days," Daniel began. "Our appointment with the bank is coming up and we need to get everything in order."

Faith leaned forward. "We should all think about heading back to Seattle. You two have a meeting with Rita, and I need to get myself organized. Plus, Nathalie needs to get back to work."

"Yeah, sorry, babe," Nathalie huffed. "But maybe you could stay at my place for a few nights when we get back?"

"Sure, I'd love to."

"So, should we talk to Bessie, then book some flights back to Seattle?" Carmen asked the group.

Molly stood. "I'll go find Bessie. No time like the present. When we get back to Seattle, we're all going to be busy, so let's get things organized and settled here first."

Carmen placed a soft kiss on Molly's lips. "Good thinking, babe."

"Ew, is this what they're like now?" Mateo interrupted. "All *babe* and *sweetie*? And smooching?"

"All the time," Enid added. "Sickening, right?"

"Are you for real?" Carmen all but shouted. "You've been pushing us together from the start."

Molly sighed. Carmen always rose to the bait. Enid had that mischievous glint in her eye that spelled trouble, and she loved to direct it at Carmen to provoke her.

"Carmen, *sugar pie*," she grinned, sticking her tongue out at Mateo, "they're yanking your chain, honey."

Carmen snapped her mouth shut, flipping off Mateo and Enid instead of speaking.

"So easy," Enid commented. "Okay, troops, let's get a drink."

"We're getting Bessie first," Molly reminded.

"Okay, troops, let's get Bessie to make drinks," Enid amended, grinning.

Well, at least life will be interesting.

How could it not with Enid Butcher as a neighbor?

Faith planted her hands on Enid's shoulders. "Let's leave alcohol out of it until we have a solid plan, huh?"

"Ugh, the youth of today," Enid replied, but agreed to stay off the booze for a little while longer. She did, however, pop a gummy.

Molly took that as her cue to fetch Bessie. She wanted to have a word with her old friend first, without anyone else listening in. Walking through the kitchen, Molly spotted Bessie in the living room, her feet up and a trashy book open.

"I've got a bone to pick with you!"

"Uh-oh, I'm going to presume Enid told you the grand plan, then?" Bessie said matter-of-factly.

"Oh yeah. Why didn't you tell me? I would have helped, or, I don't know, done something."

Bessie put her book down and patted the couch. "Come and sit here."

Was Molly acting a bit like a sulking teen? Maybe, but she already had a wedge of guilt stuck in her craw after leaving Bessie alone to chase after a girl. The reason she'd come to the ranch in the first place had been to take some of the load from Bessie, and lately, Molly felt she'd done the opposite.

"Molly, I know you're beating yourself up about leaving for Seattle, and I wish you'd stop."

"I just feel bad for leaving you."

"I get that, but I'm fine. This place is fine, and it's about to get better. Enid and I have become quite the gal pals."

Molly wanted to point out that if they went around calling themselves "gal pals," it was likely they'd be confused as an actual couple.

"We've both watched you all grow and struggle, but more importantly, you have all come together. We also knew you and Carmen needed some time to figure things out. Enid got talking about the future, and the possibility you guys wouldn't stay in Seattle."

"Really?"

"Oh, yeah. She called it. That woman is no fool."

Molly grinned. "No, she certainly isn't."

"I floated the idea of her coming here. We're getting older, and if you and Carmen did move, I didn't like the idea of my friend being alone."

"We had every intention of asking her to come along," Molly said.

In fact, it was one of the first things Carmen had wanted to discuss further–after all the sex, of course.

"I'm sure you did. But I was hoping to get her here faster, if I'm honest. The woman is a blast, and I haven't had this much fun in years."

"So, you're like besties now, huh?"

"Totally. She's going to braid me a gummy friendship bracelet."

Molly snorted, "She would, no doubt."

"So, while you guys were all dealing with your shit, Enid and I came up with a plan. We get to help each other *and* more kids."

Molly sank back. "Wow, it's all changing, isn't it?"

Bessie leaned back too, placing her hand on Molly's leg and giving it a pat. "It is, and it's wonderful. I'm so pleased you took a chance, Molly. You deserve all the love Carmen has to give."

"Oh, I hope so, Bessie. It scares me how much I love her. Jesus, we only said it to each other a few days ago, and since then, I've felt both elated and terrified. What if I get scared and run away?"

"You won't."

"How do you know that?" Molly really wanted to know what made Bessie so sure.

"Because you've just told me how much you love her. Every other time you flitted with the wind, and away from a woman, you weren't in love. You were still looking for it, and now you've found it, sweetie."

"But what if it's too fast? I mean, we've just started dating, already said those three words, and are now looking at living together."

"Okay, take away what society's opinions are. Forget timeframes—forget it all and just think about you and Carmen. Do you want to move here with her? Does it feel right for you? Does it feel rushed?"

Molly looked to the ceiling, gathering her thoughts. "No, it doesn't feel rushed, and that unnerves me. Before meeting Carmen, I was always diligent; always analyzing my feelings, wanting to make sure they were solid. Then she came along, and it's like I lost the ability to think straight. No matter how much I reasoned with my brain that I needed to be cautious, for whatever reason, my heart bulldozed over everything."

Bessie nodded. "After everything you experienced with Alan, it's no wonder you were cautious. It was going to take someone very special to break past those walls. Carmen is the person. You know it. You love her, and remember, Molly, all because you're in a relationship now, albeit an early one, thoughts and feelings will be a constant, whether they are good feelings, or ones that scare the shit out of you. As long as you continue to choose each other every day and talk when things feel scary, you two will be fine. Let her know your fears and help her with her own. That's how you keep Carmen Ruiz. And that's how she keeps *you*. Trust each other and just go for it, kiddo. Take risks, because, my darling, you both have so much to give one another."

Resting her head on Bessie's shoulder, Molly sighed. "Thank you, Bessie—for everything. You know I see you like a second mom, right?"

"And you know how I feel about you, sweetie. Everything will be okay, Molly. I promise."

"It has been a *day*, right?" Carmen said as she and Molly strolled slowly down the dirt road, meandering, taking in the quiet beauty of the land.

Molly tightened her grip on Carmen's hand. "Yeah, you could say that. I did *not* see Enid's news coming."

"She's a sly old fox. But I'm happy. I think she's going to love it here."

"I think we all will." Molly hadn't told Carmen about her brief therapy session with Bessie. She didn't need to. But she would do her best to open up to Carmen if those feelings ever arose again. She'd accept Bessie's advice, and trust that together, she and Carmen would always choose to keep each other.

"There's a lot to do when we get back. I'm sort of dreading it."

Molly cocked her head. "It's just organizing, babe."

"Mol, my dear sweet love, have you any idea of the pandemonium that is about to ensue? We have to help Mateo pack his closet. And if you think that's going to happen without a dozen runway shows, you're out of your beautiful mind. And then there's Enid. We'll need to help her, too. I'm dreading what we're going to find in her house."

Molly's shoulders shook with laughter as she listened to Carmen moan. "We can send Faith and Nathalie to help Enid."

Carmen gasped dramatically. "We can't subject either of them to that potential trauma, Molly. No, it's down to us. I think we need to make sure we have plenty of rum available for after."

"I'll put it on the list."

They fell silent as they continued to wander down the dirt track.

"Hey, isn't this where you got lost?" Molly asked, casting her gaze around the familiar area.

Carmen gave her a side-eyed glance. "Uh-huh. Have you spent any time around here?"

"Um, not really. Only to help with plowing the field. I know Bessie's land stretches beyond those trees."

"Have you ever been in the trees?"

"Can't say I have. Why? Oh, do you have a nature-fueled fantasy, Ms. Ruiz?"

Carmen chuckled, pulling Molly closer, dropping her hand to lay her arm over Molly's shoulder. "I have many fantasies where you're concerned. But no, I wanted to show you something and get your take on an idea I had."

"Sure."

The smell of pine was delightful. Just a few steps into the treeline, the world seemed to change into something completely different. Soft mulch padded their footsteps.

The light was bright but filtered, and the birdsong became so much louder and sweeter. Molly followed Carmen around a bend until they faced a small log cabin.

"I found this when I got lost," Carmen said, taking another step forward. "Isn't it beautiful?"

Molly nodded along, making no sound. The setting of the cabin within tall pine trees was something out of a movie, although the cabin clearly needed some work. "It's gorgeous."

"You really like it?" Carmen turned away from the building to face Molly fully.

"Yes, I do."

Carmen toed the dirt with her sneaker. "Um...what would you think of us making it our home? I know it needs work, and I'm happy to do it, or, you know, call someone who actually knows how to renovate. I thought it would be nice to have our own space, away from the hustle and bustle of the main house. But if it's too far away, that's fine, I'll forget about it. Or if it's too soon to be thinking about living together, I can stay in the cabin while you stay at the ranch house. You know, whatever you want. Um...you're not saying anything."

Molly grinned. "It was a little difficult to get a word in while you were rambling so hard."

Carmen scratched the back of her neck. "Sorry about that. I'm just nervous."

"Why?"

"Because I want to make you happy and feel like you have a home."

Jesus fucking Christ, this woman!

"Always the caretaker, huh," Molly smiled. "Baby, we could live in a tent, and I'd think it felt like home. But the cabin would be much warmer," she winked.

"So, you'd like to, you know, do it up and live here? Um, with me?"

"*With* you? Oh, I don't know. I'm going to have to give that some serious thought."

"Oh, yeah, of course. No pressure."

Molly rolled her eyes, snaking her arms around Carmen's neck, pulling her down. "I was joking, you dork. Let me be clear: Yes, I want everything you just said—in the cabin, together."

Carmen puffed out her cheeks. "You're just as much a jokester as Enid sometimes. I'm fragile."

"Fragile, huh? You weren't so fragile this morning."

"That's true. Maybe we could, you know..."

"In the woods?"

"There's no one around, and I think I know a very romantic spot to get a little hot and heavy."

"Lead the way."

Molly squealed as Carmen hauled Molly over her shoulder, laughing. "Carmen!"

"Hold on, buttercup."

Molly laughed all the way through the trees until Carmen finally set her down, capturing her lips. They parted a few moments later, breathless. And then Molly noted their surroundings, and the small creek babbling away. It was utterly blissful.

"Wow, this is…"

"I know. Can you imagine us coming here on hot summer days, getting naked and handsy?" Carmen said, her voice low and eyebrows wiggling.

Biting her lip, Molly ran the flats of her palms over Carmen's chest and down her abdomen. "I think I need you to show me what you mean. I'm more of a visual learner."

"My pleasure."

It turned out it was all *Molly's* pleasure. The birds weren't the only ones who sang in those woods that afternoon.

24

Faith

Faith smiled into the sun, which had followed them back to Seattle. They'd been back a week and already accomplished a lot. Molly, Carmen, and Mateo seemed to be on a mission to get the house packed up.

Enid was taking a more laid-back approach to the whole thing, which Faith felt sure had pissed Carmen off to no end. Seeing Carmen in full 'boss mode' was equally impressive, as it was terrifying. No wonder the woman had the creation of two successful companies under her belt.

Molly clearly found Carmen's demeanor a massive turn on, because Faith lost count of the number of times she'd walked into a room, only to find Molly devouring Carmen's face.

Today, though, they'd all got out of the house to visit Rita. Molly and Carmen were currently in a meeting with her, which allowed Faith to enjoy the mammoth-sized backyard. If she were honest, she'd already spent several days doing just that. Faith had spent one night at home and the rest curled up in Nathalie's arms, in her bed.

"Go for a dip, babe," Nathalie said over the top of her book.

"I plan to have a meeting with Rita of my own, so I don't want to get wet."

"But you look so...hot," Nathalie grinned.

"I'm not getting in the pool just so you can check me out for a few minutes."

"But... Please?"

Faith threw her head back, laughing. "I don't need to get in the pool to strip off, babe."

Standing from the sun lounger, Faith dropped her summer dress to the patio, showing off her new bikini. The weather was nowhere near as nice as in California, but today was warm enough to warrant fewer clothes.

"What time is your meeting?" Nathalie asked, as her eyes scanned Faith's body from head to toe.

"In about ten minutes, so don't start getting any ideas."

"Start?" Nathalie laughed. "I'm almost at the point of finishing. You look incredible. I want to do—"

"Faith, Rita's waiting in her study," Molly called, poking her head around the sliding glass door.

"Oh, great. How did it go?"

Molly smiled. "Good. Will you come to the house tonight and have dinner with us? I think Carmen wants to check in, and we can chat about the details of our meeting."

"Sure, I'll come over before five."

"Nat? Care to join us for tacos and the ensuing argument about the amount of hot sauce needed in one household?"

Nathalie chuckled. "Love to. Thanks, Molly."

"Great, see you both later."

They watched Molly disappear. Turning back to Nathalie, Faith shrugged. "Sorry, baby, looks like you need to wait a little while longer to do whatever it is you want to do to me."

"No problem. In fact, I'm going to head on upstairs, take a shower, and maybe start things off."

Pouting, Faith bent down from her hips until her cleavage was in Nathalie's direct line of sight. "Hmm, don't get too far."

Nathalie licked her lips, her eyes glued to Faith's breasts. "Maybe I'll wait."

"I think that would be a better idea. I'll make it worth your while."

"Jesus," Nathalie groaned. "Go. Now. Before I kidnap you and keep you in my bed for eternity."

Planting an open mouth kiss on Nathalie's neck, Faith enjoyed feeling her girlfriend squirm. She was really getting good at this whole seduction thing.

"See you soon." She purred.

Picking up her dress, Faith threw it over her head, straightening it out as she walked toward Rita's study.

"Faith, my darling. How are you?"

"Great, thanks."

"Sorry, I've not been around much this week." Rita waved Faith over to the couch. "Sit, sit. Let's talk. Are you ready to jump on this college application?"

"I want to go. But I've decided to take a year off first."

Nobody, not even Nathalie, knew Faith's final decision. She'd thought of little else since getting back from the ranch. After learning about Enid and Bessie's plans, plus Carmen and Molly moving, Faith knew it was the right thing to do. She wanted to be there with them, helping to set up new accommodations for more kids.

The idea of getting into college solely due to Rita's influence didn't sit right. If Faith was going to go down that road, she'd do it on her own merits. And, if she did apply for this year, it would be a rush. She'd literally be thrown into classes without any preparation.

"I think I'm going to look at summer programs for next year, before starting that next fall—if I get in."

"Okay, I'm onboard with that. And of course you'll get in, I told you—"

"As much as I appreciate your offer to help, I would like to do this myself. Is that okay?"

Rita smiled softly at her. "My darling, it's more than okay. I can still provide you with character references and such. Plus, I'm a whiz at personal statements, so feel free to pick my brain."

"I promise I will. Are you sure you're okay with it? Everything you've planned recently seems to be changing."

Of course, she wasn't just referencing her own change of heart and plans.

Rita laughed, "It's never boring working with the Ruizes and you Parsons women, I'll give you that. But, no, I'm just happy to be creating something new with you all."

"I need to fill Nat in on my thoughts. I wanted to talk to you first. I'm worried everyone will think I'm giving up on attending college."

"Don't fret, Faith. Once they hear your plan, they'll be fine. I think Molly and Carmen will be over the moon, to be honest."

"Thanks, Rita. You're such a great mentor. I'll miss you."

Rita waved off Faith's comment. "I'm only as good as my student, and I'll be making regular trips to the ranch, so don't worry. We'll still have time for a coffee and a catch-up."

Interesting. If Rita planned on visiting the ranch, Molly's meeting must have gone well, although, Faith didn't really know what Molly had planned.

"Great. Um...that's all I really wanted to talk about."

"Fabulous. I can take a lunch break before my next meeting."

"Rita, you need to be taking better care of yourself."

"You're as bad as Nathalie. I'll eat, I promise, now skedaddle. I'm sure your girlfriend is having a rotten time without you. The girl can't get through an hour without you, nowadays."

"She's a smitten kitten. What can I say?" Faith laughed.

"Off with you. We'll talk soon."

Giving Rita a quick hug, Faith skipped up the winding staircase and headed for Nathalie's room, where she heard the shower running.

"Just in time," she muttered to herself, grinning.

"Oh, hey," Nathalie said over her shoulder, the water cascading down her toned back. Faith was almost salivating. "That was a quick meeting."

"It was, and I'll tell you all about it...after!"

"After?" Nathalie cocked her eyebrows.

"Yeah, after...stuff."

"I do like stuff," Nathalie replied, kicking open the glass door with her foot.

Slipping out of her clothes, Faith stepped into the shower, shutting the door. "Mmm, I love your skin," she mumbled against Nathalie's back.

"I love you," Nathalie gasped, while Faith slipped her hands up to cup Nathalie's breasts.

"I love these too!"

Nathalie's head dropped back to Faith's shoulder as she let out a wanting moan. "Pinch my nipples."

Rolling both nipples between her thumbs and forefingers, Faith pressed her sex against Nathalie's ass.

"I want to eat you out," she breathed.

Nathalie simply nodded, her breath already ragged. Faith turned Nathalie around and pressed her back against the tiles. Dropping to her knees, Faith took a second to look at her prize.

Running the pad of her thumb over the swollen bundle of nerves so clearly in need of release, Faith feasted on the sounds of Nathalie's moans, which grew louder with every pass.

"Baby, please!"

"Hold on to my head, Nat. Guide me. Tell me what you need." Faith leaned in, swiping the tip of her tongue over Nathalie's sensitive hood. She only had to brush the hood hiding Nathalie's clit, and her girlfriend almost hit the roof.

"God, I want you to fucking eat my pussy hard, Faith."

Now that was something Faith was happy to do. Diving in, Faith consumed Nathalie with a lascivious appetite. She felt Nathalie start to shake as she continued to lavish her pussy with sucks and licks.

Nathalie's scream reverberated throughout the room. A warm gush of liquid ran down Faith's chin. Not ready to stop, Faith lapped up every drop until Nathalie pulled away, panting.

"Holy shit, that was some good...stuff!" Nathalie gasped.

The Ruiz house was alive with music when Faith and Nathalie stepped through the door just after five. Salsa music pulsed throughout every room. The sound of laughter outside steered the pair towards the small backyard.

Mateo was in the middle of the grass and sporting one weird-ass outfit. He wore neon tracksuit pants, with tie-dye shorts over the top. His upper half consisted of a tight T-shirt that had a unicorn smoking a joint on the front of it, topped with a leather vest.

Faith and Nathalie shared a quick look, both raising their eyebrows as the rest of the group carried on, unaware of their presence. Mateo strutted up and down his imaginary catwalk. Carmen wolf whistled and Molly was doubled over laughing. Daniel stood by with a large drink, giggling. Enid, dressed frighteningly similar to Mateo, performed some sort of dance on the sidelines, completely lost in her own world.

"If we back out slowly, maybe they won't see us," Nathalie joked.

"Oh hell no, I need to know what this," Faith waved her hand around, "is all about."

"Okay, let's do this then." Nathalie took Faith's hand, leading her up to the small table. "Hey, everyone," she called over the music.

"Faith! Nathalie!" the group shouted.

"Come and sit down. We're just admiring some of Mateo's more interesting fashion choices over the years," Carmen cackled.

"Wow, you actually bought all this?" Faith asked, causing Molly to double over laughing again.

"Hey, it was all the rage at one point!" Mateo defended, although his grin said even he didn't buy his own bullshit.

"Never in the history of fashion has any of that been in style," Nathalie added. "You should have just lied and said you'd lost a bet or something."

"Hey, it takes time to develop fashion as impeccable as mine. There were bound to be a few mistakes along the way."

"I say we have a ritual burning," Enid shouted, still dancing. "But I call dibs on the tracksuit bottoms. I can rock those!"

"No fires," Daniel announced. "You guys want the security deposit back, right?"

"Daniel's right, no fire. We can have a ceremonial Goodwill bag stuffing event if you want." Carmen suggested.

"God, no. People do *not* deserve to be assaulted with those monstrosities," Enid replied. "Bury them in the garden or something."

"Enid, you literally just called dibs on one of these monstrosities," Mateo argued.

"Pfft, potato, tomato."

"That's not a saying," Molly laughed.

"Are we having tacos or what?" Enid asked, sidestepping Molly's comment.

"Yes, they're on the way. I ordered so no one had to go out. Let's get the table set and drinks poured. If this is going to be the last time we all sit down together for a while,

I want it to be nice," Carmen said, already clearing the table of more clothes.

Faith couldn't explain the lump that had suddenly formed in her throat. Hearing Carmen say this could be the last time they would all be together hit her hard.

But it was true. After today, Mateo and Daniel would help load Enid's boxes into a moving van and replace them with their own. Enid was eager to get back to California and insisted the guys make themselves at home, even though the paperwork hadn't gone through yet.

When Enid's lawyer had pointed that detail out, the woman had scoffed and said she wouldn't let a 'ferret in a suit with bad hair plugs' tell her what to do. That was the end of that conversation.

Faith was waiting to find out what Molly and Carmen's plans were as they now affected her, even though her aunt and Carmen didn't know it yet.

Their food arrived fifteen minutes later, and everyone crammed around the outside table, laughing and joking. Faith sat back slightly, just needing a second to watch her family.

So much had happened in a relatively short amount of time. She thought back to the day she turned up on Carmen's doorstep looking for Molly, scared and alone. She smiled at the memory of Mateo trying to dress her up, and how Carmen acted as her rock from the very moment they met.

"Hey, babe, what's wrong?"

Faith jolted slightly; she'd been lost in thought. "Hmm, nothing, I'm fine."

"Faith, you're crying," Nathalie said softly.

Bringing a hand up, Faith wiped her cheeks and found she was, indeed, crying. The table had grown quiet, everyone looking at her with concern.

"I was just remembering my first day here," she said. "How Mateo wanted to play dress up and Carmen...was just the calm energy I needed to not feel so scared. You both changed my life that day. This house...it's been the first real home I've ever had, and I suppose it just hit me we'll no longer be living in it together."

"Oh, honey," Carmen said, moving from her spot next to Molly, walking over and drawing Faith up into a bone-crushing hug. "I can honestly tell you, the day you arrived, this house became a home to all of us."

Another set of arms surrounded them. "You changed our lives just as much, *chica*," Mateo added quietly.

"I'm going to miss this," Faith hiccupped.

More chairs scraped across the ground and more warm bodies added to the pile.

"This will always be your first home, Faith," Molly whispered close to her ear. "Nothing can take that away."

"And we'll visit each other," Mateo said. "You can come and stay with us whenever you want."

"I will, you know. I'll need my facials," Faith smiled. The group chuckle quickly became a group sob. "I love you all. More than I can say."

After several more minutes, they disbanded and sat back down. Each of them had to take a second to compose themselves.

"It's weird moving out," Carmen finally said.

"When are you actually moving out? What happened with Rita?" Nathalie asked.

"Well, it was more about Molly than me. I work remotely, so it doesn't really affect me, but Molly was just offered a new position."

"So what did you manage to work out?" Mateo asked, taking Daniel's hand. Faith smiled at the two of them.

"I'm still taking the job, which means I'll need to travel now and then, but I can use the ranch as my home base. Rita will also absorb the charity side of the ranch. It means we will have more funding and help. Bessie was more than happy, as long as she and Enid could continue with their plan. Rita had no qualms with that."

"Oh, wow, Molly, that's amazing," Faith gasped. "I mean, we're going to be able to help so many kids."

"That's the plan. It's going to be a lot of work, and adjustments on everyone's part, but I have a really good feeling about it," Molly smiled.

"It's going to be great," Carmen added, kissing Molly.

"So, when will you leave?" Mateo asked.

"I'm going to drive with Enid to California in the van," Molly said.

"And I'm going to tie up some loose ends here, so I'll probably travel in a week or so," Carmen added.

Faith raised her hand, just like Molly had done at the ranch. Mateo rolled his eyes and muttered, "Smaller nerd."

"Um...so I have an update."

"Speak, child," Enid called through a mouthful of taco.

"I've decided to take a year off before starting college."

"What?" Nathalie asked, her face searching.

"Yeah, so I thought about it and there are a couple of reasons I think it's the right call. One: I want to get into college on my own merits, so I plan to take some summer courses next year. I'll apply for next fall, but I won't be too upset if I have to wait longer. Two: I want to help at the ranch. I want to be involved, and I know I could do that while in college, but I want to dedicate my full attention to getting the new aspects at the ranch up and running. There will be plenty of things to do, and plenty of time for me to hone my skills working in the shelter." Faith took a deep breath. "So, what do you all think?"

"Why didn't you tell me?" Nathalie asked.

"I wanted to make sure Rita was okay with it first, and I wanted a bit of time to sit with the decision to make sure it was definitely what I wanted."

"Okay, fair enough. So, you'll be going to California with Carmen and Molly?"

"Well, if it's okay with Carmen, I'll stick around until she's ready to go?"

"More than okay with me. And just for the record, I'm totally behind your decision. You know what's best for you, Faith."

"Same here," Molly added. "We've got your back."

"Nat?" Faith said, turning to her girlfriend.

"Baby, you know I support whatever you want to do. I'm happy we'll have another week here. And I already planned to ask Rita for some more vacation time. I've earned it. So, we won't have to be apart for too long."

Faith took Nathalie by the face and kissed her soundly.

"So that's it then," Carmen sighed, her gaze sweeping across the group and then the house. "It's happening. We're moving on."

"We're moving *forward*. Together," Molly replied, caressing Carmen's face.

Faith smiled widely, her eyes tearing up again. "You did it, Mol," she laughed. "You figured out how to keep Carmen Ruiz."

Carmen laughed, "And you found Molly Parsons."

"Jesus, you're a bunch of saps," Enid proclaimed with a grin. "I love it! Anyone for a gummy?"

25

Epilogue

Carmen

Carmen blamed Mateo for her current emotional state. That asshole! How dare he turn up with little Lucia strapped to his chest, looking like a proud papa. Son of a bitch. And on today of all days.

Wasn't it enough Carmen was going to have to watch Faith walk across the stage to accept her honors degree without breaking down into a mushy mess of a human? Now she had to deal with the swell of unconditional love that bundle of snot and poop elicited. The baby was cute, too. Carmen snorted at her own joke.

"Doing all right there, champ?" Enid asked from two seats down. There were several rows dedicated to the people there to support Faith.

"We agreed to no more sports terms. You ruined that category of endearment many years ago."

"God, I'd almost forgotten about Ralph, the hotel manager. Yeah, okay, fair enough. No more sports references. Still, you look like you're one sniff away from a total meltdown."

"I'm just a little emotional."

"Fuck. Lesbians are the worst!"

"Hey," Carmen cut in, "it's like watching my own kid up there!"

"I'm fucking with you. We're all proud of her. She's a rockstar."

"Hell, yeah, she is," Molly announced, sitting in the chair next to Carmen, looking gorgeous in her summer dress and golden hair shining in the sunlight. Oh, God, Carmen was welling up again.

"Baby, are you okay?"

"No, don't be nice to me. You'll make it worse," Carmen sniffed.

Molly chuckled. "Alright, I'll be extra mean."

"No, don't do that either."

"Oh, boy," Mateo commented, walking up to take his seat at the end of the row. "Carmen, If I'd known you'd turn into *this*, I wouldn't have told you to continue therapy. Jesus."

"Yeah, well, *this* is what you get. I'm a well-adjusted human now, who fucking cries at things."

"Well, I'm proud of you, babe. I like that you can express yourself now."

"Even when she cries after sex?" Enid asked.

"I do not cry after sex," Carmen retorted way too loud. A few other proud parents turned in her direction. "Shit," she hissed, sinking down in the chair. "Enid, you suck major fucking balls."

Enid cackled, high-fiving Mateo. "Still too easy."

"Hey guys," Nathalie panted. "Jesus, it's warm out here. I shouldn't have run."

"How's our girl?" Molly asked.

"Nervous. I don't know why?"

"Too much attention on her, huh?" Carmen sniffed.

"Something like that. Hey, are you okay?" Nathalie asked, her face marred with concern. Christ, how bad did Carmen look?

"Fine, just super proud."

"Oh, shush, it's starting," Daniel whispered from the row behind.

The crowd grew silent as the ceremony began. Carmen smiled and clapped for every student who walked across the stage to accept their diploma. When

Faith Parsons was called, Carmen's heart was seized with unbridled joy. Not only had Faith finished college, but she'd also done it as an honors student. To say Carmen was proud would be an understatement.

Watching Faith these last five years had been a privilege. She'd grown into a remarkable woman, as demonstrated by her current achievements. Not only did Faith work hard in school, she dedicated herself to helping at the ranch and the shelter as often as possible. There was nothing the woman couldn't do if she set her mind to it. Carmen was sure of it.

When all the fanfare was over, people milled about, waiting for their kids to disentangle themselves from their overexcited friends. Carmen heard Faith squeal in delight as she pushed through the crowd and launched herself into Nathalie's arms. They kissed...and kissed, until Enid finally had enough and flicked Nathalie on the ear.

"Break it up. This isn't your dorm room!"

Faith giggled, pulled back from Nathalie, and smiled a smile that could light up an entire building. "Oh my God, I graduated!"

Carmen braced herself as Faith barreled towards her. They hugged, laughed, and cried. "I'm so fucking proud of you!"

"I couldn't have done it without you, Carm," Faith whispered in her ear.

"Okay, let's all get our hugs in and then head back to the hotel. We've got some celebrating to do," Molly shouted over the din.

Carmen took Molly's hand as they strolled to the car. It was still difficult at times to accept their happiness was permanent. She often looked at Molly, Faith, and even Enid, and just felt overwhelmed with love.

That old part of herself that would panic for a moment, making her think she would lose them, still popped its head up now and then. But with literal years of intense therapy under her belt, and utter devotion from Molly, Carmen could feel it, and then simply let it go.

Moving to California gave Carmen exactly what she needed. She'd renovated the cabin, even performing some of the work herself. It turned out Molly got hot for Carmen in a toolbelt. They'd helped Enid design and construct a small cabin for herself, and then started the enormous task of building a place for kids to live while sheltering and working on the ranch.

It had taken years, but they were finally finished. Toward the end of all of that, Mateo announced he and Daniel were looking to start a family. They'd adopted tiny

Lucia, and Carmen couldn't have wished for anything more for them. Mateo was finally getting his brood. And, of course, the little one had flawless skin and gorgeous, rich black hair, and was possibly the best-dressed baby in all of the U.S.

Carmen had to bite back another round of sobs that threatened to break free.

Molly

She shouldn't laugh, but watching Carmen try to subtly wipe away a fresh set of tears as they made their way to the car was just too much. The poor woman was a bag of emotions and hated every second of it. For Molly, it was a sign that her wife had healed.

The second they moved to the ranch, Carmen had insisted on finding a therapist. Molly had done her best to support her, even volunteering to sign up for weekly sessions. If Carmen could take the bull by the horns, so could Molly.

They'd found a practice recommended by Dr. Stark and had been going ever since. Faith jumped on the bandwagon too, which only cemented the fact they'd all made the best decision to start fresh in California.

"Babe, are you okay, really?"

"Yeah, I'm just being silly."

"Carmen, you're not silly. You're happy."

"No one else is losing their shit," Carmen chuckled.

"I think it's beautiful you can openly show your emotions. I love that, and I love you."

"You have to say that. We're married."

Molly rolled her eyes as they slipped into the car. "I do not *have* to say anything. It's true. Now, would you like a second to freshen up?"

Carmen wiped her hands across her face. "No, I'm good. Thanks, honey."

They shared a sweet kiss, that still to this day, took nanoseconds to turn fiery.

"Later," Molly panted into Carmen's mouth. "We need to welcome your mom. I cannot think of stripping you naked, and welcoming your mom, at the same time. I think there's like, a law or something."

"Ugh, fine. Stripping me naked can wait. But not too long."

The drive back to the hotel was relatively quick. Molly had booked several rooms the second Faith informed her of the date for the graduation ceremony. Enid insisted on driving herself, which worried everyone. Enid was a...passionate driver, to say the least. Faith and Nathalie rode with Mateo, Daniel, and Lucia. Molly fully understood Faith's need for baby snuggles.

The hotel restaurant was full of people by the time Molly and Carmen arrived. Mariana, Carlos, and Mia sat at the bar. Lisa, Courtney, Micah, Liam, and Bessie were already picking at the party food. It was mayhem and Molly loved it.

Faith had met so many people, and made so many friends. The place was bursting at the seams as people crowded around Faith to congratulate her.

"Molly, my darling, how is everything?"

Molly turned and smiled at an approaching Rita, who was just as proud of Faith as she and Carmen.

"Rita, it's great to see you. Everything's good at my end. How was London?"

"Wet," Rita laughed. "I get enough of that crap in Seattle. But it went well. I think we're moving in the right direction."

"Great. Carmen's just taking a second to regroup. She's a little overwhelmed."

"That's fine, it gives us a few minutes to talk shop."

"Oh, is there something wrong?"

"Not at all. I'm thinking of hiring another manager. One that would do the bulk of the traveling."

"Am I not doing a good job?"

Rita tutted as if Molly had just said the dumbest thing in the world. "Molly, my dear, you are just about to receive two babies."

Molly beamed. "Yeah, we are. I can't believe it's happening. Just two more days."

"Exactly. And I can guarantee you're not going to be happy swanning off, traveling around the country for a while. Mira and Ruben will need you, and so will Carmen."

"We discussed it, Rita. Carmen knows the work is important."

"Of course she does. Will you stop being obtuse? The second you have those babies in your arms, *you* will not want to leave. What I'm suggesting is giving you some time at home, where you can still work, without missing all the precious moments with the twins."

Taking Rita's hand, Molly leaned forward and kissed her on the cheek. "Thank you, Rita. You're right. I have been dreading the first time I have to leave. I just didn't want to let anyone down."

"And that's why *I* made the call. So, look after the babies, and your wife, and enjoy it. When, and if, you want to resume traveling, we'll talk, okay?"

Molly nodded. "Deal. Now, have a drink. I'll send Carmen over later."

Stepping around several people, Molly made her way to the bar. She greeted Mariana and Carlos, hugged Mia, and proceeded to have a long drink of water. Two days. They would have babies in two days. Sweet little twins who had been abandoned, just like Mateo and Carmen.

"Molly, where's Carmen?" Mariana asked.

"She'll be here in a few minutes."

"Ah, there she is."

Molly turned from her spot and locked eyes with her wife. They were each other's anchor points.

Carmen smiled and drew Molly in for a kiss. "Sorry I took so long. Everyone okay? Hey, Mom."

"Hello, sweetie. Everything's great. Faith looks like she's having a whale of a time."

Indeed, the young Parsons was all smiles and laughter.

"I think she's just happy she can stop studying for a while," Molly laughed.

"And you two? Are you ready?" Mariana asked with a twinkle in her eye.

She'd taken the news of becoming a grandmother with hysterical crying. Then she proceeded to decorate one of the spare rooms in the house. The nursery was ridiculously big and decked out with everything the babies would ever need. Molly and Carmen also had crates of baby stuff that had been shipped to the cabin, courtesy of the world's most excited grandmother.

"Two days," Carmen stated. "I'm petrified," she laughed nervously.

"Nonsense, you two are going to be wonderful mothers."

"They are," Mateo agreed, coming up to the group. Lucia kicked her legs out from her carrier on Mateo's chest. Molly immediately scooped her up and held her close.

"Yes, and this little one is going to be their best friend, aren't you, sweetie?"

"She's going to show them what style is all about. Because, knowing their luck, the twins will latch on to Carmen's unfortunate fashion sense."

Molly still laughed at Carmen and Mateo's bickering. It never changed. "Don't start, you two. There are enough kids to look after already."

Both Ruizes pouted. Molly kissed Lucia's head and took a second to embrace the moment. She was exactly where she wanted to be: Home.

Faith

The day had been wonderful. Finally graduating from college, after so much hard work and personal sacrifice, felt amazing. For years, she and Nathalie had done the long-distance thing. Nathalie was possibly the most supportive person on the planet. She was always there to pick Faith up when she floundered or became frustrated. Faith's frustrations usually came from the inability to see

Nathalie as often as she'd wanted. Not only was Faith in a different state, but Nathalie was also working a lot.

In Faith's third year, Rita sent Nathalie to London for six months. That extended separation had almost broken her, and them. Faith had been hours away from walking away from college and flying to the UK when Nathalie had knocked on her dorm room door. They'd spent forty-eight glorious hours catching up in bed. Nathalie had made the journey knowing it would be short, but also knowing they needed it.

That was her Nathalie, all over: considerate, and aware of Faith's every need. When the six months had ended, Nathalie requested Rita position her for a while in California. And because of all those reasons, Faith was preparing to make good on the promise she'd made herself and Carmen in that Salsa club five years ago.

What better opportunity to ask Nathalie the question she'd been harboring for years, than here and now? All the people she loved the most were gathered together in one place.

The buzzing of her phone gave Faith an excuse to step out of the room for a second. Smiling at the name scrolling across the screen, Faith took a deep breath.

"Hey, Mom."

"Sweetie, did you do it?"

Faith laughed. "Not yet. I'm trying to summon up the courage."

"Faith Parsons, you don't need courage. You need to get your butt in front of Nathalie and pop the question. I've got champagne on ice here waiting."

"Mom, it must be like seven in the morning over there."

"Half past seven. And anyway, it was Tony's idea. He's stringing up a 'congratulations' banner as we speak."

Faith laughed out loud. Tony Peters was a wonderful man and Maureen's boyfriend of two years. Tony had been on vacation in California when he literally bumped into Maureen at the local market. Sparks flew, and before Faith knew it, Maureen was moving to Ireland to be with Tony and to start a new life. Faith could see her mother had never been as happy as she was with him.

It had felt weird to begin with. Only having Alan Parsons as a role model left Faith wary of the new man, but it took just a few meetings to see how gentle and open he was. He welcomed Faith and Nathalie into his world, doting on them both, and on her mother.

Alan had never tried to contact Faith since the cemetery encounter, and after intensive therapy, Faith realized she was okay with that. She didn't wish him harm or bad will, but that didn't mean she wanted him in her life.

"I'll call you as soon as I've done it. You're still flying over next week, right?"

"Of course, sweetie. We can't wait to celebrate with you."

"Okay, I'm going in. Talk soon. Love you."

"Love you, too."

Faith took Maureen up on the offer of joint therapy sessions, and they'd worked hard to move on. It had been painful, and Faith had lost count of the times she sat sobbing on Carmen or Molly's shoulder that first year in California, but it had also been freeing and healing for everyone. Molly gained a friend back in Maureen, and although Carmen always kept a wary eye out, they got along well.

"There you are. Fucking hell, I thought you'd done a runner," Enid panted. "Bessie and I are ready!"

"Um...ready for what?"

"To do our dance. We've been practicing for days."

Enid and Bessie were glued at the hip. They were best friends and were terrible influences on each other. Faith presumed Bessie would calm Enid a little, but she—and everyone else—had been *very* wrong.

"Enid, I have no clue what you're talking about."

"Our dance for your proposal. We're ready."

"Still no clue."

Enid stopped and stared, cocking her head. "Shit, I thought we'd had a conversation. Maybe I was tripping. Well, never mind, it's happening now. You go and stand by the stage, and we'll get this thing moving."

Pulled along in a haze of confusion, Faith planted herself by the stage as Enid signaled the deejay. Bessie cleared an area at the front of the small raised platform the restaurant used for live music.

When the theme song from "Dirty Dancing" came blaring over the speakers, Faith lost it. Bending over, she laughed until she cried, as she watched her two favorite seniors reenact the famous last dance scene.

Her gaze wandered around the room where she saw Carmen and Molly looking stunned, before Carmen burst out laughing. They were going to make great parents. Faith couldn't wait to meet her little cousins.

Mateo and Daniel were swaying their hips to the music. Lucia squealed in delight, nestled in Molly's arms. Everyone else, including Nathalie, stood frozen, watching the carnage unfold.

When they gave their final bows, Faith stepped towards Nathalie. She saw Molly nudge Carmen in her side, and then poke Mateo. With her family by her side, Faith cupped Nathalie's cheeks, giving her a gentle kiss on the lips. Nathalie smiled and then went wide-eyed as Faith dropped to one knee.

Faith had found her place in the world. She'd found her home and her family, and now she was going to treasure them. Nathalie was already nodding before Faith uttered a word. But when Faith did ask, and she slipped the ring on Nathalie's finger, Faith heard the one thing no person should hear on a proposal:

"Fuck! My new vag art has been wiped off my leg. Permanent ink, my ass!"

Afterword

Thank you for reading *Keeping Carmen Ruiz*.
Please spare a few more minutes of your time by heading over to Amazon and Goodreads to leave a review.

Acknowledgements

For the people past and present who took me under their wing when I needed it most.

Other Titles By Alyson Root

A Dance Towards Forever

Diving Into Her

Always Emilie

Broken Parts Included

Love & Other Wild Things

Finding Molly Parsons

Keeping Carmen Ruiz

The Wisdom of Bug

Sleigh Bells Ring

Risking Immortality

Waiting for Eternity

Fighting for Infinity

Mob's Seduction

About the author

Alyson was born and raised in the heart of England. She moved to Paris in 2015 when she met her wife. Together they moved to the west of France, where they now live with their two dogs. Alyson spends her time reading sapphic fiction books, writing and Scuba Diving.

Alyson discovered her love of writing in her mid-thirties. Her debut book, *A Dance Towards Forever,* was inspired by her wife and their very own love story. Alyson wrote *Diving Into Her* and award-winning *Always Emilie,* which added with her first book, created The French Connection series.

www.alysonroot.com

a.rootauthor@alysonroot.com

HUMAN
AUTHORED™

THE Authors Guild®

9550378